FAST TRACK

VICTORIA DENAULT

For Kelly Keating. Thank you for being a good friend.

PROLOGUE
EXACTLY LIKE ROSE PETALS

Lucia

I've felt pain before. I've had two concussions. I've broken four fingers at the same time in a carting accident when I was nine. I had my wisdom teeth out and got a dry socket when I was twenty-one. I had a pinched nerve a few seasons back that made it feel like I was driving with a barbecue skewer speared through the left side of my neck. But burn pain is excruciating and exhausting in a way that I've never known. And never want to know again.

"Come on Lucia," Nick's voice is soft. He's never soft, but lately that's all I hear. Gentleness and sweetness and encouragement. Add that to the list of shit I hate. "Just a few more reps."

I drop the foam ball I've been squeezing and push back from the kitchen table. He stands as I do, and stares at me with the same face my dad would make if he were here now. But Dad isn't here for a reason — because I don't want to see that type of face.

"I need to go for a walk," I announce and make my way through the apartment.

All the windows are open, and both sets of doors to the

balcony that wraps the front of the apartment are also wide open. This is a great furnished rental in the heart of my favorite district, *Le Marais*, where my sister's bestie and manager Jennie found us. It's light and airy and decorated in pale pinks and seafoam greens that give it a soothing, retro feel. And yet it feels like a prison.

"Let me grab my jacket," Nick says and heads off to the second bedroom. He's been sleeping there for the last five days, as I requested. I told him it was because I get night sweats and toss and turn all the time with this stupid pain medication they have me on. But it's not the real reason. The real reason is that he is suffocating me.

"Can I do this one on my own?" I ask trying hard to keep the bite out of my tone. He's the definition of a doting boyfriend, and I should want that. But I don't. "I promise I am just going to circle the block. Maybe grab a Starbucks on Rambauteau. I might pop in the Monop and see if they have a baguette for dinner. Are you still thinking of Fondue or maybe we go out? How about Tacos at that Speakeasy around the corner?"

"Yeah. Okay." Nick says, his tone flat.

He stops moving toward his bedroom and stands there, shoving his hands into the front pockets of his pants. His hair is all over the place. He's in a faded Motley Crew tour shirt he scooped up at a vintage shop, and despite being black, it's almost see-thru. His skin is tanned from spending a lot of time on the balcony while my physiotherapist is here or I'm sleeping. Therapy and sleeping are my two main activities these days. The tan on his already dark skin makes his pale blue eyes pop even more than normal. He's a gorgeous man, and he would do anything for me, and it's making me itch like a rash.

"Don't forget to take your phone," he says, and I grab it off the console in the hall.

I stand there a minute, perfectly still, as a debate rages

inside my heart and my brain. I need to tell him. But I don't know what to tell him. Do I want him gone? Yes, but also no. What I want is for him to change. Back into that carefree, light-hearted, alpha roll guy who I wasn't even sure I could keep interested in me. I want that back. That uncertainty and excitement and *levity*.

He's at the other end of the hallway, in front of the bedroom door, just watching me. I can feel the weight of his stare pinning me the way the seatbelt did in that ball of fire. "You might want to take a jacket. It's supposed to rain at some point this afternoon."

I glance at the brass hooks on the wall beside me, next to the door. The only things there are his leather jacket, which he hasn't touched since we got here three weeks ago, and a sweater of mine. I ignore them both and leave without another word.

Outside, the streets of Paris are ridiculously busy, as always. People are bustling by, sitting in every available chair at cafe terraces and sitting on park benches around Centre Pompidou. For a city that costs a ton to live in, no one ever seems to work here. I also like that the influx of tourists means you hear at least four different languages every block you walk. Having been raised by an Italian mother and a French father with a home base in Spain, but spending my formative years bouncing around the world, it's nice. Paris is the melting pot America claims to be. It's comforting, and that's what I need right now.

Crashing my race car in an F2 practice session last season was terrifying. Not because I hit the guard rail at high speed — there isn't a professional driver in this sport that hasn't done that. But because for some God-awful, unknown reason, this time I went through the barrier. It tore the car in half and ignited its 120 kilos of fuel into a massive fireball. And I was stuck in the center of it, my seatbelt jammed, and the glove on my left hand melted, leaving my skin to get scorched as I frantically yanked at the belt clip.

"I got out," I whisper to myself now as I cross the street and open the door to the Starbucks. "I got out."

No one notices me muttering to myself. The line is six people long. The young servers behind the counter look frazzled. I turn around and leave. I can't handle the wait, and to be honest, the last thing I probably need in this uneasy mood is caffeine.

I need to tell that sports psychologist about this. About Nick. I was so skeptical about seeing someone, but Dad insisted. He says the stupidest thing he ever did was wait until Mom died to see a shrink. He truly believes that he would have been a better driver and person a lot sooner if he'd had one as part of his race strategy from the get-go. I agreed to see her because it's what everyone wanted, including the board that oversees my sport. I didn't want to give anyone a reason to not give me the open spot in F1 on the team my dad owns and my sister Frankie runs.

Of course, they haven't made it official yet — that the spot is mine. But I know it's only a matter of time. They're waiting until I have the all-clear from the doctors to race again. That's why I'm here, working my ass off with physiotherapists and doctors and Carmyn, my psychiatrist.

But Nick is here because when that crash happened, everything between us changed. It was honestly like a chemical shift inside him. As soon as he walked into that hospital room, I knew that our relationship was never going to be the same. And even high on painkillers and foggy-headed with a concussion, I didn't like it.

Nick, my sister's bodyguard and my part-time bed buddy, was not the guy looking at me with a pained expression and wet lashes like he'd been crying. The guy who walked into the hospital room was a traumatized boyfriend. And I never asked for that. I didn't want that. At least not in this way. It felt as jarring and unexpected as the crash itself.

And I'm shit with explaining myself to him, or anyone for that matter, so I've just let him do what he needed to do. Which apparently is take a leave of absence from my sister's employment and move to Paris with me.

As I walk toward the Monop, for that baguette, dark ominous clouds appear out of nowhere. The rain starts instantly and without hesitation like someone in the sky just turned on a shower full-force. Big heavy drops tumble down. People scurry off terraces and rush into stores. But I don't. I just keep walking down the street in my sandals and flowing dress and bandaged hand. Sunglasses on, like it's not throwing down rain.

It feels horrible and yet lovely at the same time. I feel kind of free for the first time since the crash. Since I first saw Nick's agonized face. That is until I see Nick jogging up the empty sidewalk toward me. He's got my coat under one arm and is holding an umbrella with the other. Just what I don't want — a knight in shining armor. Or, more accurately, a soaking wet 80s band T-shirt.

I put my hand out to stop him. "I'm not made of sugar. I'm not going to melt. You didn't have to come out here to save me."

I push past him on the sidewalk, leaving him there with my coat and the umbrella. He starts to follow me, and as I glance over my shoulder, I see him holding the umbrella out toward me, trying to cover me. I want to scream.

"You're not supposed to get the hand wet, Lou. The skin grafts are still healing."

"Fine," I grab the coat from him and drop it over my damp bandages and keep walking. Only he grabbed the wrong coat. This one was a prototype from Mirabella Racing for the new jackets for next season. Frankie left it for me to try the last time she visited. It's got a microfiber lining. It grazes my fingertips and every hair on my body stands up on edge. I don't know how to explain it, but I detest the feel of microfiber. It's a visceral reaction.

I try to swallow it down and keep walking. Nick is still behind me every step. Finally he says. "Lucia, are we ever going to talk about this?"

"About what?" I ask.

"About how you are freaking out about us," Nick replies.

"What us?" I demand as I pick up my pace because thunder just boomed above. I don't want to get electrocuted, and besides, he's ruined the fun of the walk now anyway. "I am not freaking out about the version of us I agreed to, which was casual sex and snarky comments and occasional dick pics."

"I never sent you a dick pic."

"Yeah, but you could have. That was in the scope of our arrangement," I explain.

"And this isn't," Nick is stating the obvious, not asking a question. He knows he's crossed all the lines. "Me caring about you breaks our unwritten contract. Not because you don't have feelings, but because we agreed not to talk about them. Or show them."

Huh... my pace slows. He just hit the nail on the head. He does that a lot. Verbalizes my feelings when even I can't. But still. "I don't like to be forced into change."

"Yeah well, it wasn't exactly my plan to admit to myself or you that you're a hell of a lot more than a bed buddy," Nick says simply as he falls in step beside me on the narrow sidewalk so we're both under his umbrella now. "But you almost died, and watching that happen kicked me out of my blissful ignorance. I'm sorry. I wish the transition to reality had come less violently for both of our sakes. But fuck it. This is the hand we were dealt, and thank God you're still here so I can tell you I have feelings for you."

I can't handle the feel of the microfiber a second longer, because this conversation is all the uncomfortable I can take. I shove the jacket into his free hand. "It's microfiber. I can't stand it."

"Right... like rose petals."

"Exactly like rose petals," I reply and almost shudder just thinking about the texture. I hate them, which is a real pain in the ass when you almost torch yourself and everyone you know sends you get well flowers.

My apartment building is just past the next intersection. I wonder if he closed the windows and door before he came looking for me. So I ask him. He chuffs out a heavy breath and squints his eyes at me. "I just told you I have real feelings for you, and you want to know if I closed the windows?"

Is he... are his eyes... is he crying? No. He wouldn't dare. But his eyes are definitely watering. Oh my God, I am fully and completely not okay anymore.

"It's a rental!" I bark back. I'm starting to get cold, which makes sense because I'm soaked. The city is starting to smell. Paris smells like an old basement when it's wet, likely from all the ancient stone buildings. As we wait for the light to turn so we can cross the street, I watch a shimmer of oil ripple across the top of a puddle.

"If you don't have real feelings for me, Lucia, I'll back off," Nick says quietly. "I know you hate change. And surprises. And this is all of that, and you've had more than your fair share of change recently. And trauma. So say it. If this isn't real. If you really want a bed buddy and not a thing more, just say it."

The light changes, traffic stops, but we don't cross. I turn so we're facing each other, and look up at him. His thick, dark hair is damp, but not soaked like mine. His t-shirt is clinging to his very defined chest and abs. Rain drops pepper his dark skin. I have feelings. And I've known it for a while, but when he walked into that hospital room, I felt... the responsibility of his heart. And I didn't like it. He is falling in love with me, and I know that because I think I am falling for him too. But, he's right. Change is not my friend. It's my worst enemy, and there is so fucking much of it right now. He reaches up and runs the pad of his thumb over the curve of my cheek, probably wiping at the rain drops. "You get me. Always. Like on levels no one else ever has."

"I know."

"How?"

I don't expect him to answer that. In my head, it's a mystery of the universe. So I close my eyes when he kisses my forehead and relax a little. But then he does answer. "Because I'm very familiar with neurodivergent conditions."

What?

"What are you talking about?"

"I heard the doctor in Mexico mention that you might want to take depression medication because it can help with ASD symptoms. And I know about ASD firsthand. I have family..." Nick's voice trails off as he looks above my head. "Shit we missed the light."

"You think I have Autism?" I sputter back at him and step back. It feels like some kind of betrayal. I know he was there when the doctor made the flippant comment, but I didn't think he agreed with the doctor. I certainly don't. I mean... I would know about this already, right? I'm almost fucking thirty! I just thought it was a mistake, and I refused the prescription. "You heard me tell that quack doctor I didn't need meds, right? You think I do? Because my brain is...off?"

He blinks. "I don't think anything is *wrong* with you. And I never said you need meds."

"But you think I have some disorder?"

"I think... I mean it might be worth looking into. The doctor made the comment because he saw signs, and thought you had already been diagnosed" he says, his voice so calm and placating that it makes me itch. "Have you talked to your sports therapist about the whole aversion to certain things, like microfiber? Or the way you kind of meltdown with change? Like when your dad and Adelaide announced they were having a baby?"

Now that tanned color is slipping off his face and into the gutters of Paris. Along with my ability to cope. This feels like a last straw situation, and I'm a camel. Something in me definitely breaks. "She's there to help me get back into my sport. Not to help me deal with my daddy issues. And I don't have autism."

"ASD. You shouldn't call it autism or Asperger's anymore. Also, neurodivergent conditions are really common, and talking about them with a therapist can help you in life and racing, Lucia."

"If you don't like me as I am, then you don't have to be around me," I snap, and I have no idea why I'm suddenly absolutely furious, but I am.

I charge right out into traffic, which is basically gridlocked, so I'm not going to get smoked by a car on top of everything else. Nick calls my name, but I keep walking. He catches up to me at the apartment door. I didn't bring my keys, so I have to wait for him. Fuck. He unlocks it. "If I didn't like you the way you are, Lucia, I wouldn't be here. I'm sorry. I didn't mean to upset you. You've been off since the doctor said that, and I feel like... you should talk about it."

"I've been off because I'm tired. Tired of doctors. Of therapy. Of physical therapy. Of everyone looking at me and treating me like I almost died. I just want everything to be normal again," I tell him, and as soon as the door to the building is unlocked, I barge through it and storm toward the staircase, ignoring the elevator because the idea of being in a confined space with him makes me feel like there are fire ants in my veins. "And now you think I need some stupid opinion on my brain on top of everything else I'm dealing with?"

I hold up my bandaged hand as if he needs proof of what I'm currently going through. "I'm not... I don't have some disorder. There are a ton of women that don't want relationships. Or that don't like unexpected change. That don't like the feel of a certain fabric or whatever. Fuck, Nick, back off."

"Whoa," he says, and for the first time since the crash, he's got his bodyguard voice back. It's fifty percent foreboding, twenty-five percent snarky, and twenty-five percent placating. All of which I used to get so turned on by, but now I hate it. "First of all, don't act like I'm insulting you or calling you deficient because I certainly am not. Being on the spectrum doesn't make you less. It makes you different, but that's not less. And I'm sorry if I think the doctor might be right. But I also think that you're perfect. And amazing. And that if you decide to get a second opinion on the ASD diagnosis, it changes none of that."

"I am not on any spectrum!" I yell and it echoes through the stairwell. Great. We're going to get a noise complaint. I reach our floor and stop in front of the door to the apartment. He hands me the keys instead of opening the door himself, so I let us in. "We haven't hired you to hand out medical advice. So stick to what you know, Nick."

"You didn't hire me at all," his voice is deep and with hard edges on every word. "I worked for Frankie. And I'm not here now because of that. I'm not even getting a paycheck. I'm here because I am in l—"

"You shouldn't be here at all," I interrupt because I can't hear the end of that sentence. Not now. My brain is swimming in too many emotions, and I am sinking fast. "I think it's time you went back to work. This isn't helping me. You aren't helping me."

The words are like little daggers, and I hate myself for throwing them at him. He looks absolutely miserable. It's the first time I've ever seen him look sad, and it's brutal. I hate myself right now. "I just... I can't do this right now."

"Yeah. I think that's clear," Nick disappears down the hallway.

I stand there, shivering, dripping puddles onto the herringbone hardwood until he reappears. He's carrying the simple black bag he brought with him when he moved in. He grabs his black leather jacket off the hook and comes to a stop in front of me. "I've called Mick. He'll be here tomorrow in time to take you to your doctor's appointment."

He stares at me, but I stare at the puddles between us. Then he says. "Go change. Get warm. Call me when you're ready."

And then, he leaves. And I let him.

ONE

FALSE START

Lucia

THIS WAS SUPPOSED to be the best moment of my life. This was my redemption. My lifelong dream come true. I was going to show everyone who ever doubted me that they were wrong. Full stop. And I would smile in victory and self-satisfaction. But I'm not smiling. I'm sweating. Sweating so profusely that big, salty drops slip off my forehead under my helmet and land in my eyes. They mix with the tears I'm trying — and failing — to fight off. And no matter how hard I grip the steering wheel, my hands tremble. My legs feel like they are made of spaghetti.

I can hear Frankie in my ear. My sister's voice is firm without being hard. It's even, her words slow and sure, but also a pitch higher than normal. A minute tone change that only I would notice, thankfully, because the T.V. stations have access to any radio conversations they want.

"What?" I spit out, sounding annoyed. I'm annoyed, but not at my sister, the Team Principal at Mirabella Racing. I'm annoyed at the thumping sound that is happening in the car. It's so fucking loud that I can barely hear Frankie.

"Is everything alright?" Frankie repeats. "You slipped a spot again and... Logan is worried about overheating?"

She is outright lying. I hate lying. "No. It's not overheating it's this sound..."

I pause as I hit the chicane in this fairly tricky Australian course. I brake too late and I lock up, but just for a second. Still, I fight harder than I should for control. I almost slide right off the track. Fuck! The banging is louder than ever. I slow up. Another driver zips right by me.

"What sound?" Frankie asks. "Lucia, is there engine trouble?"

"Yeah. Yes. I can't... this thing is not working. There's a—"

"Pit. Pit now." Frankie interrupts. Again, her voice is even. Calm, albeit a little firm.

"Fuck." I hiss but I focus on the track, the light rain spitting down, the spin and grip of the tires on the pavement, and the looming light that signals the pit lane.

It's only as I veer off the track and down the pit lane that the banging sound lightens. And that's when I realize — that sound is not the car. It's my heart. The sweat turns cold on my skin, and I start to visualize my name, slipping down the standings on a television broadcast. Because I only started in seventh and by now, with this stop, I'll be last or close to it when I get back out there.

Only I am not getting back out there. When I come to a stop in the pit, there's no crew waiting with new tires or anything. They start to move the car into the garage.

"No!" I call out, angrily. "I can head back out! The sound is gone!"

That's a lie. My heart is still hammering.

Logan walks out and shakes his head. He lifts his left arm

and draws a line. I'm out. They've called it. My first Formula 1 race is over, and I officially Did Not Finish. I want to scream and cry and light the universe on fire. But cameras are on me. So I grit my teeth so hard my jaw aches and unclip my harness. It's super annoying how much shit you have to unhook or remove to get the hell out of an F1 car. I just want to be free.

I swear under my breath as they wheel the car into the garage and I finally get everything untied and off me. I am a full-on brat about this, and I know it. After all, this crap that I'm cursing is the only reason I'm alive right now. It kept me from drying in that F2 crash last year. Thanks to fire-retardant gear, my helmet, the harness, head and neck support system, and the halo (steel bar around the top of the car) I'm still alive with nothing to even remind me of that crash except the skin graft on my left hand. And my brain, which won't forget. Unfortunately.

I pull myself from the car. There are three guys with cameras just outside the garage all clicking away and a dude with a television camera. Because as if the pressure of my first F1 season wasn't enough, there's a documentary being shot on the sport, and I have to do interviews and crap for that on top of my normal press duties. Frankie pulls off her headphones and hops off her stool on the pit wall. She's marching toward me before I can leave and make it out of here and to my private room at the paddock.

She stops me by standing directly in front of me and leans in. "You stomp off to your room, it's the equivalent of an actor on set storming off to their trailer. It's all everyone will talk about."

"And that will be worse than them talking about the fact I didn't even finish my first race?" I whisper back, yanking off my fire-proof balaclava. My hair falls out with a plop as the braid I tied it into hits my left shoulder blade.

She smiles. It's fake but looks so calm and consoling. And

then she drops a hand on my shoulder and squeezes. Frankie has gotten good at this whole Principal thing. "I need you to chill at the pit wall for a minute. Talk to Logan and Rocco and whoever the hell else you want like it's no big. Then Clara is going to walk over, and you're going to follow her. Into the back. And she's going to check you out."

"What? No. Why?" The words are flying from my mouth faster than the raindrops bounce off the pavement outside the garage. "I'm fine. There was a sound."

Frankie knows. I can see by the way her hazel eyes soften and her eyebrows pinch ever so slightly. She knows the sound wasn't the car. She tilts her head, and her hair, as long and thick as mine but with no curl, creates a curtain blocking out cameras. "I am not asking. Your gloves are why your race is over. You need to get checked out."

My gloves? My mouth falls open and then snaps shut. Right. Our gloves, on top of being fire retardant, have sensors that monitor our breathing and our heart rates. So, yeah. She definitely knows it wasn't the car making a knocking sound. Fuck.

I clench my jaw again and nod before moving out of the garage to the pit wall. I feel like I'm made of lead and Jell-O-o at the same time. And all that sweat that was pouring off me when I was driving has turned cold and is leaving me with the need to fight off the shivers. That's also probably from my adrenaline plummeting so quickly.

Why couldn't today go the way I'd intended? Frankie drops back onto her stool, hooking her feet clad in sparkling beige flats onto the rung and plopping her headphones onto her ears again. As she adjusts the mic, I hear her say, "Yeah. She's fine. Car is acting up. Logan is on it, but she's out."

I'm guessing that's Billy, her boyfriend and my teammate. She's informing him he's now Mirabella Racing's only shot at points. Logan walks over and leans in, holding up a diagnostic iPad. I barely look at him. "Is this the part where you show me the data that isn't there on the car that isn't broken?"

"I'm mic'd," Logan says as his hand covers a small metal clip on the front of his shirt.

I glance over at the camera crew which has full view of us as they congregate outside the garage, across from our pit wall. Fucking hell. I hate this part of the job. I clench my jaw again and turn back to Logan. He's new. We hired him when my dad and Frankie dismissed my dad's longtime business partner and all the people loyal to him. It was a move the sports world is still curious about since it's been clear it wasn't an amicable break. Logan came to us from Mayflower Racing, an American-based team. He's Canadian though, and only thirty, which is young to be the chief engineer on an F1 team, let alone have done the job on two teams. He is no stranger to media or cover-ups at this point, I'm sure. And his reaction solidifies my thoughts.

"I know drivers always want to blame themselves," Logan says smoothly, uncovering his mic. "Especially rookies. But we have a real problem with the water pump, and the engine was struggling to stay cool. I'm sorry we let you down on your first race."

I can only nod. I mean, fuck. He looks so sincere in this lie to protect my reputation that I almost want to kiss him. Or cry. Probably both. So I just nod and see Clara over his shoulder walking toward me. She's technically Billy's trainer, but I don't have my own yet, so we're sharing. She gives me a soft smile and waves me to her. I step around Logan and away from the pit wall and walk over to Clara. Without a word, she leads me back through the garage, past everything, back to the kitchen room, which is empty. No one is foraging for food or making tea in the middle of the first race of the season. She lifts a finger to her lips as she closes the door.

At first, I have no idea why she's being so James Fucking Bond but then I remember, as she reaches for it on the collar of her Mirabella shirt, that she's mic'd up too. She gently yanks off her mic and drops it in the sink and then turns on the tap, drenching it. When she turns off the water, she looks up at me with a smile.

"Oops!" Clara says without concern and then walks right over to me and grabs my arm. She presses a thumb to the middle of the inside of my wrist, and her jovial attitude evaporates. "Sit down."

There are a few plastic chairs, in Mirabella colors of course, against the wall, and so I sit. I want to argue, because I always want to argue when anyone tells me what to do, but I have to admit, I'm feeling weak. She grabs a bag she must have put in here before she came to get me and she pulls out a blood pressure cuff. "Unzip."

I undo the top part of my suit and pull my arm out of my long-sleeved undershirt with our sponsor logos plastered across the front. She takes the cuff and wraps it around my bicep and pumps. I wait, knowing the results won't be great. "I can't take lorazepam during the season. I don't want to risk a drug issue. But I'm seeing a sports psychologist."

"Since the crash? Same one?" Clara asks and her dark brown eyes examined my face as I nod. "How often?"

"Once a week, minimum," I reply. I hate sharing this info with Clara, but I know I have to. She's part of the team. Billy trusts her, so I should. I just don't know her all that well, and I'm pessimistic as fuck. "But she's on-call too."

"Is this your first panic attack?" Clara asks bluntly as the cuff deflates and she frowns at the results.

"Yes. During a race," I clarify. "I've had a couple before. Like at night. And no, this isn't just because of the crash. I've had them since my mom died when I was a kid. Randomly. Like, not often, but maybe a couple times a year."

Clara nods and leaves my side to walk over to the row of bar fridges under the counter. She pulls out a Coconut water and hands it to me. "Drink this."

"I hate coconut water."

"It has much-needed electrolytes," Clara explained. "And it will hide this well."

She pulls a little packet out of her pants pocket and holds it up. It's filled with powder. "Ashwagandha. It's an herb that helps with stress and anxiety. And before you refuse, Billy takes it all the time as part of his regular vitamin protocol, and it's not a banned substance."

"So why are you slipping it to me like this is a clandestine drug deal?" I have to ask. She smiles. Clara has a great smile. It overtakes her whole face and makes her angular cheekbones puff up into apples.

"Because you are the media magnet right now," Clara reminds me. "First female F1 driver who survived what looked like an unsurvivable crash. They're over-scrutinizing everything you do, and no one needs to figure out that you had a panic attack in your first race which caused your sister to pull you out. Am I right?"

"So right," I mutter and take the packet. She twists the lid on the coconut water and walks over and dumps a little down the drain. When she walks back, she holds it out to me, and I dump the powder in.

Clara replaces the lid and gives the bottle a vigorous shake. When she hands it to me, she says, "So you'll schedule an appointment with the shrink before the next race."

"This isn't your concern," I tell her as I stand up and take the bottle. "Trainer. Not agent, manager, team principal, sister, or even friend. No offense."

"No offense taken," Clara replies with a small shrug. "I've watched you for years. You have walls like a freaking Game of Thrones castle. You also like to shoot down a lot of the people that dare to try and scale them. Must be lonely."

"No. Not really," I reply tersely. "I don't have time to be lonely. And I get what I need when I need it."

"Okay, well, I'm not going anywhere, and you don't seem to be in a rush to hire your own trainer so..." Clara shrugged again and then walked to the door. "I'll scale those walls, Castera."

I don't answer her with words. I just shrug back at her, because whatever. Clara isn't the enemy. She's just not inner circle. And she never will be, but she's welcome to try. My inner circle hasn't changed in decades. It's my sister Frankie and my dad. And at one point Nick, but that ended by my choice.

Clara opens the door, and we head out into the garage. The director of the documentary is standing there waiting for us with a sound guy and frowns on both their faces. Clara does the best fake clueless look I think I've ever seen. Girl could win an Academy Award. The director's name is Steve, I think. If I remember right. "Your mic, Clara?"

"What about it?" She lifts a hand to her collar and her eyes get wide. She looks down and back up. I want to smile, but I bite it back. "Shit. Where is it?"

She looks around like it might be on the floor at her feet. The sound guy, whose name I've never bothered to learn, walks past her into the kitchen. He grabs the mic out of the sink and glares at Clara. She blinks. "Oh crap. It must have fallen off when I was grabbing Lucia a drink. Sorry!"

They turn to me, and I hold up the coconut water as if showing off an evidence bag at a trial. Then I turn to Clara. "Thanks. Later."

And I leave, making my way through the garage to the pit wall, ignoring Steve, who is calling for me to get mic'd up. I am not in the mood for it. And besides, they have boom mics they use when we're wandering around. If they want to eavesdrop on me, they will. I steady my breathing as I walk, concentrating on deep breaths in and slow breaths out. But by the time I get to the pit wall, I'm feeling less weak. By no means one hundred percent, but better.

Frankie looks over her shoulder and hands me an extra set of headphones.

"How is he doing?"

"Billy's in fourth. By the next turn, he'll be within DRS of Allard," Frankie says and motions to Logan to get up, but I shake my head.

"I want to stand," I reply. "I'm fine."

Frankie frowns but says nothing and goes back to watching the screens in front of her. The race goes on, and I'm shocked at how painfully slow it is when you're not in the car. God, I hate this. I hate today and how it turned out and how I can never fix this once-in-a-lifetime moment. I will never have another first F1 race, and this one ended in one of the worst possible ways.

Clara shows up just as the race is on the last lap. She hands me my phone. "This is blowing up."

Of course it is. I shake my head. "Don't want to talk to him."

"Your dad or Nick?" Clara asks.

His name causes my heart to drop like a deflated basketball. "Nick?"

"Yeah. He's called a couple of times too," Clara replies. "But it's mostly your dad."

"I'm not talking to anyone right now," I reply and gently push her hand, holding my phone, away from me. "They want to hear what I have to say, they can watch the presser."

"Speaking of which, you might as well get a head start," Frankie mutters and motions for me to head toward the reporters. "And don't make this day worse. Keep your inside thoughts inside."

I sigh. My sister knows me too fucking well. Clara walks off with my cell, and I make my way to the vultures. They ask the typical questions. "What happened?" And "Are you disappointed?" But luckily, I don't give them much of a chance for anything deeper because the race ends. Billy landed on the podium in third, and so I announce that I need to go congratulate my teammate and leave.

And that's what I do. I make my way over to the cool-down room to hug Billy. "You okay?" He asks me in his heavy Aussie drawl.

"Yep. Sometimes things just overheat," I tell him, and when our eyes connect, it's impossible to ignore the concern in his. He's not just looking at me like his teammate but like a family member. He's that in love with Frankie. And I know she loves him, and that makes me happy for them but a little annoyed for me. He's going to want me the lower those walls Clara mentioned. Ugh.

"My first race, I lost grip in the rain and nearly hit a wall. Finished twelfth," he tells me. That's not a consolation because at least he finished. But I smile like it's helpful and leave him to mingle with the other winners and deal with his own media.

I decide not to watch the podium ceremony. I don't even care how it looks. I mean, I'm exhausted and humiliated, and I'm sure Frankie can make up some kind of excuse for my absence. I go to my private room in the Mirabella paddock. I lock the door behind me and drop down onto the couch and let the tears finally fall. But only a little, because I can't risk being caught on camera later with red eyes.

There's a buzzing sound, and I realize Clara put my phone in here. I'd asked her to keep it on her before the race when I narcissistically thought I'd want to hear praise from my dad about my stellar finish when it was over. She must have left it here after I refused to take it back because all the calls and messages were making her nuts. I sit up, wipe at my eyes and grab it off the small round table in the corner.

Forty-freaking-seven missed calls, mostly my dad. But yeah, Nick phoned three times. There's only one text because my dad hates texting. He can speak four languages but barely writes in one. His typos are insane. So I know the text has to be from Nick. I don't want to open it because I told myself I was done with him — on every level. No more friendship. No more sex. No more contact.

But I open the message.

> Eminem was right. Success is your only mother fucking option. Failure's not. So do whatever it is you need to do to shake this off, Lucia.

I should have blocked his number, but I have to admit, this is exactly what I needed to hear. I don't respond though. Instead, I pull up Spotify on my phone, choose "Lose Yourself" from my playlist, and hit play. And then I sing it at the top of my lungs while I get changed.

Fuck it. There's always the next race in Barcelona. And I'll do so damn well there that no one ever even remembers this false start.

TWO
RUDE. BUT VALID POINT

Nick

I SEE she's read the message, finally, but she hasn't responded. I'm not disappointed. Well, okay I'm totally disappointed, but not because I wasn't expecting it. Because I wanted to be wrong. But when I don't see any bubbles, I know she's not even contemplating writing me back, so I just shove my phone in my pocket and stare out at the ocean. It's this unreal blue color here in Greece. I'm impressed.

Sadly, though, I can't stare at it all day. I have to keep an eye on my client, who is behind me in a lounger at the private pool. I scan the nearby homes — all white stucco mansions — as I turn to find her on her back on the lounger, buck fucking naked. That is not what she looked like when I turned toward the ocean to check my phone. Jesus Christ. I am so over this woman.

"Saffron!" I bark.

"Yes, baby?" She purrs like she's a cat drunk on the sun. Her lean arms raise over her head and she points her toes, stretching.

"Where is that thing you told me was a bathing suit?" It was honestly two minuscule pieces of fabric. It was like someone took the world's tiniest bikini and cut it in half. It was obscene, but I was quickly learning Saffron Kent's definition of that word and mine were miles apart.

"On the ground, over there," she points behind her lounger. "I have a tour coming up, and I have no idea what my costume designer is thinking up, so I can't have tan lines."

"And I can't have naked pics of you all over the fucking internet," I remind her and walk over, grabbing the towel off the lounger beside her and dropping it over her naked form.

She shoves her ridiculously large sunglasses up into her dirty blonde hair made that way by thousands of dollars of highlights and stares at me with big, brown unbothered eyes. "You have Boomer energy. It's a real mood killer."

"I'm thirty-one, Saffron," I remind her. The towel thankfully covered all of her from the waist down, but those large and in-charge breasts of hers are still on display. "We're only two years apart. Technically."

Mentally, it's like I'm babysitting a toddler, not protecting a full-grown woman who has produced two platinum albums and four top ten singles in her ten-year career.

"I said Boomer *energy*," Saffron repeated. She wiggles to a sitting position, and the towel is now at her knees. I grab it again and reposition it to cover her crotch. "I've asked my Crystalist about you. She said I need to get you something in aquamarine.... Or was it Topaz? I'll message her again."

Saffron leans over to grab her phone, which is beside a tall glass filled with some kind of crushed ice cocktail. The towel moves again, and I contemplate quitting.

"Jesus, I've dated women for years and seen their pussy less than I've seen yours," I snap. Is it polite no? Professional? Also, no. But those two things aren't on my resume and never have been. I tell every person considering hiring me the same thing—I will keep you alive and avoid trauma or problems at all costs. That's it. "I've only been working with you for six and a half weeks, and I don't even know if you own anything more than see-thru underwear and bikinis."

"I do," Saffron replies without even a ruffle of one egotistical feather. "You'll see me covered head to toe once the tour starts. You should see some of the shit they put me in. Leather, taffeta, and sequins to name a few."

Saffron starts making gagging sounds. I roll my eyes. "Seriously. I need you clothed. Your manager and your father didn't hire me so that a tabloid could plaster your tits across a magazine cover."

"It's the internet nowadays, boomer, not a magazine. They aren't environmentally friendly," Saffron tosses her sunglasses over her eyes but thankfully grabs the scrap of fabric I'm still not convinced is an actual swimsuit and starts to put it on. "And my dad and manager would only be disappointed if my tits were on the internet if they didn't get a fifteen percent cut."

Well if that's just not the saddest damn thing I've ever heard. I change the subject, because I do not want to get close to this one. I was close to Frankie and all the Casteras, and look where that got me? "What the hell is a Crystalist?"

"A professional who is in charge of curating your crystals to give you maximum positive luck, health, and energy," Saffron says thoughtfully, like she isn't talking pure gibberish. "Crystals saved my life, Nicky. I swear I wouldn't have made it through the last tour without my lavender tourmaline."

"Oh yeah, I should get me some of that," I roll my eyes again and she frowns.

"Boomer."

I chuckle. "You have a meeting on Zoom in twenty-two

minutes," I remind her, looking at my Apple Watch. "And it's with the record execs, so maybe put on some real clothes."

She sighs dramatically like a teenager being told to clean their room but gets up off the lounger. "I'm going for a quick dip first. Care to join?"

She is standing at the edge of the infinity pool, blinking her false eyelashes at me. I shake my head. She cocks hers. "Aren't you all hot and bothered in that stuffy outfit in this heat?"

My stuffy outfit is a pair of black shorts and a black T-shirt. "I'm fine. Swim and then get ready."

I turn back to the ocean and hear a splash behind me. I yank my phone out of my pocket and scroll through my contacts until I find Mick. Well, technically Michael. He hates being called Mick, but Lucia insisted on calling him that. I punch the call button.

It rings so long I assume he's not going to pick up, but he does. "Yep?"

"Hey Mic... Michael, Nick here."

"Who?"

I worked with this guy for three years, I've only been gone less than one, and I'm forgotten? "Darcy. Nick Darcy. Frankie Castera's old bodyguard."

"Oh hey! Yeah. Hi," Mick says with a looser tone. "How ya been? Did you watch the race?"

"Yes. That's why I'm calling," I say and clear my throat. I hate that I'm resorting to this. "How is she?"

"Not sure yet," Mick replied. I could hear people in the background, and considering the race ended less than half an hour ago, I'm assuming he's still at the track in the paddock area. "Haven't seen her."

"What do you mean you haven't seen her?" I question, my voice stern.

"She didn't finish, so she sat at the pit wall and watched the race then did press, and I think she's now in her room," Mick replies like this is not a big deal. "I'm on my way there now to check. If I can't find her, I'll text her. She's not far."

"You're her bodyguard. Paid to have eyes on her at all times," I shouldn't be lecturing him or scolding him, even if he's doing a shit job. I'm not his boss. It's Sebastian 'Bash' Castera, Frankie and Lucia's dad, who insists they have bodyguards. He pays our... I mean *their* wages.

"It's never been like that with me and Lucia," Mick argues. "If I'd had eyes on her at all times last year, I could describe your dick better than you."

Rude, but valid point.

"Look, just a bit of unsolicited advice," I start trying to sound casual. "She's the first female driver in decades, and there's going to be a lot of assholes coming for her and a lot of overeager fans with crushes. And I'm not there, so unless she's fucking another person trained in protection, she's vulnerable if you aren't around."

Please dear God, may she not be fucking someone else. Protection or not, the idea makes me want to vomit. I'm not over Lucia. I don't even try to pretend that I am.

"Yeah. Okay. I'm not going to let anything happen to her, mate," Mick promises in his heavy Geordie accent. "And if this is also your way of checking up on anything else... just know I haven't had to pretend I don't see a guy leaving her hotel rooms since you."

My heart wraps that news around itself like a heated, weighted blanket. But it shouldn't. Mick isn't the most perceptive, and if he's lost her now, in a contained space, lord only knows what he's missed at a public hotel. God, I wish I could be the one protecting her. But she made it clear she wants me gone in every way. So I am.

"Don't mention I called," I tell him. "And good luck. She's going to be a lot to handle after this."

"She's always a lot to handle," Mick replies, his voice tired. "Later mate."

I end the call and realize there's a lot of sloshing water sounds behind me. I turn and my heart seizes when I see Saffron in the deepest end of the pool flailing and gasping. Holy shit! I drop my phone with a clatter on the pool deck and dive into the pool, shoes and all. As soon as my arms wrap around her middle she stills. And then curls her arms around my neck.

I breach the surface, shake my head like a puppy trying to get the water out of my hair, and glare at her. "Was that a fucking joke? Are you okay?"

"No joke," she whispers and I feel her fingers play with the hair at the base of my neck. "Acting. I was believable, right? You thought I was drowning?"

"Yes," I grunt and try to pull away from her, but she's holding on and not letting go. "Saffron. Don't."

"I know you slept with your last employer," she says flatly as I manage to untangle her from me and start to wade my way to the other end of the pool. It isn't even that deep. She can touch the bottom with her tiptoes, I'm sure.

"Well, if you think I slept with my last employer, then you think I'm gay," I reply tersely. I learned long ago that when you work with celebrities, there are no boundaries. Saffron isn't talking to me about this personal shit blatantly and without tact because she's a bitch. She's doing it because no one has ever told her not to. "Because my last employer was Bash Castera."

"You know what I mean," Saffron argues as she breast-strokes to the side of the pool opposite me and grabs hold of the ledge. "The daughter. I've got it on good authority that you were bumping not-so-uglies with her for a while."

"I worked for Francesca, not Lucia," I remind her of that razor-thin line that makes a difference. "And I know a lot of bodyguards get involved, and I know your last one did, but that doesn't mean it's mandatory with any job. And to be blunt, I'm not interested. But it's not because you aren't gorgeous or talented or any of that crap so do *not* take this personally and make this a thing. "

She spends a long time looking up at me under that curtain of false lashes as I walk out of the pool and grab the towel I used to cover her up to wipe down. I fucking hate pools. It fucks with my hair, and I can never get that smell of chemicals off my body even with a shower. And I might be showering at the airport on my way home if she's about to fire me.

Finally, as I level my eyes back at her, Saffron blinks and says airily. "Shame."

She gets out of her pool, the minuscule bikini still in place, thank God, and wanders over to grab her towel off the lounger she was sitting on. She pops on her sunglasses and grabs what's left of her melting alcoholic slushy. "Can't blame a girl for offering."

"I don't blame you."

"Cool," she smiles and it seems sincere. "I'm gonna do the Zoom out here on the deck."

"In the living room is best," I correct gently. "There's a blank wall in there, won't give away the exact location of this place. I know someone at that studio is leaking shit about you every chance they get. The longer we can keep your vacation a secret, the better."

"Okay," she agrees without a fight, which is typical. Underneath it all Saffron trusts me, and that's key to this job.

She bounces off into the house. I walk over to the other side of the pool to grab my phone and then slump down into a chair by the small outdoor table to dry off a bit. She won't need me in the meeting, so I'll shower and change then. I open up my phone and look at the text I sent Lucia. Still no response. I expect nothing, but yet, I'm still disappointed.

I fucking miss this stubborn, fiery woman with every single part of me. And I think I've given up on that ever changing.

THREE
BIG BALLS FOR A MAN WITH SUCH A TINY DICK

Lucia

MICK STOPS to chit-chat with the valet at the hotel, but I keep walking. The doorman nods as he holds the door open. He looks like he wants to say something, but I level him with a curt thank you nod and a look that says 'I don't need placating, thank you very much,' and to his credit, he seems to get it. I note that his name is Earl and make a mental note to leave a tip specifically for him at the front desk before I leave.

Frankie is standing in the lobby, with Billy and her bodyguard, Jack. Billy is smiling. His blue eyes are bright. His honey yellow hair tousled. His stance relaxed. Confident. Cool. Everything I had hoped to be at the end of this day. I feel a drowning wave of jealousy, and I fight it off. Because Billy is a kind, empathetic, good guy and he deserves his success. And it's certainly not his fault I'm a failure.

"Hey! How do you feel?" He asks me as I try to breeze by the group.

"Peachy," I reply and try to keep walking, but my sister

hooks me by the elbow. "Frankie. Go fuck your podium driver. Leave your DNF to sulk."

"My DNF driver can sulk," Frankie says. "But my sister isn't going to wallow alone. Let's do dinner together. In your room. Or mine. We'll order from your favorite Italian place. We'll get Cacio e Pepe and risotto balls."

"They don't deliver," I remind her.

"I'll pick it up for you guys," Jack volunteers, and I turn an icy stare on him. He's a bodyguard. He doesn't scare easily, but he does look away.

"Thanks, new guy, but I'm on my in-season diet," I reply and tuck a piece of hair behind my ear that's escaped my braid. "I don't need the media reporting that I can't fit in my car anymore."

I gently yank my arm back from Frankie as her perfectly smooth forehead creases and her eyes shift to the front door. "Where is Michael?"

"Mick is yakking with the staff," I tell her. "And I need to shower this day off my body. So thanks again for the dinner offer, but I'm sticking to salad and poached salmon off the room service menu. See you all on the plane to Spain tomorrow."

"Lucia, come on..." Frankie calls after me, but I just give her a wave over my shoulder and keep on moving.

Of course there's a cluster of people at the elevators, because it's the last thing I want and that's all today has on the menu, apparently. I shove my hands into the pockets of my hoodie and keep my eyes glued to the marble floor in front of me as I wait for the elevator to come. Someone else already punched the button, so I don't even get that satisfaction.

The doors open on the first elevator, and people start surging forward. About five, but it's more than enough strangers for me. I don't move. I'll take the next one. It's partly because I don't want to deal with being confined with people who may or may not figure out who I am and start talking to me. And it's partly because Nick always told me not to get into elevators alone with strangers. He told me that whether or not they know who I am, it's a situation I should avoid.

I hate that I think of him every day. Multiple times a day. It's not just work-related. In fact, that's the least of it. I think about how he smelled when I had my head buried in his neck before I would come. I think about the way I could feel his eyes on me, across a crowded room, and it would make me wet. I think about the smirk he had that was just for me. The one that took that intimidating, aggressive look he always had on his handsome features, and somehow it turned intimate when he looked at me. And more dangerous, but in the best possible way.

It annoys the shit out of me because he was always just a bed buddy. Someone convenient and capable, not a boyfriend. I don't do those. I can't do those. I'm not capable of an intimate, long-term relationship. I've tried, and I don't succeed at them. And I don't repeat things I can't win at. It's not who I am.

I look over my shoulder as I wait impatiently for the next elevator. Where the fuck is Mick? I don't see him. My sister, Billy, and Jack have disappeared too. Probably into the bar having a celebratory drink with my dad on FaceTime. He's in London while his young bride, Adelaide, cooks my future sibling in her belly. I notice a man standing off to the side of the alcove where the elevators are located. He's on his phone, oblivious to me, but when the elevator arrives and I step inside, he does too. Quickly. And his eyes are no longer on his phone, they're on me. And something about his stare instantly makes me uncomfortable. I'm about to step off the elevator, making a mental note that I've already punched my floor, and he's seen it. But the doors are starting to slide shut, and then Mick shoves a meaty hand in between them to keep them from closing and steps in.

"You didn't wait for me?" He says, like he's shocked.

"I'm not supposed to wait for you," I remind him sharply and stare at him with wider-than-normal eyes. I need him to take notice of the guy over my left shoulder.

Of course he doesn't. "I was talking to the manager. Someone left something for you with a bellhop, and I was explaining we don't accept unsolicited, unexpected gifts. There was no name or return address either."

It's probably a bad sign I'm shocked Mick was doing his job and not just gabbing about football scores or something. He shoves both hands in his pockets.

"Well, thanks for taking care of that. I pressed your floor for you."

In my peripheral, I notice the guy is still staring at me. Only at me. My eyes shift back to Mick and mentally beg him to bring his A game. The dude was hired because he is one of the best. Seriously. Where did that guy go lately? "Your floor t—"

Bing! The lightbulb goes off just a little too late. But at least it goes off. Mick's eyes land on the guy behind me. Then they slide back to the elevator panel. "You need me to press your floor, sir?"

The tone is polite. Calm. Cool. Sadly not as menacing as Nick's tone always was when he was dealing with potential threats. The guy who is maybe close to forty and bulky but not in a buff way still has his eyes focused only on me. "Tough day for you, huh, Miss Castera?"

"Yep," I reply. "And it's just Lucia. Or Castera, like the other drivers get called. No Miss required."

"But the other drivers don't have tits and an ass that fills out that suit so damn perfectly," he says without even hesitating over his classless, inappropriate remarks.

Mick moves, pushing me behind him and stepping up into the guy's face. I look at the elevator screen on the panel. We're approaching the ninth floor. My floor isn't until the fourteenth, so I hit nine on the panel so we can get the fuck away from him.

"You need a lesson on how to talk to a Formula One driver, my fists are more than willing to teach you," Mick tells him. "Now I suggest you apologize and then get the fuck off this elevator."

The elevator stops and pings. The doors start to slide open. The guy doesn't move. He still won't even glance at Mick. His blue eyes are laser-focused on me. "The only person who needs to apologize is her. She's fucking up the entire Mirabella team with her nepo-baby bullshit. She should have made a career out of flaunting her body on Instagram instead of pretending she can do a man's job."

"Wow, you've got big balls for a man with such a tiny dick," I reply. And if Nick was here, he would be furious, but Mick won't be.

I step out of the elevator, and this dude tries to follow me, but Mick blocks his way and he is at least smart enough not to put his hands on Mick. He puffs out his chest though and stares daggers at me. "Give the seat up, bitch. You suck."

"Go fuck yourself," I sit back and the doors start sliding closed. I turn to Mick. "Take his picture!"

Mick pulls his cell out of his pocket and immediately fumbles, but I yank mine out of my pocket and snap a pic of the dude, getting most of his face before the elevator doors close.

"Good job," Mick says sheepishly. Fucking hell. Nick would have twelve shots of the dude and I wouldn't have had to prompt him. "Send it to me and I'll call the front desk and give them the details and photo for their security team. This dick will be booted if he's a guest. And the cops will be informed."

I nod because complaining about Mick's handling of the situation isn't going to solve anything now. He motions for me to follow him, and we walk over to another set of elevators at the opposite end of the hotel. We take one down to the lobby, and after he chats with security and the manager for half a fucking hour and I sit on a plastic seat in the cramped security office, we're finally able to go.

"We need new rooms," I remind Mick, who stares at me with confusion. I want to explode at him for being an idiot, but I don't. "The dude saw what floor we hit. We need new rooms on a different floor."

"Right. Yeah," Mick looks over at the manager. "Can you make that happen?"

"I'll send someone up to your rooms to pack them immediately, and we'll move you," he promises. "Let's see what else I have available."

I roll my eyes and plop back down in the uncomfortable plastic chair.

AN HOUR LATER, I'm in a new room three floors down, and there's a hotel security guard assigned to just patrol our floor twenty-four-seven. I should feel better, but I don't. After a steaming hot shower, I cocoon in the plush hotel bathrobe and throw myself down on the bed. My phone starts to buzz with an incoming FaceTime. It's my dad. I know I have to take it. If I don't, he'll just keep calling.

I hit accept, and my dad's handsome face fills the screen. Like *fills* it. I could examine the pores on his nose. "Dad, hold the phone farther back."

"It's not a phone, it's my iPad," he says, and now I can count the hairs on his unshaven face, individually.

"Back away from it, please," I request trying not to sound annoyed. "Unless you want me to start naming your nose hairs."

He chuckles, and then there's nothing but his fingers over

the camera for a second before his whole face comes into proper view.

"There you go, darling." The voice is Adelaide's — his wife and my twenty-nine-year-old stepmom. Then I see her float by behind the chair my dad is sitting in. She kisses the top of his salt-and-pepper head. I give her a small wave. "Hey, Adelaide."

"Hi Lucia," She smiles and it's genuine, which is insane because we are not exactly friends. I've been a bit of a cow to her. "Sorry about today."

"Thanks," I say and she walks out of screen — belly first. And it is quite the belly. I have to wonder how the waif-like woman can stand upright with a belly that seems to be the size of two basketballs. "Are you sure you aren't having twins?"

She laughs off-screen. My father smiles. "I wish!"

"Don't you dare!" She calls out, still laughing.

I hear a door close, and Dad turns back to me. His smile starts to dissipate. He's going to make me talk about the race. So I deflect. "I'm happy for you, Dad. You seem happy."

"I feel young," he admits, almost sheepishly. "Not having the weight of being Principal for the team is a huge relief. And this baby... well I'm over the moon. My heart feels like it's the size of the Eiffel Tower, and the little one isn't even here yet. It's exactly the way I felt when I was waiting for you and Frankie to be born. That's why I feel young."

I smile. How can I not? That revelation warms even my lifeless heart. "I'm looking forward to the baby shower."

"Good," he replies and his smile is still fading. "But let's talk about the race."

I groan and tip my head back into the plush pillows. "I wish we wouldn't."

"What happened to your car?" He asks. "I was texting with Logan, but he was very vague. I don't like vague and neither will the press."

"They pulled me because my heart rate was spiking, according to the gloves," I admit, and I feel a wave of shame. My dad had a bunch of crashes when he was a driver, and I'm sure he never got panic attacks over them. I mean, they didn't have the same gloves that could record that shit back then, so who knows?

"So it was malfunctioning gloves?" He asks, and the hope in his voice is so apparent I have an overwhelming urge to lie to him. I have total Daddy's Girl Syndrome and always have. His opinion, his love, and his acceptance are all I've ever truly wanted. And I've always had it. Hopefully, this doesn't change that. We're just staring at each other, and my lack of verbal response becomes the response. He nods a little. "Okay. How are you feeling now?"

"Okay. I mean physically," I reply. "Emotionally, I hate myself. I'm embarrassed and humiliated and so disappointed I could spit fire."

"Yeah, well that will happen with every race you DNF," he assures me, which is anything but reassuring. "Of course the first race is an extra kick in the teeth. But have you talked to a physician? Or your therapist?"

"Got a Zoom meeting with her first thing in the morning," I assure him. "The time difference and all. Besides, I need a little alone time to process."

He nods again and scratches the scruff that now lives permanently on his face. The beard makes him look like the guy who used to pimp beer and claim to be the most interesting man in the world. "*Louloutte*, I have the utmost confidence that these jitters won't get the best of you for long."

"Thanks," I say and I try to absorb that confidence he has, because I have none. Zilch. Zero. Nada. "Tell the fans that. They still think I shouldn't have a seat. And wouldn't if it wasn't for my last name."

"That's bullshit," Dad declares with anger in his tone. "Two other teams were interested in you. You won the F2 championship twice!"

"All of that was BTC," I reply and shift to prop up my pillows more.

"BTC?" He repeats, bushy brows pinching in confusion.

"Before the crash," I say, and he rolls his eyes.

"I hate text talk, use full words, Lucia," he lectures like the boomer he is. "And fuck that. We all have crashes. Part of the job."

"Do you know that some people refer to me as Fire Ball?" I ask him. "I read it online."

"Oh for fuck's sake what are you doing reading about yourself online?" He demands and frowns. "If I read about myself online, my self-esteem would be in the toilet. And so would Adelaide's. And they're still saying cruel shit about Frankie even though she led James to a World Championship last year and we finished top three in the Constructor's standings. Trolls, Lucia. They are all trolls."

"I know. But one of those trolls got in my elevator here and told me to my face," I admit. "And to say I didn't handle it well is an understatement."

All the fury and frustration leave his face. He stares at me with eyes that are dead with shock and a slackened jaw. "What?"

I tell him the bullet points about what went down in the elevator. He hangs on every word, and then, like a pin has been pulled in a grenade, he explodes. He pounds his fist into the desk his iPad is balanced on, causing it to tip, and now I'm staring at the coffered ceiling of the home in London he bought with Adelaide just a few months ago. "How come Mick didn't call me to debrief me already? How did the guy get into the hotel? Why did you and Mick get into an elevator with other people?"

"It was a clusterfuck, but I'm fine," I assure his ceiling. "Please calm down and pick up your iPad. Also, I'm sure Mick is sending you a report as we speak."

I make a mental note to remind Mick to send my dad a report ASAP. God, now I'm my bodyguard's secretary. I see his fingers cover the camera again and hear him cursing as he fumbles with the iPad. Then the sound of a door opening and closing again.

When Dad comes back into view, Adelaide is with him again. She looks like she's amused by his buffoonery when it comes to technology. He thanks her and then pulls her down to sit on his lap in the chair he's in. He recounts the details I gave him about the incident to Adelaide. Who looks at me through the screen and says. "I hope you told him to go fuck himself with that tiny penis of his."

"Yeah I did, pretty much," I admit and smile at her.

"You know that they wouldn't give a male rookie this kind of scrutiny," Adelaide goes on as she wraps her arm around the back of my dad's neck and shifts to get comfortable. I'm sure it's nearly impossible with that belly. Oddly, her arms are still stick-ish and her face not at all puffy. Other moms at her OBGYN office must hate her when she walks in. "Even if they were nepo-babies. Isn't there a dude on a team who is the son of the biggest sponsor? And he isn't shit on for every move he makes. That kid didn't even earn points last year did he?"

"Gabriel Allard? The designer French kid?" Dad pipes in.

"You make him sound like a handbag," I laugh. "Yeah. His family paid a shit ton of money to be the main sponsor of Mayflower Racing when they were in financial trouble last year and he got a driver's spot. And you're right, Adelaide, he gets some grief over it, but not the same level of animosity I get."

"They also don't ask him asinine questions like 'What will you be wearing to the team kick-off dinner?'" Adelaide barks. "And his family owns a fucking fashion house."

"You saw that press conference?" I ask thinking back to the one last week where I got that awesomely ridiculous question. Meanwhile, they ask Billy what he thought of the new engine design for the car.

"*We* watch all the press conferences," Adelaide informs me. She emphasizes the we in that sentence. She wants me to know that it's not just my dad.

This woman really is difficult for me to understand. She's a bucket of contradictions, or at least she feels that way. And in general, she seems to react the exact opposite of what I consider 'right'. Like if I was married to a dude and his daughter acted like a vicious bitch when I announced my pregnancy, the last thing I would do is be even nicer. But that's Adelaide's chosen route.

"Anyway, they should ask you the same questions they ask the men," Adelaide announces.

"If only," I reply and my dad is nodding. "Anyway, I wanted to reassure you I'm seeing my therapist. It won't happen again. And I'm okay."

"Okay," my dad doesn't look like he's cool with that, but he accepts it. "If you need anything — day or night — I'm available."

"And you're still coming to the baby shower?" Adelaide asks, her inquiry gentle.

"Wouldn't miss it," I promise and give her a genuine smile. "Thanks for having my back. Both of you."

"Of course," Adelaide is beaming now, and I can see my dad squeeze her a little tighter. God, she truly better have the best of intentions with him because he's the best man I know, and he's in love with her. I can't help but still be a little leery of her.

"If Mick lets something like this happen again, I am getting you a new bodyguard," Dad threatens, and I nod because I honestly don't give a shit who follows me around. I don't feel I need protection. I'm fine on my own, but this makes him feel better, so whatever.

"Okay," I say. "Love you, Dad. Bye."

"*Bisous ma louloutte*," he says, and as I move my finger to hit end, I hear him say to Adelaide. "How the hell do I turn this off again?"

I close my eyes and immediately pass out because I'm exhausted.

FOUR

YOU'VE ADAPTED WELL

Lucia

DOCTOR CAMRYN ROMERO'S dark brown eyes blink as she stares at me through her glasses, which have thick, black frames. Her hair is short, like super-short. Like a few people have suggested I should do with mine since it's always under a helmet anyway. She's wearing a deep purple blazer and a cobalt blue turtle neck sweater under it. That's all I can see of her on the video call. This is my twenty-second meeting with her, and the one thing I am certain of about her is that she has never met a color that scares her.

"Lucia?" She prompts because I haven't answered her last question.

"I'm sorry. What?" I say and flash her a sheepish grin.

"You slept like shit last night didn't you?" She says and sighs. "You are never this unfocused if you've slept well."

"Yes. Of course I slept like shit," I reply tersely and adjust my legs on the couch, pulling them up. "I failed to complete my very first race in the big leagues, and then I was made fun of by a fan. It was a shitty day."

"You've got the tools to shake those things off," she reminds me calmly and pulls off her glasses to clean them as she continues. "Go back to that workbook I gave you. Journal your thoughts. Do one of the guided meditations I also gave you. If you don't use the tools, there will be no growth. I can't do this part for you."

"I know. I know," I sigh.

Carmyn puts her glasses back on. "I think it was more than disappointment and frustration that was keeping you awake last night."

"It was also crushing self-loathing," I tell her.

She smiles, sadly. "Yes. But Lucia, you have that in bucketloads, win or lose. And we'll get back to that. But I think it was also guilt. Because, as you recounted the story to me about the asshole in the elevator, I felt like you were downplaying it. This means you downplayed it to your dad, and you're wired in such a way that you feel guilty when you mislead or downplay things. It's flat-out lying to you."

I make a growling sound. "It rattled me more than I let on. Yes. But not the idiot, himself. The way I had to remind Mick to do his job."

"That would worry me too," She replies without hesitation, and I stare at her, making sure she isn't just placating me. She smiles and it's knowing this time, not sad. "You don't need validation, Lucia. You are entitled to your feelings even if they are different than mine. Or anyone else's."

"So you agree he should have been quicker to handle it?"

"Yes. And whether I do or not, if you feel that way, say something."

"I don't feel things the way a lot of other people do, so I second guess myself. We've been through this," I remind her, and my words are hard and cold. "And my whole goal, if I made it into Formula One, was to keep my head down. Not make waves. Be noticed for my talent and nothing else."

"That's impossible with or without being on the Spectrum, Lucia," Carmyn replies.

I feel a wave of anxiety wash over me with that label. "Spectrum." I swallow it down like bile that has risen in my throat. Before I can respond, Carmyn continues speaking. "You're a woman. You already stand out for reasons you can't control. Because the sport is a misogynistic cesspool, and no one, from the media to the drivers to the fans, will let you forget it. Even if you'd won the race yesterday that wouldn't change."

"And so you must understand why I can't tell anyone that you diagnosed me with Autism Spectrum Disorder, right? Because I don't want to give anyone yet another reason to discredit me."

Carmyn opens her mouth to argue, but our eyes lock through the screen and she closes it. She nods. "I disagree profusely that having ASD is something you should be ashamed of, but I will admit that people in this sport will look for any excuse to discredit a woman, and this could be used as one. It would be wrong, but it could happen."

I didn't pick Carmyn as my sports psychologist. I don't even know who did. I think it might have been my dad or someone at Mirabella, but the fact is, I stuck with her because of two things. Because she seems to hate Formula One, and she swears. There's no bullshit with this woman. And she can treat me without prejudice. She's not helping me get over my trauma because she wants to see me in a race car, succeeding as soon as possible. She's doing it because she wants my mental health as a human being to be the best it can be.

I asked her about ASD after Nick and I imploded. She knew something was horribly wrong in our session after Nick left me alone in Paris. I broke down and told her all about the doctor in Mexico assuming I knew I had ASD. And Nick agreeing with him. It was then, after more and more conversations and asking questions, Carmyn made the official diagnosis of what she said would have been labeled 'mild Aspergers' in the past, but now is just called ASD.

"I'm not ashamed. I'm just... I'm shocked and I need time to process this diagnosis before the world weighs in," I reply and she nods in agreement. "Anyway, as for Mick, my dad said he has no problem replacing him. Maybe there's a female bodyguard I could work with."

"Or maybe Nick could come back," Carmyn says casually, even though she knows it's far from a casual statement. I glare. She smiles again. "You know my thoughts on that. He cares about you, and you alienated him because he showed it."

"We will agree to disagree on that," I tell her and add. "I can't work with Nick,"

"You said he's the best at what he does."

I nod. "He is. But it's too messy now. And I don't want to see him. For more reasons than I care to tell you about."

"You're supposed to tell me everything. That's how this works," Carmyn's tone is pointed.

"In time," I reply, and there's a knock on my door.

"You can get that. Our session is just about done. And I think we should schedule another one on race day, before warm-ups," Carmyn says. "So email me later with when that is. Okay?"

"Yes," I say and there's another knock. Louder. It's Frankie. I know it. "I'll email from the plane in a few."

The screen fades to black as Frankie knocks, *again*. I shut my laptop and holler. "Jesus woman, learn some patience!"

I pull myself off the small couch in my hotel suite and march over to the door. I'm about to unlock it and fling it open when the asshole from the elevator's face swims into my brain. Right. I look through the peephole and see my sister's best annoyed expression. So now I swing open the door without doubt. "You need to calm your tits."

"I should punch you in the tits for not telling me about the elevator thing," Frankie replies barging past me into my room.

Jack is leaning on the wall across from my door, looking at his phone. Without looking up he says. "I'll leave you two alone while you threaten each other's tits. Be right here if you need me."

"You've adapted well," I tell him and shut the door.

Frankie is pacing the tiny living room. She's wearing a pair of pink pants and a silky cream tank that looks like it's supposed to be under clothes, but as usual, she is flawless. Her thick chestnut hair is loose and waving slightly as it skims her shoulder blades. Her skin holds a tint of bronze from the off-season, which she spent in Australia with Billy, probably naked and fucking in the sun. I'm not judging. I'm jealous. I haven't fucked anyone since Nick.

"Lucia, Jack had to tell me about the creeper in the elevator with you," Frankie says, annoyed. "And he was told by Dad, who asked him to keep an eye on Mick because he doesn't think Mick is doing a decent job."

"He isn't," I reply. "But he will. I think yesterday was his wake-up call."

Frankie stops pacing and puts her hands on her hips. She's the taller of us. And the one with bigger boobs, lighter hair, skin, and eyes. She made a truckload of cash as an influencer before she took the job of Mirabella Principal. People like her. She says and does the right thing all the damn time without hesitation. I've always admired her for that, but I've never been jealous. We have never had any time for petty emotions between us because we lost our mom so young, and we both knew we had to stick together. "Why are you still so distant?"

"Frankie, stop pushing me," I reply like I always do when she asks this question. The first time she did was when she showed up at my rental in Paris where I was doing rehab for my burned hand. She actually left Australia and her romantic vacation time with the love of her life and flew across the freaking world to find out why I wasn't returning her texts and wouldn't pick up on video calls. "I promised you a long time ago it wasn't personal. I'm not mad or whatever. I just need to focus on me."

"I'm not a boyfriend you're breaking up with," Frankie reminds me. "I'm your best friend. Your only sibling, and now your boss. You can't escape me, and I need you to stop trying. I gave you space. I headed back to Australia and didn't call you once during those six weeks."

"However did you distract yourself?" I ask facetiously. "Poor Billy's massive cock must have been sore."

"Shut up," Frankie snaps, but she's smiling just a little bit. "I gave you space. Now, when the season's on, it's my job to be up in your business. And as your sister, I need to be. Because I thought I was going to lose you last year, and quite frankly, I'm not over it."

A heavy silence fills the room. We've done a fairly decent job of not talking about it since my car burst into flames and I barely got out. But that unofficial moratorium has apparently ended. And that's fair. Even I understand that. "I'm not over it either. Clearly."

I flex my hand. I hate how tight the skin feels even more than I hate the way it looks. And it looks like an absolute horror show. The skin on the back of my hand just past my wrist is streaked with angry red patches. Frankie is looking at it too, I realize, as I lift my eyes to her.

"What are we going to do about that?" Frankie says as she meets my stare.

"I'm working with my psychologist. And I'm scheduling an appointment for her on race day. I didn't do my meditations on the morning of the first race, and I probably should have, so I will at the next one," I promise her. "Other than that, I don't know what to say. If it happens again, I'm open to your suggestions. But let me try this my way one more time."

"Okay," Frankie says without hesitation. God, I love her. She walks over and hugs me. "I know you hate hugs, but I had to. I need it. Now let's go. We have to catch the plane."

I walk over and quickly pack up my laptop. Frankie stands there watching me as a sister, not a team principal, and I know there's going to be some remark coming about my appearance. As I zip my laptop into its case and shove it into my messenger bag, it comes. "You know you don't have to wear track wear on days off. No need to be a walking billboard with all those logos and crap."

"I know. I can wear jeans. Or a dress. Or anything else," I look down at my Mirabella Racing sweatshirt and warm-up pants. "But looking like a girl just further proves their point that I am a girl. And you of all people know what an albatross that is."

I roll my eyes, and she shoots me a sympathetic smile as we make our way to the door to rejoin Jack and hopefully Mick, who should also be outside. "You know that giving in to their bullshit is worse than rebelling against it. It took me a bit to realize it no matter what anyone said, so I am just gonna let you figure it out on your own too."

"Who was telling you to ignore the bullshit? Dad?" I ask as I open the door.

Jack is exactly where we left him. Mick is nowhere to be found. I frown as Frankie steps into the hall too, and the door swooshes shut behind her with a soft click. "Nick," she announced. "He had the best advice last year of everyone, and he did the best job of calming me."

Fuck. Of course Nick. Of course.

"Where is Mick?" I ask Jack, angry about his absence but also about how Nick is popping up in my life yet again.

"I'll text him and tell him to meet us in the lobby. Now." Jack tells me and reaches for my bag, but I shake my head. The male drivers don't have people carrying their luggage. I purposely scaled down my luggage this year too. I only travel with one mid-sized suitcase and one messenger bag. That's it.

We get into the elevator, and we get to the lobby before Mick. We have to wait. I am beyond unimpressed. Frankie scowls at him as he finally rushes across the lobby, his bag dragging behind him with a broken wheel. Jesus, was he always this much of a putz, or is something up? Sadly, I don't have much to compare it to because I'm so focused on the season that I don't know Mick all that well. Nick used to be the one to talk to him the most.

"Sorry. My wife just doesn't know when to shut up." He grumbles out as a form of apology. "Problem with the kid."

"You have a wife? And a kid?" I chirp, and Mick nods, not at all surprised I'm clueless. Jack, on the other hand, looks shocked.

"I have an about-to-be ex-wife and a fifteen-year-old whose favorite hobby is doing the exact opposite of what I say," Mick grumbles.

"His name is Liam, and he's in his rebellious phase," Frankie informs me as we start out the doors of the hotel.

Sterling Samuels's brother and rookie driver, Spencer, is out front signing autographs for a few fans who have figured out the hotels we stay at while in Australia. Some fans notice us as Jack hands the valet the tag for our car, and a few of them start calling out for me and others for Billy. More for Billy, which isn't a surprise. He walks over immediately, a broad grin on his already gregarious features as he eats up the attention.

"Go," Frankie urges.

"I always feel like a fraud giving out autographs after sucky races," I mutter, so no one but Frankie hears.

She reaches out, takes my hand, and gives it a small squeeze before I can pull it away, which I always do. I'm not big on acts of affection like the hug earlier but especially not in public. "They aren't just here for the now, Lucia. They've probably followed you from carting days. They're judging you on your entire career, which includes a mountain of wins, or else you wouldn't be here. And they know that, so give 'em some love."

I swallow down the urge to argue, and I walk over. After all, there's no car to climb into anyway, so what am I going to do? Just stand there and ignore them? The first autograph I sign is for a young girl, probably about ten. She's with her dad who looks almost as excited as she does. Her hand is trembling as she hands me a jersey. It's not a Mirabella team shirt. It's red and gray, and I see the name of a carting team on the front. "It's my carting team," the little girl says to me. "I'm gonna be you one day."

She sounds so fearless and confident and excited. I fight the urge to tell her to be careful what she wishes for. Instead, I ask her name. She says it's Charlotte, and so I pause and write her a special message on her shirt. "I wish you all the success in the world, Charlotte."

"Thank you," she beams. "And thank you for clearing the way."

I smile and move to the next person holding out a Mirabella hat at me. It's a guy in his early twenties, and Billy has already signed one side. I can tell just by looking at him this guy isn't a race fan, he's a professional autograph collector who will go on to sell this online for cash. But none of that annoys me right now because as Charlotte walks away with her dad, I hear her say "Dad! She wrote that she hopes to race beside me! See! Oh my God, this is the best day of my life! Lucia Castera wants to race beside me!"

I keep signing everything and anything shoved at me and pose for a few selfies because that little girl's happiness is giving me strength. I even manage to bite my tongue at the few snickers I can hear and comments like "Rough start, Lucia." and "Hope you can shake off those jitters." and other placating comments.

When I get to the end of the line, Spencer is signing something, and someone holds out another baseball cap with our team logo on it. I reach for it, but the guy snatches it back. "I just want Billy's signature. No offense."

Ouch. Offense taken. I turn without a word or making eye contact with the dude, but I hear Spencer say, "If I were you I would have taken all the signatures I could get. Lucia is making history, and her siggy is going to be worth more than gold. More than my brother's."

That has me turn, and I notice he's pointing to his brother's signature on the Mayflower hat that the guy has in his other hand. The guy's eyes find mine, but I turn away and continue back to my sister. Jack is loading our luggage into the extra-large SUV with Mick. Spencer leaves the line of fans to head to his car. Our eyes meet, and he smiles at me. I smile back. We were adversaries in F2 and technically still are in F1, but both being rookies at the same time and siblings with something to prove seems to have created an unspoken bond. And I'm grateful for it.

And whether it makes me petty or not, I'm also grateful when Billy leaves the crowd before reaching the dude and ignores him as he calls out. Inside the car, he slides in next to my sister as I crawl into the very back row of seats, and he winks at me. He did that on purpose. "Fuck that guy."

"Yep."

Frankie doesn't say a word, because her nose is in her phone. The drive to the airport is uneventful, and I drift off into sleep and have to be shaken awake by Frankie. When I crawl out of the car, I'm shocked to see my dad standing on the tarmac in front of our private plane. He is grinning proudly. "Surprise!"

I blink away the sleep. "What are you doing here?"

"I needed to have a budget meeting with Frankie and Logan," Dad says and he opens his arms for a hug. I don't know how I ended up in a family of touchy-feelies. I step into his embrace, and he kisses the top of my head. "And I wanted to see you in person."

"Your wife is about to pop out your spawn," I remind him. "Don't want to miss the birth of your first son."

"We have almost two months left," he reminds me as he lets me go. The air swirling around us, rising from the charcoal-colored tarmac is hot. "And we don't know the sex."

"I do," I assure him as Frankie motions at us.

"Let's get going," she urges.

For the first couple hours of the flight on the team plane, I am blissfully unconscious. When I do wake up again, I'm alone on a couch at the back, the seatbelt cutting into my side because it's too tight for my slumped-over position. And my neck is killing me. I'm going to need a massage. I undo the seatbelt and wander toward the front of the plane to get a drink and some kind of snack. I don't see Estelle, our flight attendant.

I pass Billy and Frankie, who are sitting side-by-side and both asleep. Her head is tipped onto his shoulder, and his arm is around her. Then I see my dad sitting in one of the solo chairs, leaning forward. Mick is across from him in a chair facing him, and he is leaning forward too. And the looks on both their faces are intense, to say the least. So I slow my walk and study them, managing to hear the tail end of their conversation. "I told you that this year was going to be tough. And she's not the—"

Mick notices me and stops dead. I rest a hand on the back of Dad's chair as he looks up too.

"She's not the easiest person to protect." I can tell by the guilty look on both their faces that I finished that sentence right. And I should care, but I don't. Anymore. I've heard it all before. Mick isn't my first bodyguard, and he clearly isn't going to be the last. "Are you quitting?"

He shakes his head immediately. So I turn to Dad and grip the buttery leather under my fingertips. "Are you firing him?"

"Not yet," Dad says with brutal honesty. Mick doesn't flinch, so he already knows where he stands.

"Well, whatever you do, don't consult me on anything," I mutter and continue to the front of the plane where the fridges and snacks are. Estelle is up there and offers to help me, but I tell her I just wanna scrounge, which she knows means look around and find something to eat and drink myself.

I've been on private planes since birth. And Estelle has been the flight attendant for Mirabella for almost a decade. She grabs a wicker basket filled with snacks and heads out of the small galley kitchen to offer it to the other passengers. I putter around and take extra time making myself a Speculoos flavored latte and then lightly brie a croissant. As I pull it out and smear some butter into the middle, Mick appears in the doorway.

"I just want you to know that I'm sorry," he says.

"Sorry for what? I hate when people apologize for the truth, Mick," I tell him, my eyes staying on my croissant.

"I'm not sorry for calling you that. You're not the easiest client," Mick replies and leans on the door to the bathroom. "I'm apologizing for dropping the ball yesterday."

I nod and pop open a tiny jar of marmalade. "Are you

distracted by your wife and kids that you got without telling me? Kudos for adopting a fifteen-year-old. Most people go for infants. And a mail-order ex-wife is a new one. Again, most people go for the brides."

He chuckles and I smile as I look up. "I never bothered to tell you about them because that's not the relationship we have. And it doesn't have to be."

"Okay, but like other people know," I say, and I don't know why this irks me so much. "And you probably know if Jack is married or whatever."

"Girlfriend. She's Norwegian and models," Mick replies.

I roll my eyes and take a bite of the croissant. It's crumbly and warm, and the bitter marmalade and rich butter oozing out of it is heaven. "My God, why is everyone all up in each other's business?"

He chuckles again. "Look, you and I work without the warm and fuzzies. But here's the thing... I am not as focused as I should be. I think I can regroup and make it through this season. But I'm resigning after that. And it has nothing to do with you. I just have to shift my focus now with the divorce and the kid. But I'll make sure to help Bash pick my replacement."

I nod. "Because I'm not the easiest."

Mick rolls his eyes, but his smile is sheepish. "There are worse problems than being a complicated client. And that's the thing, Lucia. You're complex but not a nightmare by any means. I've had nightmare clients before, and trust me, it's not you."

"Like who?" I ask as I break off another piece of croissant and pop it into my mouth. "A Rockstar? A movie star? A head of state with the morals of a wild dingo?"

He grins. "Popstar Oh my word, they are the worst. And even though I warned him, now Nick is finding out for himself."

"What?" I almost choke on the first sip of my latte. I wipe the foam from my lip and struggle not to cough.

"He asked me about any gigs when he left here, and I warned him that he didn't want to work for her," Mick says, and he has no idea why I am so confused. Or even that I'm confused. He's telling me this story like I know where Nick is and who he works for. "I worked for Saffron when she was young on that silly kid's program, and she was already a nightmare. So I was shocked when I found out he took the gig anyway."

"Saffron? Kent? The British singer?" I picture the twenty-something woman in my head. She's pretty and curvy with big boobs and big doe eyes, and something bites into my heart the way the seatbelt was biting into my side. "Nick works for her now?"

"Yeah. And he's lasted longer than I would have guessed," Mick replies and plucks a bag of cheese and onion potato chips off the counter. "I knew that guy was tough, but shit, that train-wreck of a girl can break just about everyone."

"Maybe he's fucking her." The words flew out of my mouth.

Mick freezes for a second, and his eyes soften a little. "We both know he's smarter than that."

"Do we?" I grab my latte and toss the napkin my croissant was on into the trash bin under the counter. "Anyway, thanks for being honest with me. And I'm sure the rest of the season will go smoother."

He nods as I start out of the kitchen area. But his words stop me. "He checks in, you know."

"What?" I heard him, but my stupid brain, or maybe heart, needs to hear it again.

"Nick checks in," Mick says like it's the most casual announcement ever. Maybe it is. I mean, if I didn't still think about Nick naked all the time, it wouldn't be a big deal.

"That's ridiculous," I reply hoping my voice sounds calm and level to him even though it doesn't to me. "Tell him I said that next time you talk."

"Sure thing," Mick says, still casually, but now amusement has seeped into his tone, and I do not like it one bit. So I leave him in the tiny kitchen and march back down the aisle with my latte and a scowl on my face. A scowl so intense, Billy lifts an eyebrow when he sees it.

This might be amusing small talk for Mick, but for me, it's like catnip. And I do not need anything to trigger the obsessive qualities my brain likes to grab onto. Not if it isn't about racing. But it's too late. I'm slipping down the rabbit hole already as I drop down in my seat and put my latte on the side console table. I spend the rest of the flight wondering why Nick keeps checking in.

Is it because he still feels loyalty to my dad? Is it because he is a fan of the team? Is it because he's invested in Frankie doing well since he worked for her and left on great terms? Or is it because he still thinks about me naked all the time too? Why do I both fear and need it to be that? Ugh.

By the time we get to the hotel, I'm in a foul mood because I've thought more about Nick than racing, and I need to focus. I get my room key and head straight to the elevator so quickly that Mick is left chasing after me. He yells for Jack to bring my bags up, we don't use bellhops if we can help it, and slips into the elevator with me. He sweeps my room and sees the complimentary amenity on the desk by the minibar. Having the race team stay in your hotel brings a boatload of cash, so they always leave us something extra. This Four Seasons went above and beyond with a fruit tray, a bottle of sparkling cider, and a big bouquet.

"Nice," Mick notes and then leaves as I glare at him adding, "I'm in the room to your left. Do not open the door for anyone but me and the usuals. I'll bring your bag as soon as Jack gets it up here."

"Thanks," I drop my messenger bag onto the chair in front

of the desk. I'll be here watching last year's race and making notes."

I don't watch him leave, but I hear the door click. And right after that is when I notice the card in the flowers. It isn't common for the hotel to add a card. I mean, there's usually a welcome note, which my eyes land on beside the fruit tray. So what is this? I pluck the card off the lily it's balanced on and read it.

It's typed, which means the florist transcribed it so the sender must have ordered online or over the phone. It says. *The pressure isn't going to lessen. Can you handle it? I'm watching.*

I read it over and over, and my emotions swirl together and short-circuit my brain. I don't understand who it's from and why it was sent. It's not a threat, but is it a positive message? I don't know. I just know it's unwanted. I don't need it, and I don't want it. Even if it is a bouquet made up almost entirely of my two favorite flowers — lilies and white jasmine. Who knows that? Frankie. She wouldn't do this. Dad. He wouldn't do this. I doubt he told Adelaide my favorite flowers. And she would sign a card.

Nick.

Nick knows.

In a scramble, I grab my cell out of my messenger bag and flip through my contacts. I never deleted or blocked his number. I never had to because he never tried to contact me after he quit. But now I know he was keeping tabs on me through other people.

I text him a short, concise and brutal message.

> Don't send me flowers. Don't watch. Forget I exist.

FIVE

SHOULD WE FIND OUT, BOB?

Nick

BILLY DOESN'T PICK up when I call him, so I text him. And he sees it, according to my iPhone, but he doesn't respond right away. There's not even a thought bubble, and as I pace my furnished rental apartment in London, I want to punch through a wall I'm so frustrated. But then a moment later my phone lights up, and it's a video call. From Billy.

I hit accept, and Billy's face fills the screen. "Hey, mate!"

He looks and sounds so relaxed and upbeat, but then his blue eyes take in my expression and his smile slips. His expression darkens. "You okay?"

"No," I reply tersely. "I got a text from Lucia."

Billy's expression lightens. He runs a hand through his golden hair and moves. The background behind him is definitely a hotel room. "Is she asking for a booty call or something? Are you even in town?"

"No. I'm in London, and she isn't asking for that," I reply and heave out a heavy breath. "She told me not to send her flowers. The thing is, I didn't send her flowers. And she said don't watch."

"Don't watch the race?"

"I didn't bother to text her back for clarification because I don't want to freak her out," I explain as I pace my boxy, plain living room. "But how come she has flowers in her room and she doesn't know where they are from? How come Mick didn't check that? How come I'm the one on high alert about this?"

"I don't know, mate. I think we should ask Mick. Or Jack," Billy says.

"Who the hell is Jack?"

"Frankie's new you," Billy explains.

"If you tell him, then he'll tell Frankie, and I don't want her to worry about this," I tell Billy, and he stops walking and smiles at me, sheepishly.

"Too late for that, mate," Billy explains. "We share a hotel suite now."

There's a jostling of his phone, and for a millisecond I'm looking at the lush carpet until Frankie's pretty but concerned face fills Billy's phone. "What's this about flowers?"

I explain the whole thing again, begrudgingly, because I really didn't want to put the family into panic mode. Bash Castera is overly protective of his daughters because he became a single parent when they were pre-teens, and a big chunk of his heart is wrapped up in them. More so than others because it's the last part of his beloved wife Mirabella that he has left. I understand him. I understand the whole family dynamic. It's why I worked so well with them for so long. That, and because the girls are really easy to work for. Most of the time.

"We have to call the police. Between this and the fan in the elevator, I am freaking right the fuck out right now."

Both my eyebrows reach for the ceiling. "What fan in the elevator?"

With every word Frankie speaks recounting what happened to Lucia, my heart struggles to beat. It's like every word is heavy, wet cement filling my chest cavity. Hardening in the space around my heart, making a cold, impossible chamber of fear around it. "I'm calling Mick."

"Wait! No! Dad already had a talk with him on the flight over," Frankie explains. "And besides, no offense Nick, but you don't work for us anymore. This isn't your problem."

She's right. Her words aren't harsh, they're just facts. And she's got such a soft, understanding smile on her face I can't be offended even if I wanted to be. And I kind of do, but I have no one to blame for this but myself. I decided to leave. I could have stayed on as Frankie's bodyguard even when things between Lucia and I ended. That girl would be the absolute best at ghosting me to my face. I knew that. I just also knew I couldn't handle it. I needed to protect my heart. She wanted it over, fine. But I had to leave to make sure I was able to get over her.

That should be happening any day now....

"To be fair about this, Mick could have easily assumed the flowers were an amenity," a voice I'm unfamiliar with comes over the phone, and Frankie tilts it so I can see a beefy, dirty-blonde-haired guy in all black standing by the window of the hotel suite.

"Nick, meet your replacement, Jack," Frankie says. Jack gives me a curt nod.

"Tell me you haven't just glanced at the welcome package on the desk," Jack says to me.

"Does Frankie have flowers in her welcome amenity?" I ask him, and he shakes his head.

"Can someone call Mick and get her the hell out of that room?" I demand.

"I already texted him while you were talking to Frankie," Jack replies simply. Okay. I don't hate this guy.

"Thanks," I say, and he nods. Frankie's face fills the screen again with Billy next to her as she sits on a small couch. I know just from the furniture and years of working with them that she's at the Four Seasons in Monaco. The Castera family only stays at the Four Seasons if there is one wherever they're going. And Mirabella Racing has a contract with them during race season for all their top-tier staff. "Frankie, whoever is doing this knows you guys always stay at the Four Seasons."

"Do we need to switch hotels?" Billy asks, and he looks depressed. I don't blame him. The luxury chain is the best one out there in my opinion.

"I would switch it up for the next destination if possible. Just for Lucia," I advise.

"I'm not letting her stay in a hotel all by herself," Frankie declares.

"She has Mick," I hear Jack say from elsewhere in the room, but Frankie just rolls her eyes.

"Great. Now I need this guy caught," Billy remarks, frowning. "He's costing me my late-night swims at the Madrid Four Seasons. Dick."

Frankie glares at him, and he looks instantly remorseful for that joke. He leans in and kisses her cheek. "She'll be fine. She survived a ball of fire. This rando isn't about to ruin her."

"I know how tough Lucia is better than anyone," Frankie replies. "But I still don't want her to know the depths of this issue. Because she obsesses like it's an Olympic sport, and the only thing I need her obsessed with is driving."

I don't think that's a bad idea. "She doesn't need to know this at this point. I haven't responded to the text, and I won't. But get on Mick and the hotel thing. And let security at the track know too, will you Jack?"

"My best call," he says.

Yeah, I like him. Frankie turns her hazel eyes from Jack, off-screen, to me. "Mick didn't want to come back this year either. He has some personal stuff he's dealing with, but Dad convinced him to stay for one year so we weren't training a whole new team."

"Yeah, well if he agreed, then he has to do his fucking job," I growl. "Your sister has a target on her back for simply existing in this sphere with the misogyny around your sport and in the world, in general, these days. And we all know that she has those demons from last year to slay."

"I wish you could come back," Frankie tells me, her voice tight. "I know how weird it would be, but I also know you wouldn't let your previous relationship get in the way. And she listens to you and trusts you. We all do."

"Well, I'm employed," I reply and drop down to sit on the edge of the Ikea coffee table in my apartment. "Unhappily, but employed."

"And involved," Billy adds.

"What?" I rear my head back. "Involved in what?"

"Not what, who," Billy says and his blond eyebrows furrow. "With your girlfriend-slash-boss."

"Saffron?" I say and twist my face up at the thought of being involved with her. "Are you mad? No. I'm not dating her. Have zero interest in that."

"Tell that to the tabloids," Billy replies.

Frankie turns her head to her boyfriend so all I see is a curtain of thick, chestnut hair. It reminds me a little of Lucia's. Same thickness but Lucia's curls every which way. God, I miss grabbing it while we fool around. "What are you talking about?"

"I saw pictures of you and Saffron in Greece. She was basically butt-fuck naked and you were all over her," Billy explains and gives me the name of the online site that published the pictures. "They've blurred out her private bits because they know enough to not get sued. But those unburied pics might leak for the right price. You know how it goes."

"Mother fucker," I hiss. "I have to go."

"Bye Nick. We miss you." Frankie says.

"Keep me updated on this Lucia thing?" I ask even though I regret it as the words leave my mouth. It's not my problem, and I shouldn't make it mine.

But Billy and Frankie both nod and I end the call before I can say something else that's stupid. Then I google the site Billy mentioned. Some mid-level, trashy gossip from the United States. Just as I warned Saffron when we were there, they must have rented a neighboring villa or paid off a neighbor to snap pictures of her.

I immediately call her publicity team, who are on it, and already told her lawyer. Tim, her private publicist, not the one for the record label, advises me to not let her talk about it. Anywhere. For any reason. Act like it doesn't exist. I don't know if that's the strategy I would go with, but I'm not in PR. I'm in protection, and I feel like I failed by not getting her to take the risk seriously. I apologize to Tim because of that.

He chuckles. "Buddy, we knew Saffron would get herself into trouble whether she had a fleet of bodyguards or not. This isn't on you. I'm just sorry the bottom-feeding press involved you on a personal level. You got a girlfriend you have to warn about this?"

"Nope," I say.

"Okay well, bonus there," Tim replies. "You going to Glow with her tonight?"

"Where?"

"She's on her way to Glow. The new bar in Notting Hill?" Tim explains. "She didn't tell you?"

"She said it was a night in with Netflix," I explain. "I'm at home." I look down at my torn jeans and old ratty t-shirt.

"Huh. She must be skipping, which is weird because her ex is going, and we all know she loves to show up where he is."

Fuck a goddamn duck. Saffron lied to me. I know it in my bones. "Well, if she does pop up at the club, she won't be alone."

Part of the reason I was hired was that Saffron and her ex had a very nasty breakup. They both wrote some really heinous lyrics about each other and have gotten into some public screaming matches. The record label wants to hold onto whatever remnants of a clean image she has left, and brawling with her ex—a perpetually drunk lead singer of a rock band who makes terrible decisions more often than he produces hit songs —is the last thing they want.

I don't even take a second to change. I grab my leather motorcycle jacket and helmet off the coat rack by the door because that will get me to her place quicker than the car. I cursed her the entire twenty-minute ride there. And of course, she's climbing into a hired car with two of her soul-sucking fake besties as I pull up. I lock my helmet to the bike and pull open the passenger side door as she is about to slip into the back after her friends. Our eyes meet and she looks mildly disappointed. "Oops."

"Yeah. Oops," I growl and get in next to the driver.

I did not want to spend what was supposed to be my night off watching Saffron and her two best bimbos getting hammered on a four hundred dollar bottle champagne. Messy drunk girls are a big pet peeve for me. I have to keep reminding myself I'm being paid to be here.

Her ex is here, across the room with a bunch of dudes. He's a few years older than Saffron and has more tattoos than I.Q. points. Don't get me wrong. I love tattoos even though I don't have any. I get hard just thinking about the one on Lucia's rib cage. I use to love to run my fingers over the Lily and Jasmine tattoo when I would worship her perfect tits.

Someone snaps their bony fingers in front of my face, bringing me out of my reverie. I'd be grateful for it since the last thing I need to do in a crowded club is get hard thinking about my ex, but the person doing the snapping is Axl Black. Her ex. Also known as Robert Nichols on his birth certificate, but he once threatened to stab a reporter for bringing that up. So I do. "Yes, Robert?"

I see the anger explode behind his eyes, swimming in tequila. "My name is Axl. And who the fuck are you?"

"I'm no one you need to know," I reply without moving even though he's trying his best to intimidate me. He's standing over me, shoulders back, chest puffed out as much as a dude who exists on cigarettes, narcotics, and booze can puff. "You want to talk to her, try. If she says no, leave."

He looks over at Saffron, who is watching us over the top of the Marie Antoinette champagne glass hovering in front of her mouth. I slide my eyes to Axl because he is still glaring at me.

"I don't want to talk to her. She's a whore who dumped me for your geriatric ass, apparently."

"Why does everyone think I'm older than dirt?" I ask the universe, exasperated.

Saffron untangles herself from her useless girlfriends and stands after some intense wobbling. She points at Axl with the hand holding her Champagne so half of it sloshes onto the floor between us. "Did he just call me a whore?"

The girlfriends almost pretend to care as they watch the scene in front of them. Axl turns his drunken rage on her. "You leave me and start fucking this old fuck face in Greece like five minutes later? If it talks like a whore and acts like a whore, it's a whore."

"You've been broken up for months," I remind him, because drunk people hate facts. "And I work for her. I'm not involved with her."

"Stop calling me a whore, you whore!" Saffron yells back. Like a champ. I roll my eyes. This is going to get ugly. She points the champagne glass in my general direction. "Deal with him!"

"Not my job to keep your feelings from getting hurt," I remind her calmly. "Just your physical person. And this moron isn't putting a hand on you, are you Robert?"

"My name is *Axl*," he spits out through clenched teeth. "And no, I don't hit women."

"Probably because they'd hit you back, and you don't look like a guy who can take a punch," I reply and stand up. "Should we find out, Bob?"

"Who the fuck is Bob?" Saffron squeaks, baffled.

"He's going to hit me!" Axl bellows and his security guy marches over.

We look at each other, and I can tell neither of us gets paid enough for this shit. I turn and take her arm and pull her closer. The champagne glass tumbles to the floor, which is carpeted, so it doesn't break. What idiot carpets a floor in a bar? Her fake besties are both filming. "Cameras off or I will drop your phones off the balcony."

They both immediately put their phones in their laps. Saffron is slurring some words of protest but I ignore them and pull her up next to him. "You want this guy's attention, you got it thanks to a moral-less photographer in Greece. So what now?"

"I didn't want his attention," she lies. "Now punch him."

"Nope," I snarl at her and then drag her out toward the exit. She doesn't fight me, and thankfully, Axl's bodyguard ignores his demands that he punch me.

Once we get outside, the car is waiting for her, and I open the door and tell her to get in. She doesn't object. Her friends come stumbling out behind us calling her name. "Saff! Wait! Honey, wait!"

She pokes her head back out of the car. And here's where it gets ugly. Because Saffron is smiling with all the energy of a puppy at the dog shelter. Pick me! Love me! Blah blah blah.

"I'm okay," Saffron assures them.

They both blink. "Yeah. But, like, you gotta pay the bar tab. We drank two bottles of that champagne."

And the puppy at the shelter begging to be loved face morphs into the puppy who just got kicked face. Hell, even I feel for her now. "Of course. Nick?"

"Handled," I reply, and she slams the car door.

I turn to the bouncer who is guarding the VIP entrance and hand him a business card. "Saffron Kent owes you for two bottles of champagne. Can you call me to clear it up tomorrow?"

"Yeah." He nods. They're used to this kind of shit when they cater to celebs.

I turn to the girls and back to the bouncer. "Only two bottles of champagne. Not a fucking thing more."

His eyes slide to the two users and back to me with a nod. I push past the girls. "Wait! We need a lift home too."

"Call Uber," I snap and climb into the front seat next to the driver.

The drive home is mostly silent until we're about five minutes out. And then her gentle sobs reach my ears. Fuck. I turn my head and see her cradling her head in her hands. "Y'okay?"

"No." She manages to whisper between sobs. When she lifts her face, there is make-up everywhere but where she put it to begin with.

"Those girls are not your friends," I tell her. "And that guy is not the love of your life."

"I know both of those things," she replies, her voice suddenly sounding very sober, which makes her words even more sad. "But they're all I've got."

I sit with that for a minute. When we get to her house, I get out and open her door and even reach in to take her hand and help her onto the sidewalk. I look at her. "Do you need me to stay? In your guest room?"

I've done it before. On nights she's been too drunk or we've come in super late from a flight. But somehow offering right now feels like I'm opening up some kind of can of worms.

"You can stay," she nods, like I was asking to do it not offering. "Those girls will make their way back here though. Because they were supposed to spend the weekend. So, like, no guest room available. But my bed is big."

She steps into me, dropping a palm on my chest, near my heart. I shake my head. "I do not date clients."

"I've googled you, Nick," she reminds me. "The race car girl. Fireball."

"Using other people's unflattering internet nicknames means that yours are free to be used to," I warn her. And I'm irrationally annoyed by the fact she's trying to insult Lucia more so than the fact she's hitting on me, again. "So what will it be, Auto-tune Barbie? That's the one that's been plaguing you for a while."

"Fuck you."

"Saffron, this is not a working relationship I'm going to be able to continue if you don't figure your shit out," I warn her as she shoves me. "Or at the very least keep me the fuck out of it. I will lose my life if it means protecting yours, but I'm not going to lose my sanity dealing with your unsorted mental health. Got it?"

"Did you just call me insane?"

"No. I called you unsorted."

"What the fuck? You're fired!"

"Okay then," I unlock her front door and hold it open. She

stomps up the path and manages to stay upright despite the drunkenness and the four-inch heels.

She stops, only to slap me across the face. My whole body fills with so much rage I freeze. And then I close the gate behind her and make my way back to the street and my motorcycle.

I'm willing to bet that she won't even remember firing me in the morning. Or that if she does, she will beg my forgiveness. And I'll probably give it to her, because there's only one other job I want, and I can't have it.

I tug my helmet on and straddle the bike as my phone starts to buzz. I yank it out of my motorcycle jacket and see the name Bash Castera.

Or maybe I can have that other job.

"Bash? What is it?"

SIX

KLUTZY GIRL TRIPPED RUNNING

Lucia

"MISS CASTERA, CAN YOU REPEAT THAT?"

"Do I fucking have to?" I ask, and Frankie glares at me. So I sigh and look over at the two cops in the corner of the hospital room. "I went for a run. I noticed the car about a mile from the hotel. It was crawling along the road about twenty feet behind me. Headlights off. I think it was electric because it was completely silent. I only noticed it when I stopped to tie my shoelace and glanced behind me. It had also stopped. And I thought that was weird. But then it got creepy when I started to run and it started to move."

"Cars move when they are on the road," the police officer on the left says. Like I'm a fucking moron.

"Yes. So I stopped again. And it stopped again," I say, trying hard not to spit the words out through gritted teeth but this police officer is getting on my last nerve. "Is that normal? I was running on a sidewalk. Not in the street. Not in his way. And the sun had set. Is it normal for cars to drive with their lights off at night and stop at the same time as every person on the sidewalk does?"

"No," The second of the two cops says, and he looks almost apologetic. Or maybe just scared that I'm crazy. I'm not. I know what happened.

"And you didn't alert anyone?" The first, more skeptical, bigger-dick-energy cop asks.

"I texted my bodyguard as I was running," I explain and shift on the hospital gurney. The paper crunches under my butt. "And told him I was circling back and asked him to track my phone, just in case."

"Why wasn't he with you?"

"Because I wanted to be alone," I snap. The answer makes me look like an idiot, because it was an idiotic move. "Anyway, then I turned onto a small, dark street. Not on purpose but to get away from the car. I figured that the more side streets I took and turns I made, the less likely this guy would follow because it would be too obvious. But he did follow. And I was in the process of Google mapping the police station so I could run to it when I fell. The car immediately stopped so I just started screaming my head off, drawing attention so if he tried anything, I would have witnesses.

"And that's when people came out of their homes and the car drove away?" The second cop asks and I nod curtly.

"Perhaps next time you take him running, the bodyguard?" the first cop says. "Just in case."

"Are you going to do something about this or not?" Jack says stepping in between the officers and my bed. "Feel free to say no, but do it in writing so we have something for the lawsuit if she's attacked, followed, or hurt in any way between now and Monday when we leave your city."

Frankie's approving eyes land on her bodyguard. She is thrilled with him, and who could blame her? Mick is nowhere to be found. But I know he's in the hospital because he did show up at the place where I fell, and he's the one that alerted the police and drove me here to get my knee checked out.

The cops scowl at Jack, who doesn't look the least bit bothered, and ask to speak to him outside. He glances at Frankie, who nods. They leave the tiny room, and I'm envious. The place smells so strongly of cleaning products that it's giving me the beginning of a migraine. Frankie drops her purse on the floor and climbs up on the bed I'm sitting on. She sits right beside me and tries to side-hug me, but I jump down. My knee throbs a little, but it's nothing. I know real pain now since the burns from the race car crash. This knee ain't it.

"I'm not some panicked little girl with an over-active imagination. That car *was* following me," I insist and she nods.

"I believe you. I do. So does Jack and Billy and Mick," Frankie assures me calmly. "And Dad."

My heart plummets. I spin to face her, my braid flying. "You told Dad?"

"Of course, Lucia," Frankie's looking at me like I'm the insane one. She told Dad! He's going to drama-queen all over this. "And yes he's freaking out, but that's normal."

"Fuck." I hiss and shut my eyes so tightly I see stars. "He's going to fire Mick. Because I gave him the slip."

"Yeah probably, but that's on Mick. You shouldn't be able to give him the slip," Frankie says. "You wouldn't be able to give Jack the slip. Or Nick."

"Do not bring his name into this and make everything even worse," I moan. I start to walk aimlessly around the small room. It helps with the dull ache in my knee. "Well, at least I didn't have to get stitches. There's that."

Frankie looks down at the butterfly band-aide on my knee, right in the center of the kneecap. "You're still going to have to get approval from the F1 medics to race Sunday."

"I know," I turn to the door because Jack has opened it and is stepping inside.

"So the cops are filing a report. They're putting one undercover cop in our paddock, and I'm moving into the new hotel, with Lucia," He announces, blindsiding me.

"What new hotel? What about Mick?"

"Mick will stay at the old hotel, with Frankie," Jack advises, and he's texting on his phone at the same time.

"So we're swapping bodyguards?" Not the worst scenario. I just don't want to be responsible for Mick being fired. It really wasn't his fault I ditched him. I have a habit of making sure I get what I want, even when it bites me in the ass.

"For tonight, yes," Jack says. "Doctor has discharged you. Police are gone. Car is waiting in the loading bay. Frankie, Billy is out in front of emergency distracting the media that somehow found out she's here. You can meet him there and give a statement or whatever."

"Thank God for a boyfriend that enjoys being the center of attention," Frankie says with a grin. She grabs my hand before I can pull away and squeezes it. "Text me when you're settled in the new place."

I nod, and as we step out into the bland, bright hospital corridor, I follow Jack one way and Frankie heads the other, blowing me a kiss and calling, *"Baci!"*

Jack is blissfully silent the whole ride to the new hotel, and I just follow him like a well-trained pet. I assume my stuff has been moved, but I don't ask. And I'm right because when I get to the room I've been given, it's all there. "Mick moved your stuff."

I nod. Jack jerks a thumb toward the room to the left of my hotel room door. "I'm in here. Do not open the door for anything or anyone. I will text you before I come to get you in the morning. And if you feel like leaving this room, at any hour, for any reason, text me, and I will be outside your door before you can open it."

He turns and walks to his door without waiting for any kind of okay from me. Because it's not a request, it's an order. "You remind me of her last bodyguard."

"Judging by the way everyone still talks about him, I take that as a compliment," Jack gives me a small smile and motions for me to go back into my room.

I do and lock the door. This day can't end fast enough. The fact that media was at the hospital means every reporter in town is going to ask about this at the presser after practice. I'm going to have to think up an excuse that leaves out the mystery vehicle. Because that opens up a whole shit storm I do not want to deal with. And it makes me look like the hysterical, helpless girl. Which is how I felt looking at that car, squinting in desperation to read the license plate and being unable to make it out.

I text Frankie that I'm settled and heading straight to bed. I don't sleep for hours though, as I think about a story I can tell. All I keep circling back to is 'klutzy girl tripped running'. So I guess that's what I have to go with. And then I start thinking about Jack. He is confident and alpha in that subtle way like Nick. It's what attracted me to Nick from the start. The Alpha Male vibes that buzz like electricity off of him even though he appears as calm and placid on the outside as a sloth taking a sunbath.

Nick... with his dark hair, smooth, tanned skin, and shockingly light eyes. The broad shoulders and the torso that's rippled with muscle cut into muscle and... the look. The way his eyes said everything without his mouth getting involved... He could make me wet with just *that* look.

Great. Now I'm fucking horny. I flip over onto my back in the dark hotel room and open my eyes. Then I close them and let my hand slip into the only thing I'm wearing under these sheets - my underwear. I re-live, in my memory one of the times Nick and I were together. Not the last time.... That one is painful to think about. But the first time.

I'd been thinking of him a lot. More than I'd ever thought of anyone who had ever worked for our family. He started guarding Frankie when she was twenty. The problem was she was out in the world on her own at that point and steering clear of all things racing, so I didn't see him much. I thought about him a lot, though. The alpha-vibe thing he emanated felt like it was tuned to just my frequency, even though he didn't really act like I existed. Other than a hello or a good-bye, he didn't talk to me.

So I started talking to him, the way I talk best — like a smart ass. And that's when the smiles started coming. That's when I would catch him eyeing me from across a room. But it wasn't until the weekend my dad announced he had married Adelaide that we connected. Frankie and I lost our shit, obviously. Me more than Frankie, which was normal. I was always labeled the over-reacter even though I don't think I do it. I just don't sugar-coat my feelings to make them easier for others to swallow.

Anyway, I was furious and called Adelaide a gold-digger and questioned my father's morals because of her age. Okay, yeah, but she was... *is...* young. Frankie's age. He could have given birth to her. Well, my mother could have. Anyway, Dad demanded I leave the party he was hosting to surprise his nearest and dearest with the news. I refused, and he ordered Nick to carry me out, which Nick did. I screamed and yelled the whole time, but he took me down to the parking garage of the restaurant, tossed me in the back seat of his SUV, and I grabbed his jacket and pulled him in with me and kissed him like a wild animal. And he kissed me back the same way. And then he flipped me over, lifted my dress and slapped my ass before he turned me around again and went down on me.

Right there in a dark corner of fucking parking garage. It wasn't the first orgasm of my life, but it was the best. At that point. I let my mind take me right back to that moment now. Years later in this darkened, lonely hotel room. I try to remember exactly how the leather of the seat slipped against the silk of my dress. The way the expensive fabric of the blazer felt against the back of my legs as he threw them over his shoulders. The sting of his palm against my bare ass. My fingers do a feeble job of mimicking the heaven that was his tongue against my clit but it's enough tonight to get me there. I moan out his name and the memory and the orgasm are enough to relax me into sleep. Finally.

SEVEN
YOU'RE NOT JUST ANY BODYGUARD

Lucia

WHEN I WAKE up in the morning, I'm so eager to get the hell out of my hotel room before my father shows up that I fly through the shower, throw on my team logo clothes, and text Jack without wasting time on hair or the minimal make-up I dare to wear. True to his word, Jack is outside my door when I open it.

"Morning," he says. "Didn't think we'd be moving this early."

"I want to do my meditations and everything at the track," I tell him as we head down the hall to the elevator.

"And you're trying to avoid your dad, who is a late riser?" Jack asks, and I bite back a smile.

"Maybe," I mutter as we get in the elevator.

He doesn't respond, which I appreciate. Nick would throw some therapist-level words of truth at me right now, like I can't run from my problems or whatever. I lock myself in my private room at the paddock and start my meditations immediately.

Then I have a Zoom call with Carmyn, and then I jump right into the car for the first practice session of the Monaco GP.

I walk into the pit with my headphones on and sunglasses because, for some reason, that helps with my nerves. I don't take either off until it's time to put my helmet on. Out of the corner of my eye as I strap into the car, I see my dad starting to walk over, but Frankie stops him with a gentle hand on his arm. I focus on my breathing, and before I know it, I'm out on the track, and it goes well. I feel it in my bones, so when Frankie announces in my ear "Third fastest time on the track, Louie. Nice work!" I'm not surprised. I'm pumped.

"Awesome news!" I reply and I'm grinning.

Until my car is backed into the garage and I see him.

Nick.

Just behind my sister, shoulder-to-shoulder with my dad. Everything inside me crashes, like my car did when it hit that barrier last year. My insides burst into flames. Anger, lust, and longing all ignite. I yank off my helmet as Frankie jumps off the stool in front of her monitor and pulls off her headphones. "Lucia! Fantastic results."

"*Ma louloutte! J'ai tellement fière!*"

I ignore my father's praise entirely, partly because I can't stop looking at Nick. Holy hot tires, he is sexier than ever. I jump out of the car and storm out of the garage. My father tries to step in front of me, but I use my helmet as a shield and get around him. I hear Nick say, "I'll handle it."

I keep walking, right back to the paddock, into the building, and back to my room on the left. I open the door, but of course I can't close it because his body is in the way. I toss my helmet onto the couch and turn to face him. "Do not tell me that they fired Mick and hired you again."

"No, I won't tell you that," he replies, his voice as calm and casual as ever. He shoulder presses into the doorframe as he uses it to prop himself up. "I've never had to explain the obvious to you, Lucia, and I'm not about to start now."

"I do not agree to this!" I snap.

"That's fine," he replies. "No one is asking for your opinion."

I let out a strangled sound that's something between a groan and a scream and throw myself face down onto the couch. I figure he'll leave, but that's wishful thinking. I hear the door click closed, and his voice is closer than before when he speaks again. "Look, this is some Grade A serious stuff happening to you right now. I didn't send those flowers. Maybe the guy from your elevator incident did. Maybe it's someone else entirely. And maybe the person who followed you in a car is one of those two or some new psycho, but here's the deal Lucia. You have a target on your back. You know it. People think you can be played with. I am here to make sure it doesn't happen. So you can focus on the job and prove them all wrong."

"Mick was doing that."

"If Mick was doing that, I wouldn't be here," Nick replies calmly. "Don't make this a problem. You have enough of those as it is."

Blunt. And painful. Because he's essentially saying he's only back for the job. Not because he misses me. I mean I don't *want* him to miss me. Because I can't be with him, and it would be useless. I hate useless when it comes to emotions or anything else. Loathe it. But for some reason, it hurts anyway to know he didn't come back for me but for the job. And now I feel shame about masturbating to him last night because he probably hasn't even thought of me since he left, let alone got off to my memory.

"What is running through your head right now?"

I blink and roll over to face him, only I refuse to make eye contact. "I'm thinking I have a press conference in ten, so I should get my ass out there."

"Okay then," Nick nods, and I sit up and run my fingers through my hair, and it's only then I realize I drove with it loose. Well, pulled back in a ponytail but not a braid. "It's fine. There's no rule that it has to be braided, Lucia."

I hate that he knows what I'm thinking. I huff, disgruntled, and storm into the bathroom to braid it. I rub some serum on my face to massage out the lines from the helmet and straps, and I allow myself a light, natural layer of mascara and some clear gloss. I don't know if I'm doing it for the cameras or for Nick. That's a lie. I know I'm doing it for Nick. I don't want him to look at me all disheveled and think he made the right decision not missing me.

I leave the bathroom and breeze right by him. He follows behind, wordlessly. The other drivers are already taking seats, so I rush up on stage and grab my usual spot in the middle next to Spencer Samuels. He smiles at me and looks over my shoulder. "New guy?"

"Temporary," I reply.

"There are rumors floating," Spencer says. "You were at the hospital last night?"

"Yeah. Tripped running," I reply and look at him, figuring I'll find a smirk or a roll of his eyes. But his brown eyes are sympathetic.

"I once tripped on the treadmill," he tells me. "Went down like a bag of flour and flew off the back of it. In a gym filled with people. It was not my finest moment."

I smile. This guy continues to surprise me with how chill and decent he is. And nice. His brother, Sterling, isn't exactly warm and fuzzy. Or even polite. Speaking of, Sterling stands up. He's positioned on the other side of his brother. He turns to Billy. "Switch seats with me, dude?"

"Why?" Billy asks, confused. We're in a line, and someone positioned us the way they want us for the cameras because I guess that matters to someone. No one has ever argued before because who gives a shit where you sit?

"Because I want to sit there," Sterling says doing his best toddler impression. "Why does it matter? Can you just do me this solid?"

"Yeah. But if it doesn't matter, why move?" Billy asks again.

"Because he doesn't want to sit next to me," Spencer says flatly, his eyes straight ahead, not looking at his brother or Billy, or even me.

There's a heavy silence now. But Billy gets up and switches spots with Sterling. I have to wonder if the brothers had a tiff or if this is something deeper. It sure as hell feels deeper.

The press conference starts, and Spencer and I get the majority of questions, which I can tell — hell, everyone can tell — irks the shit out of Sterling. Sterling won the Championship the two years before Billy won last year. And he was Billy's only real competition. He's itching to get back on top, and Spencer, his kid brother just had the fastest time in practice.

"Lucia," some guy with an ESPN hat says. "You're not feeling any pain with your knee injury?"

"It's a scrape, not an injury," I correct him, hoping my face looks less bothered than I am. I hold up my hand, with the red, tight, angry skin. "This is an injury."

"I heard the police went to the hospital to speak with you?" A French reporter interjects in his heavy accent. "This does not usually happen for a scrape."

"There were police in the hospital that I happen to chat with," I reply without missing a beat. "Everyone in Monaco is a Formula One fan, it seems."

There's a dusting of guffaws around the room. The next question, blissfully, is for Billy. Sterling is getting tenser and tenser as the questions continue, and there isn't much for him. The guy is not comfortable with his role as second fiddle, that's for sure. If I acted like that, Frankie would put me back into media training asap.

Finally, the conference is over, and we can all leave. Sterling blows past everyone hurling his water bottle into the trash by the exit with such force the can almost tips. Reporters stop and stare. Spencer walks over and fishes the bottle out of the trash. "He's into recycling, I swear. He just forgot."

Some chuckles. I make eye contact with him, and he turns to me when I walk by. "I'm envious of your sibling not being a driver."

"You really want Sterling as your boss?" I lift an eyebrow and he laughs.

"On second thought..." he winks.

"Lucia," I turn and see Clara standing next to Nick. She's smiling. He's scowling. They look like a weird human version of drama masks. "We need to stretch your hand so the skin doesn't stiffen and the medical team wants to see your knee after being in the car."

"Okay," I walk over, and Clara's eyes flitter up to Spencer.

"Clara-Nita," he says with a nod as he passes her. Clara nods back, and her brown skin pinks just the slightest.

"Clara-Nita?" I repeat as we head out of the room behind him but head left instead of right. He's leaving the track. We're heading to the offices so strange doctors can stare at my knee.

"It's my full name."

"It's pretty," I tell her. "How does Spencer know it?"

She shrugs. "He must have heard Billy say it once."

"Lucia..."

"No talking," I snap at Nick. "I am not talking. To you. Unless my life is in imminent danger."

Clara's massive brown eyes somehow get bigger. But then she turns to Nick and smiles. "Good to see you again."

"You too," he says, and I don't need to turn around to know

he's smiling back at her. His voice changes when he's smiling. It's softer. It makes my heart jiggle in my chest like it's using a hula hoop.

The doctors that represent Formula One hmm and haw over my knee for way longer than necessary, but half an hour later I'm making my way out of the place and to the car with Nick. He's in step beside me, just a little more than arms-length away. The air is warm, but the vibe between us is chilly, to say the least. He has his aviators on so I can't see those stunning baby blues, but I know they're scanning everything around us.

"Lucia!" My father's voice comes from behind us.

Nick stops. I keep walking. Dad calls my name again. Then Nick says it. I keep walking. A few steps later Nick falls back into step with me. He doesn't speak, but I know he's unimpressed. His shoulders are a couple of inches higher than they should be. His mouth set in a flat line. He looks tanned, I note. Like he's been on vacation or something.

It's a long, uncomfortable drive to the hotel. The silence is suffocating. I pick at a thread in the back seat upholstery and stare out the window. Monaco's mountainous terrain that is covered in glitzy apartments most of the world can't afford blurs by. As Nick slows to a stop before turning off the main road and onto the hotel driveway, he shoves his aviators into his brown hair and finally speaks. "Do you want me to bring you a snack before your nap? Some grapes without the skins or apples with chunky peanut butter?"

Our eyes lock through the rearview. "What am I a toddler?"

"Sure seems that way."

"Fuck you," I snap.

"Do you know how many people would kill to have a father so concerned about their well-being that he pays a trained professional to keep them safe?" Nick asks, but I don't answer, so he keeps talking. "Stupid amounts of money, by the way. And you throw a tantrum over it?"

"You're not just any bodyguard," I spit back.

"No. I'm not," Nick retorts. "I'm the best. The absolute fucking best, so stop being a toddler and show some gratitude to your dad."

I get out of the car and slam the door. He follows, of course, but we don't say a word, and it feels really good to slam my hotel suite door in his face when we get up there. In all honestly, though, I'm feeling more humiliation than rage. And panic. How am I going to cope with him back in my life? It feels impossible.

EIGHT

BEAUTY, GRACE, AND HELLFIRE

Nick

I ADMIT CALLING her a toddler was a bit over the line. But she was acting like one. I run my hands through my hair as I lean against the wall next to the door that adjoins our suites and wonder if I should let them know I can hear them. I decide to just let her go. I know Lucia. When she's bent out of shape about something, she needs to vent. Otherwise, she gets all twisted inside like a pretzel. And there will eventually be a Chernobyl-sized emotional explosion.

I wonder how Bash hasn't figured her out by now. He's obviously known her much longer than me. But yet he still handles her like he's fumbling a football. Like right now when he tells her to calm down.

"Calm down?" Lucia parrots. "Would you calm down if someone on your staff called you a child?"

"He's not on your staff," Bash barks back. "He's on mine. When you pay for your own security, you can be offended."

"You want me to pay for security? I will pay for security!" She bellows. "Gladly."

"No," Bash replies. "Because you'll just fire him."

"Exactly! Because I am sick of being trailed by someone everywhere I go. No other driver on the grid has a bodyguard. I've been dealing with this for far too long," Lucia says, and I can feel her wrath through the wall. "And Nick left for a reason. That reason hasn't changed. He shouldn't be here."

"Lucia, I am going to put it to you simply," Bash says and his voice drops an octave but still filters through the wall. For a five-star hotel, it's sure got thin walls. "No other driver is female. No other driver has a stalker. And Nick is back because he's the best, and I am not risking your life with anyone who isn't the best."

"It's not a stalker," Lucia argues. "It's some... I don't know, stupid fan. Misogynistic loser. But he's not serious. He could have run me over easily the other night, and he didn't."

My chest feels tight as she says that. I want to scream at her over that. It really isn't Michael's fault she ditched him. Lucia and Frankie are very good at sneaking around. I learned early with Frankie, and luckily, she never seemed to mind my presence after the first year. I'm mad that Lucia isn't taking this threat seriously.

Their voices lower a little bit and become murmurs I can't make out. But then Lucia is yelling again. And this time, I don't think she's overreacting. "I can't even believe you would say that! Give up racing? What the hell is wrong with you?"

"Lucia, you had a crash that should have killed you. And now you've got someone who wants to do God knows what," Bash argues back. "Your luck will run out, and let's be honest, you've accomplished what you wanted. You *are* an F1 driver. The first female in decades. Probably the last one for decades.

We can get you a position on the team that doesn't put you in danger."

"No. I'm a driver, Dad. Just like you were. That's what I am, and I'm nowhere near past my prime," she argues, and her voice is loud. But trembling now. She's so angry she wants to cry. I get it. I would be too if my parent was telling me to give up on a dream I had just barely achieved. "I am not retiring. And it breaks my fucking heart you don't believe in me."

"I believe in you, Lucia. I also believe that this sport can and will kill you," Bash yells. "And I am not going to survive losing you."

"I am not going to die because of driving or because of this loser trying to scare me," Lucia insists. "And don't worry because you've got a new kid coming to replace me if I do. Now leave."

"How can you say that?" Bash sounds as wounded as I figured he would.

"How can you say what *you* said?" She yells back.

Okay, time to play referee. I twist off the wall so I'm in front of the door that joins our rooms. I knock once — hard — and then turn the knob and step into her suite. Bash is standing with his arms folded across his barrel chest by the door to the hall. Lucia is standing hands on hips by the bar. They both turn and glare at me like I'm the problem. I guess that's fair.

"This has gone on long enough," I announce. I turn to Lucia because even though she is the less rational one in this argument, if I talk to Bash, it will only make things worse. "Can you and I have a moment please?"

"No."

I was expecting that. I keep staring at her. Bash grumbles something.

"Bash, I have to quit if Lucia really wants that," I tell him, head still turned to his daughter. I need to see her reaction.

"This is ultimately her life, although I appreciate your vote of confidence. And it's a fair assessment, I am the best. I know other people who can handle this and would be excellent. I can give you their names and numbers and make sure someone takes this gig. Lucia isn't exactly the hardest person to work for."

"Are you sure about that?" Bash grumbles, a dig at his daughter, and I sigh. He sure knows how to throw gasoline on a fire.

"If I'm such a pain in the ass, Dad, feel free to stop talking to me forever," she snaps and storms into the bathroom, slamming the door behind her.

"I can't keep doing this," Bash announces once she's locked away. He scrubs his silver beard angrily. "I love that girl with all my heart, and she's never been easy, but this… I don't know how to communicate with her at all anymore."

"I think it's easier than you think," I reply softly, hoping she doesn't overhear. I know Lucia hates when people talk about her instead of to her. "Number one, don't tell her to quit racing. She just made her lifelong dream come true, Bash. And I know what you think. You think well, I made it to F1 too, but if I'd had a crash like that and a stalker, I would have bowed out and happily jumped into the back end of the business."

"Exactly!" He gestures with his arms out of pure relief at being understood.

"But you aren't a female," I remind him. "People would give you the win. They'd say 'he had a tough couple of obstacles, and retiring makes sense, but no one can say he didn't make it.' But for her, the narrative will be 'poor girl couldn't cut it. It's too much for a woman to handle. It's a shame she couldn't make her mark.'"

He opens his mouth to argue but quickly snaps it shut. Then he scrubs his face again and lets out a low hiss of French swear words. I nod and give him a sympathetic smile. He swears again, but it's directed at himself, I can tell. His shoulders sag as the fight slips out of him. I grab his shoulder and squeeze it. His eyes cloud. "I can't let you quit. I made you leave another job to come here."

"You didn't make me do anything," I assure him. "But if she really doesn't want to work with me I am not going to make her. And you shouldn't either. Lucia has got the best but toughest year of her career ahead of her. We don't need to make it more stressful."

I mouth the words, "She won't fire me" without a sound because I would bet my life she's got her ear pressed to that bathroom door. Bash nods reluctantly. "Well, I'll leave you to discuss with your boss."

He claps my shoulder, turns and leaves the hotel room. I exhale slowly and walk over and throw myself down on her couch. I grab the untouched tray of amenities and start to peel a banana. The bathroom door opens, and her beautiful face pops out.

Lucia Castera is a stunning woman. She reminds me of a wild horse, and I could never tell her that because being called a horse isn't exactly a woman's idea of a compliment. But I was really into Westerns as a kid. Still am, actually. And I have seen footage of wild horses in America. They're mesmerizing. Sometimes I watch YouTube videos of them to relax at the end of a shitty day. I watched this one video of wild mustangs on Pryor Mountain in Montana around the same time I met Lucia.

The horse was on top of a ridge, at sunset. A gentle breeze had the wildflowers at its feet swaying and the sky behind it was a fiery pink. Everything about the scene was tranquil. The horse was lean but muscled and was a color called Rabicano, which is the color of Lucia's hair. And this horse was bucking wildly, like a phantom rider was on its back. But there was nothing else on that ridge, not even another horse. And for some reason watching this stunning Mustang fight the breeze or whatever it was agitated with, reminded me of Lucia. And that image is what I see every time I look at her. Beauty, grace, and hellfire all rolled into the prettiest package the gods could think to create.

"You're still here?" Her tone isn't as confrontational as it's been most of the day.

"Yup." I take a bite of the banana.

"Just chilling? Eating my amenities?" She steps completely out of the bathroom and folds her arms like a prissy schoolmarm.

"You hate bananas," I remind her and take another bite. "Unless they're in a smoothie and hidden by other fruits."

She makes a hmpf sound and unfolds her arms. "I guess you need sustenance before you have to pack all your shit and leave."

"If you're firing me then yeah, I guess I do," I reply without moving. I finish the banana with one last bite and toss the peel into the trash a few feet away. I don't miss. "It's your call."

She stares at me. I still love the feel of her eyes on me. The woman is formidable, to say the least, and it kills me that people gleefully try to tear that out of her. I try to focus on the job. I'm not here to give her orgasms anymore or protect her ego. Unfortunately.

"Why do you even want this job? Everyone says you had a gig with that pop star named after a spice. Sage or Cumin or whatever the hell."

I smile. She knows Saffron's name. Her last hit song was on Lucia's favorite workout playlist last season.

"She's a nightmare. You aren't." That softens her. I can see it in her eyes. "I didn't quit because I didn't want to be around you, Lucia. I quit because *you* didn't want me around you. And with Frankie working full-time for the team and you racing on it, I couldn't keep working and stay away from you."

"I didn't say you couldn't be around," she argues because semantics are important to Lucia. She sees the world as black and white. "I just said we couldn't keep..."

"Fucking?"

She makes a face and her cheeks get rosy. "Yeah."

"Well, it is..." I stop and stand up. I need a second to stop myself from saying the truth and find a way to make the lie believable. "I needed breathing room. But I had it. And now you are in some serious shit whether you want to admit it to yourself or not. And your dad is terrified. Frankie is too. She just knows better than to tell you. And they think I'm your best bet at making sure whoever this person is doesn't get to you further. And they're right. You know it too. So you can fire me. I will go if you do. Because I want you to be happy. But someone else will protect you, and I'll make sure it's someone who doesn't let you sneak out."

"I'm never doing that again," she promises.

"Cool. So do you prefer a male or female bodyguard?" I ask. "I have incredible candidates either way."

"What will you do?" She asks and her voice is private-Lucia. The softer, sweeter, relaxed woman that very few people know exists.

"I'll find work elsewhere."

She takes a couple of deep, slow breaths and I wait, patiently because I already know I'm not going anywhere. She doesn't want to get rid of me. She just wishes she did. "You can stay. I mean, clearly, it doesn't rattle you, so it's fine."

"It seems to rattle you, though," I reply. Her eyes find mine. They're so dark and endless, and I could look into them forever.

"No. I'm just... I was blindsided. No one told me they were firing Mick," she admits. "And I feel like I cost him a job."

"He already had one foot out the door," I tell her as I walk around the coffee table. "That was part of the problem. And I spoke with him today before he got on his flight. He doesn't blame you, and he knows this is for the best."

"If you talk to him again, tell him I'll give him a good reference. Always," Lucia says, and I nod.

"So it's settled," I say.

"Settled."

We stare at each other. There's so much to say, but she doesn't want to hear it. She is over me. I'm not entirely sure she felt enough for me to even require getting over it. That stings, but I knew that was the risk I was taking when I let myself fall for her. I clear my throat. "I'll be in my room if you need me. And do not set foot out of this hotel room without telling me. If you order room service, I'll be the one answering the door. Then I'll leave you to eat in peace."

"Okay." She sounds a little defeated, but mostly I hear acceptance in her tone.

Without another word, I head into my room and shut the adjoining door. Fuck. This is not going to be easy, and it has nothing to do with her attitude.

I text Bash and tell him I'm sticking around and then I start to peel out of my clothes for a shower. Lucia will likely be taking one too if her routine is similar to last year on practice days. And then she'll order room service or maybe head to the hotel restaurant.

I have time at the moment. Enough to rinse off and jerk off to thoughts of her so when I'm with her again I can be more focused. I hope.

NINE

GET OFF ON THE ELEVENTH FLOOR

Nick

I'VE GOT my eyes closed. The spray from the shower is warm as it pelts my chest. My left hand is curled around my rock-hard cock and the right is pressed to the tile as I lean into it to keep myself upright. Behind my eyelids, all I see is Lucia. Sometimes I focus on one specific time we spent together. But other times, like right now, my brain mashes all the best times into one high-light reel.

Lucia that first time I ate her out on the backseat of that SUV. The way her legs trembled on my shoulders and she arched her back as she came. Lucia spread out, perfectly and totally naked on my hotel bed. It was before Frankie started working for Mirabella Racing. When she was still an influencer and doing an event in Prague. It was the off-season for F2, and Lucia decided to surprise Frankie with a visit. But talked her way into my hotel room and spent the night there with me before ever telling Frankie she was even there. That was the first time we spent an entire night together. I still remember waking up in the morning and finding her sprawled out next to me, and thinking it felt *good*.

But I digress, and if I'm going to come, which I want to — desperately — I need to concentrate on the naked parts, not the feelings part. My brain fast-forwards to another memory. Lucia on all fours while my dick pounds into her and she begs me to go harder.

Yep. That will do...

My balls tighten. The hot tingle of an orgasm starts its way up my shaft and...

"Oh shit!"

My eyes fly open. Lucia is standing on the other side of the shower door, both hands clasped over her mouth. Our eyes connect. It's too late to shove my orgasm back down, so I come, even though my grip has loosened and my hand isn't pumping. I groan, then growl in frustration and turn away from her.

"Fucking hell!" I hiss and fight to keep my knees from buckling. At this point, I'm not even sure they're buckling from the orgasm. It might be from embarrassment.

I take a shuddering breath when my body is done with the worst orgasm of my life, and rinse off as quickly as possible before I get out of the shower and march into my bedroom while tying a towel around my waist.

The adjoining door to Lucia's suite is ajar, but she's not there. She's on my couch, with her face buried in her hands. I run a hand through my dripping hair, shoving it back off my forehead. The style is great, dried. Short on the sides and long on top. But when it's soaking wet, it's like being a sheepdog in need of a close encounter with some clippers.

"What the hell are you doing?" I sound angry, but I'm not. I'm just embarrassed.

"I got a DM, and I freaked and I didn't think..." Lucia croaks out through her hands. She finally lifts her face, but just long enough to make brief eye contact and then she drops it into her hands again. "I'm sorry. I shouldn't have barged in here, and I definitely shouldn't have wandered into your bathroom. You didn't close the door, so I mean I saw... I just... I shouldn't..."

"What DM?" I ask rounding the conversation back to something other than the fact my ex-bed buddy just watched me shoot a load onto the shower door. "Show me."

She pulls her phone from the side pocket in her leggings and holds it up to me. The screen is black, and of course, it wants facial recognition. To be honest, I don't want to look her in the eye again, so I take a chance that her password is the same as it was when we were hooking up. It is. The screen opens, and I pull up Instagram. It's the only social media Lucia has. I go into her DMs and find the message she must be talking about easily.

It says *Where are you jogging next? Watch out for traffic!*

They sent a picture next. It's of Lucia getting into the SUV at the track after practice and media today. I'd say it's not complimentary because she's frowning and is half in the car, with her ass in the air. The account is a burner. No picture. No posts. No followers. But they are following every single Formula One driver and one Team Principal — Frankie.

I spit out a few swear words and then walk over to my bed, and grab my phone from the nightstand. I take a screencap of the whole thing and this account and send it to myself. Then I message Frankie and tell her to block the account and I will explain later. And then I pull up my dummy social media account and follow the dude. I have one with a picture of the back of my head in a baseball cap and a fake name so that I can investigate people that follow my clients without suspicion.

"What are you doing?' Lucia asks.

"Handling it," I mutter. I'm going to talk to each driver at the track tomorrow, and tell them to block this putz. Yeah, the person can just make a new account and do this all over again, but at least it'll create work for them. Sometimes, if the person is just a harmless troll, the work isn't worth it to them, and they go away. I don't think this one is harmless, though.

"Handling it like you handled yourself back there?" Lucia asks.

She's sort of smiling, like she's testing the waters to see if this is something we can kid about. It's not. So I ignore her comment and toss her back her phone. "I blocked him for you. And I'm having Frankie block him because he's likely using other drivers' accounts and her to help track you."

She nods, and I notice she's changed into leggings and a workout top. She's got a hoodie on, but it's open, and her bare stomach is the first thing my eyes go to. I used to love to kiss my way down her flat, hard abs. Lucia is in the best shape because of the job, but she's also incredibly delicate looking with narrow hips, and a tiny chest, and little hands, but I know she could probably wrestle a bear and have a shot at winning. The contrast of her delicate looks and her fierce abilities is a sexual mind-fuck I never got tired of.

"Hello!" She waves her hand in the air like a student trying to get the teacher's attention.

"Why did you change?" I ask.

"I was going to go to the gym," Lucia replies, and I'm about to blow up. She knows it and holds up a hand to shut me up. "I was going to tell you. And I wasn't going alone. I texted Clara, and she said she'd go with. And I was fine with you standing there watching us if you wanted to join. I swear I wasn't going to sneak off. But then I opened my Instagram and... I freaked. It's why I rushed in there. I'm sorry. Again."

I take a deep breath and will myself to shove down all the embarrassment. "It's fine. Nothing you haven't seen before. I don't think you should go to the gym."

"But I can't stop training!" Lucia argues, and I know she's right.

"Let me make a call and clear the gym so you and Clara are the only people in there," I say. "And then I'll get dressed. Because you aren't going anywhere without me."

"I didn't think I was," Lucia replies. She stands up and walks over to the adjoining door, but she pauses on the threshold. Her eyes are on the carpet, not me, when she adds. "And for the record, I haven't seen that before. You've never jerked off in front of me. Shame."

And before I can do anything more than let my jaw drop, she's gone and the door is closed. And I'm fighting another hard-on.

TWO HOURS later I'm listening to Clara and Lucia talk about some television show they're obsessed with. I don't watch television unless it's live sports, so I have no fucking clue what they're talking about. But I think that this Alex woman has to be a bit of a nutter if she's running away from her fiancé in the middle of the jungle to be with some American leopard hunter. Clara doesn't find it nuts. She's absolutely mooney-eyed as she talks about the storyline. I don't know Clara well, so I guess I had no idea she's a hopeless romantic.

As soon as we leave the gym, which is on the third floor of the hotel, Clara hits the down button, and I hit the up one at the elevator bank. She hugs Lucia. "Thanks for calling. I needed the distraction. See you tomorrow at the track."

Lucia waves as Clara gets into the elevator. "Bye, guys!"

Our elevator opens as hers closes, but it's not empty. Lucia steps forward, but I grab her wrist and smile at the older couple inside. "Go ahead."

The elderly gentleman nods and punches the close button.

Lucia moans in protest. "You really think that couple old enough to be my grandparents are going to give us trouble?"

"No, but what if he has one too many neat whiskeys at the bar after dinner later and mentions he saw that female driver get off on the eleventh floor?" I ask quietly.

She doesn't answer, and when I look down at her, she's fighting a smile. She looks up at me through her lashes. "I haven't gotten off on the eleventh floor yet. But you have."

A new elevator in the bank of three opens, and it's empty, so she steps in. Still grinning. I barely recover from her snark before the doors start to close. I manage to squeak in next to her before they do. I fold my arms over my black T-shirt. No need for the whole bodyguard outfit, which is usually black T-shirt or button down, black jacket, and black pants. I'm only wearing the T-shirt and a pair of charcoal grey joggers. She is still smiling.

"Is there any way I can convince you to forget you ever saw that?"

"No." She replies and looks up at me again. "That's gonna stick with me a while."

"Great," I mutter as the doors open on our floor. Once again, I have to reach for her wrist and hold her back so I can get off first.

She doesn't complain or argue. Not even one of her trademark huffs. And for some other reason I'm not looking to decipher at the moment, I don't let go of her wrist as we walk down the dimly lit hallway to our rooms. I can feel her pulse under my fingertips, and it's slightly elevated. Not abnormal as she was just working out. And her skin is dewy from that. And warm.

We get to her door, and she swipes the key card. I step in and she follows. I let go of her wrist to do a quick tour of the place and make sure it's empty and there are no new packages or gifts. The staff have been told to hold anything at the front desk, but I don't rely on someone listening to orders. The place is just as we left it. I turn to her. She's pulling a bottle of blueberry smoothie out of the bar fridge. "Are you ordering in or going out for dinner?"

"Was going to order room service," she says between sips of the purple juice.

"Order it to my room," I tell her. "I'll bring it to you."

"Okay. I'll order later," she says. "I'll order dinner for you too when I do."

I don't give her an order because the woman is familiar with what I'd pick from a room service menu. We've shared enough meals.

Something between us is different. It's like her walking in on me cut the tension between us on top of humiliating me. Oh well, I'll pay that price if we can continue to be on good terms. Even though it kind of hurts a little to be nothing but professional with her.

I head to the door that connects our rooms and pull it open. As I'm about to close it, she asks. "Can we leave it cracked a bit?"

"Yeah," I say. "Sure."

It's rare that Lucia shows a sign of weakness. This woman nearly burned to death, and to this day, she hasn't cried in front of me about that. And when I did, well fuck, that was the death of us. Or proof there never really was an us. Anyway, if she's willing to say something vulnerable in front of me, I am not about to shoot it down. "No problem."

It's only ten minutes later that I realize I misread the situation. I'm on my couch reading the five different text messages from Saffron. All of them grow in anger and rudeness as she expresses how pissed off she is that I 'just up and quit' for 'no reason at all'. She must be day-drinking.

I toss my phone onto the cushion beside me and cross the

room to get sparkling water out of the minibar. I'm a foot from the cracked door, and that's when I hear her. A gentle moan.

Is she stretching? She and Clara went pretty hard on the weights. She must be sore. But then Lucia moans again, and my dick twitches. Because it's *that* kind of moan. I slowly move until I'm just over enough from the bar to see through the sliver of open space into her room. The view is the hallway, corner of the couch, open door to the bedroom, and bed. And on that bed is Lucia Castera. She's naked, on all fours with her ass up and pointed directly at me, and she's got her left hand between her legs.

Holy shit.

She moans again. Louder. And the moan ends in a word. My name. She wants me to catch her. She's asking me to. I push the door wider and walk through it, crossing the living room in five long strides. As I get closer I hear another noise. A gentle hum. And then I see it. The hot pink toy she's holding, and working in and out of herself.

Now I'm leaning on the door frame to the bedroom, because I swear to God I will tip over if I don't. This is... *so fucking hot.* She pants a little and whimpers and then says my name again. "Nick."

"You rang?" My voice is thick and as hard as my cock. I sound pissed off, but I'm not. I'm frustrated. Sexually.

She startles a bit, obviously having no clue I was already there. But she doesn't stop, which proves it's exactly what she'd hoped would happen. She drops her chest and shoulders onto the bed and her legs slide down too. Her hand stays between her legs, pressed between her and the bed, and the toy keeps humming. She pushes her hips into the bed.

"What are you doing?" I demand but my voice is anything but ferocious.

"What you did," she says.

I walk right up to the edge of the bed. Her head is tilted to the side, right cheek pressed into the mattress just under the pillows. Her dark hair has been released from its ponytail, and a few curls are splayed across her cheek, blocking her pretty face from view. I reach down and brush them back. Thick, jet-black eyelashes flutter, and those big, endless brown eyes find mine. She is going to come. I can see it in the serious glint reflected back at me. Lucia takes her orgasms very seriously.

And something in me crawls up from the ashes. Something wild, and raw, and impossibly naive. But she wants me here. She's calling my name. I know that none of this makes sense. Our relationship always had an expiration date. And now, protecting her and fucking her, that's a whole new level of complicated. And, in the end, she doesn't want me for more than sex. She made that abundantly clear. And that crash made it crystal clear to me that I love her. So, yeah, I should turn and walk out of the room, and pretend this never happened.

But I don't. I kneel beside her and when her mouth opens in a gasp as her orgasm begins, I kiss her.

TEN

BOUNDARIES SUCK

Nick

"YOU SHOULDN'T BE HERE," she whispers against my lips when she's done coming.

"You were calling my name," I remind her.

"Oops," she murmurs and then I kiss her again.

It's long and hard and a battle. Our kisses are always a battle, and it's the hottest thing ever. Lucia is an alpha female in bed. She knows exactly what she likes and isn't afraid to demand it. I have never been with someone who doesn't pretend to be a delicate flower or a cutesy vixen. Lucia is neither. And both. It depends on her mood, and that's the thing, she is authentic. And it makes me come harder than I ever thought possible.

As our mouths break apart so we can do that silly essential thing called breathing, she starts to roll over. I'm still kneeling by the bed and my eyes devour every naked inch of her that's now exposed to me. Her perky tits, her erect nipples, her neatly trimmed little bush. The dark red pigment of the skin on the hand that's still holding the toy that's still inside her but no longer vibrating.

I reach forward and grab that tiny wrist of hers again, before she can pull the toy out. She stills and her eyes shift to find mine. "Did that satisfy you?"

"A little."

"Do I satisfy you more?"

"You used to," she admits. "But maybe I'm remembering wrong. It's been a while."

I slip my hand between her legs. Moving her fingers away, I take hold of the toy. Her eyes flutter and her legs widen, giving me more access. My dick is rioting in my pants. "Want me to remind you?"

"Yes."

I pull the toy from her and toss it across the room, then I yank my t-shirt up and over my head as I climb onto the bed, and onto her. Her hands wrap around my neck and her fingers thread themselves right into my hair. Lucia loves my hair and doesn't try to hide it. I'd be lying if I said I didn't think of her every damn time I walked into a barber and led with "Just a little trim. Don't change a thing."

She yanks gently on the strands, and my balls tingle. I balance on one forearm and try to grind into her at the same time I'm pulling down my joggers. It's not my smoothest trick but I manage to get it done and play with her clit a little too. Win, win.

She's kissing my chest and then my neck and finally my lips again. Then, when I manage to get my pants and boxer briefs to my ankles, she wraps her legs around my waist and tilts her pelvis, bringing all the right body parts together. I grunt and rub my shaft against her smooth skin, wet center. Still balancing on a forearm, I wrap my other hand around her long, delicate neck and pull my lips from her. Her eyes flutter open.

"One question."

"And then you'll fuck me?" God her voice is so needy, I almost skip the question. But it's important.

"Have you been with anyone since me?"

She blinks and I can see the lust slipping out of those wide brown eyes like sand slipping through an hourglass. "Does it matter?"

Yeah, it fucking matters. I couldn't think of touching someone else. That's what I want to say. But the fact is even if she told me she'd fucked forty guys in the three months I've been gone, it wouldn't stop me from wanting her. "I'm fucking you until you're good and satisfied no matter what Lucia. But whether or not it's with a condom is the debate."

We have never used condoms. She told me she'd been on the pill since she was fifteen thanks to Bash being a terrified, over-protective, but sensible single dad. And I was her first in a year and she'd been tested twice in that time frame as part of her regular physicals. And I hadn't been with anyone in longer than that and had all the tests too.

"That vibrator you just hurled across the room is the only thing that's been below my belly button since you left," she replies.

"Good," I shouldn't say it, but I guess tonight is a night of shouldn'ts.

"Now can we get to the fucking?" She requests. "Or do I have to go get that toy again?"

I shut her up by kissing her.

I honestly didn't take this job with the hopes that I'd be in this position again. But I also knew when I accepted that if she wanted sex again, I would give it to her. I don't consider myself weak for that. I love her. She doesn't love me, but I will take what I can get. For now. I know one day, this won't be enough. But for now, it's something. And I need it.

And as she snakes a hand between us and wraps it around my cock without a second of hesitation, it's clear she's more than happy to oblige. She gives my hard, aching shaft a long, slow tug and I arch my back and nip her bottom lip.

She smiles, but her hand stills, and I drop my eyes.

"My turn for a question."

"If I'd been with someone else, I would have just gone and gotten a condom," I tell her.

"That's not my question," Lucia replies and squeezes my cock. I grunt again. "What were you thinking of in the shower? When you came?"

"You," I confess and nip at her jawline. "And all the things I've ever done to your perfect little pussy."

"Time to give you more material for future showers," Lucia murmurs.

She's wet, which is expected after the session with her littler battery-powered helper. I want to tease her and taste her and make this long and deliciously drawn out, but I'm also impatient as fuck. And this is an opportunity I honestly didn't think she would give me again. So I yank her one leg up over my shoulder, and as she lets go of my cock I slide right into her. All the way in one glorious thrust. Lucia's hands move to her tits and she pinches her nipples. "Fuck I've missed this."

That is the hottest thing she could say to me. She reaches up and rakes her fingers through my hair again. My lips crash down on hers and our tongues tangle. I let myself drown in the feel of her hot, wet heat around my cock. And I realize, I don't just want to feel it, I want to see it.

I pull back, kiss her calf which is still up, over my shoulder, and drop her leg to the bed. I lean back on my heels, grab her ass in both hands and yank her up into my lap. She sits up, wraps her arms around my neck, and slides down onto my cock again.

"You're..." *beautiful, perfect, heaven...* But I can't say those things. They aren't what Lucia wants to hear when she's naked. Or ever. "Fucking hot."

She smiles and throws her head back. I use it as an invitation to worship her perky little tits with my mouth. As soon as I bite down on her nipple, I feel her pussy clench and stars erupt behind my eyes. I fight them off. I will not come before her. I refuse.

She's whispering my name now. Over and over, more and more urgent with each pass. She's close. I give her left nipple the same bite I gave her right before pulling back and letting my hand slip down her smooth torso to where we're joined. I rub my thumb over her clit and her back arches as her fingernails dig into the back of my neck and she comes so hard she almost takes me with her. Almost.

I fight it off again, just long enough to watch Lucia finish coming apart and then I flip us down onto the bed, her back hitting the mattress with a bounce, and I get four or five more thrusts in before I come so hard I almost black out.

I stay on top of her for a while, just struggling to catch my breath and have my muscles solidify again. As soon as I roll off of her, she jumps off the bed and grabs a hotel bathrobe off the bench at the end of the bed. She's smiling, and since Lucia doesn't do fake, I know it's sincere. "That was..."

"Incredible?"

"Yeah. As always." Her smile starts to wane. "But... I mean, should we chalk it up to a walk down memory lane? Because you work with me now, not my sister. And so this is... well, I want to say it just makes it more convenient to pick up where we left off. But it's also more complicated if we keep doing this, right?"

I put my hands behind my head and watch her. She's staring right at me. Her expression is calm, but her fingers are relentlessly twisting the tie on the robe. "Yeah. It would be more complicated. Plus, you didn't want to keep doing this."

I sit up and try not to remember that last night we spent together in Paris. I don't even realize that she was holding onto hope until her face falls flat. "Yeah. I didn't. For a reason."

She walks over to the bathroom but pauses on the threshold. "Okay well, can we just forget this happened?"

"Can we?"

I stand up and yank my pants and underwear back up, since they were still at my ankles. She watched me do up my belt. "Okay well, like, not forget but... move on. Go back to being just driver and bodyguard? Like we were an hour ago?"

"Whatever works for you, Lucia," I reply and I say it as gently as possible.

"Okay. Cool." She nods, but she looks a little shaken. Like she wanted a different response. Did she want me to argue? Lucia isn't one for games. "I'll shower and order dinner."

I nod and head back into my hotel room. This time I push the door so it's not closed, but almost. She pops her head in ten minutes later to say dinner is on its way up. I get a knock at my door fifteen minutes later, wheel in the cart, and tip the room service guy. She ordered a steak salad for her and a Cajun chicken one for me. I knock on the door. She's curled up on the couch watching race footage for Monaco from other years.

"Awesome!" She says, sitting up. Lucia changed into her pajamas, which are a grey tank top and matching pants with little white stars on them. She's letting her hair air dry from the shower, which means it's starting to form loose ringlets. It's my favorite look of hers — natural. Wild. Free.

I put her salad and the jug of lemon water they brought down on the table in front of her. She notices I don't have anything else in my hands. "Are you... going to join?"

She knows the answer is no, which is why her question is

clouded with confusion. I smile at her reassuringly. "No. I kind of left my last job in an abrupt manner, and the client is texting me non-stop."

"Saffron Kent," she says.

"The one and thankfully only," I reply. "The world does not need more than one of her."

That gets me a small smile. I walk back to the adjoining door. "See you in the morning, unless you need something."

"Okay. Sure."

And then I spend the rest of the night alone, wishing I was next door. Boundaries suck.

ELEVEN

LITTLE SAMUELS

Lucia

IT'S NOT WEIRD. I mean... it's so not weird that it's weird. And I hate that. But I refuse to let it distract me. It's been two days since Nick and I had sex. Nothing more has happened. He is just my plain, old bodyguard. I mean, I talk to him more than I did Mick, but that's the only difference. Enjoyable actually. I look forward to seeing him every morning.

But he hasn't opened that adjoining door once. And I haven't asked for it to be open because... well, I am feeling rejected. And that's insane because I'm the one who ended things with him, and I'm the one who insinuated that this relapse shouldn't happen more than once.

I hate complicated feelings. Luckily, I have Carmyn. She explains to me that there is nothing wrong with casual sex, and I shouldn't feel guilty for having it — with anyone. I knew this, but it's still nice to hear. She also, unfortunately, agrees with me that because Nick is working for me now and not my sister, and he's my ex-bed buddy, it makes it complicated sex by default.

And I was right to think twice about continuing it. It made for quite a depressing therapy session last night.

"You seem off today," Nick says as he pulls up beside me on his own electric scooter at a red light. Monaco, with the street track, is a nightmare for driving during a Gran Prix weekend. We don't even try, which is fine by me. I love electric scooters.

"Not what I need to hear the morning of qualifying," I tell him and give him side-eye, which he can't see because I'm wearing sunglasses.

"Sorry. I just thought I would mention it," Nick says with a sheepish smile. "In case you think you're hiding it. You aren't, so someone else is going to ask. Probably media."

"I'm fine," I reply and hesitate before adding. "Had a bit of a deep therapy session last night."

"Oh," He looks shocked by that. "You're still seeing a therapist?"

"Yup." I immediately start to feel defensive. Because would I still be seeing Carmyn if she hadn't confirmed his accidental autism diagnosis? Probably not.

"I think that's good," Nick decides to tell me.

"I didn't ask what you think," I remind him, and God, even I can see how bitchy that is. I take a beat to rethink how I want this to go with Nick. I don't need to purposely make things between us difficult. "Look, this isn't just about the crash. Although, I am still dealing with that, emotionally. I have a lot of pressure and situations in my life that I could handle better, and Carmyn is really good at giving me tools for that."

He just nods. 'You don't need me or anyone else to pat you on the head like a good little girl. I'm sorry."

"It's fine. I know that's not what you—" My words stop short as I suddenly sense someone behind us. We are in a bike lane, so it figures there would be other people. I glance over my shoulder and see the front wheel of a bike. As I lift my eyes, Nick turns to look too. "Hey Cedric."

"The guy on the bike, which has inched its front tire between the back of our electric scooters, is Cedric Pagtakhan. He's our reserve driver at Mirabella, meaning he drives in races only if Billy or I can't.

He smiles cheerily. "Hey! I didn't realize it was you! How are you? Big day!"

Cedric is always so smiley and perky, but he hasn't had the easiest career. He was a driver but lost his seat this year when his team, Janson Racing, dropped him and picked up Antonio De Luca, who we dropped like the rancid piece of garbage he is. He's not a bad driver. Probably even better than Antonio, but Antonio came with more sponsorship money, and Janson is barely hanging on financially. I think Frankie was right in signing him as a reserve driver, and I know he might still be at Janson if Mirabella hadn't dropped Antonio. So guilt might have factored into her signing him, too.

"Yeah, looking forward to it," I tell him.

"You definitely seemed comfortable out there in practice," Cedric smiles again as the light turned green. I put my feet back on the electric scooter and hit the power. Nick is in front of me, Cedric behind, and we follow the bike path all the way to the entrance of the paddock area. There are paparazzi everywhere, as expected, and they call my name, but I only wave and keep going. I have a meditation to get through.

"Stay and talk to them," I encourage Cedric. "For the team."

He nods. "It's you they want, though."

"Don't sell yourself short," I tell him. "You were the only bright spot at Janson last season."

"Didn't podium," Cedric notes.

"It was only your second season with a team that didn't give you a car worthy of a podium," I tell him. "You watch, Antonio won't do better. And you'll get a seat somewhere next year, I bet. We're just keeping you warm for a better spot."

"Or you might retire?" Cedric says, and I let my jaw drop. "That's the rumor anyway. I don't think you should, for the record." Cedric looks panicked as he takes in my face.

"Yeah. I don't think I should either," I say trying to sound light. In reality, I'm super pissed that there's a rumor going around about that. I just fucking started my F_1 career, why do people think I'd end it?

I wave good-bye to Cedric, ignore the reporters, and scoot to our paddock. I fold up my scooter and hand it to Nick, who has already folded it up too. He carries them in and when we reach my door, I tell him. "Can you grab breakfast and I will meet you up there after meditation?"

"No," he replies. "But I can wait outside after I sweep the room and go up to the cafeteria when you're ready to grab breakfast.

Right. Of course. I nod and motion for him to enter my room. He does, and a moment later he's back out. "Take your time."

BY THE TIME we get to qualifying, I'm ready. At least I feel more ready than I did for my first qualifying race of the season. I walk to the pit with my earbuds in and sunglasses on. Nick is a couple of feet behind me. He's good at his job, and that's all I am. A job he's seen naked. But still, just a job.

When it's time to get in the car, I hand him my shades and earbuds and slip in. The weather is unseasonably warm and dry right now, and today is no different. Rain is not uncommon for the Monaco GP. This weather is rare. I flip down my visor as soon as I'm strapped in. I feel like I'm in the zone, and I'm desperate to stay there.

There are three rounds of qualifying. After round one, the five drivers with the lowest times are dropped. At the end of round two, the slowest five drivers are dropped again and only the ten remaining drivers will battle it out. Where you finish is where you start for the race tomorrow. We get a couple of laps each round, which is a timed period, but so many things can happen to screw up your laps that have nothing to do with you. Other drivers crashing is a big one. My crash that ended in a fiery wreck happened in a qualifying round.

I flex my hand. The glove is rough on the tender, new flesh, so I have the hand wrapped in gauze under the glove. I also have brand new, better gloves that hopefully won't melt into my flesh like the last ones did. At least I know for sure the rest of the layers of protective equipment we have works well. It's my turn to leave the garage and start a lap, and I head out without a hitch. The tires are more grippy than I'd anticipated, and the track, although extremely challenging, isn't beating me.

"Nice pace, Lucia." Logan's voice fills my ears. "The car is responding okay?"

"Better than okay," I reply.

"Nice job on turn eight," Frankie's voice is the next one in my ear. "You're matching Billy for pace."

"Can we just talk at the end, please?" I ask, hoping I don't sound bitchy. I know they're just being encouraging, but I need silence to focus.

"Will do," Logan says.

It doesn't take long to get around the track, and I pull into the pit lane. No one speaks as they work on my car and then give me the okay to go back out. I don't know how I did that first lap, and I don't care. I just focus on doing the best I can, not beating myself up over the last lap. Or cutting myself slack if it was good.

When I finish that lap, Frankie's voice is in my ears again. "You're fourth! Fourth!"

I want to squeal with delight, but I don't. I am smiling ear-to-ear, but I keep my voice level. "Billy? Any other still on an out lap?"

"Billy is second. Sterling and Antonio still out."

"Thank you."

I get into the garage, but I refuse to leave the car. Billy gets out of his for a second while they tweak something on his back end. He lifts his visor and winks, giving me the thumbs up. I nod but that's it. This isn't over. I still have time to fuck this up, and I will not relax. I glance around the garage, but I don't see Nick. I wonder where he is watching from? Maybe he isn't. Maybe he went back to my room in the paddock or something. Why does that bother me?

Round two goes almost as well, but not really because of my efforts. I have a really shaky first lap. But we do a quick tire change, and I get out there ahead of Antonio De Luca, who somehow oversteers on turn four and ends up in the barriers. He's fine, but there's debris on the track behind him, and me, so several drivers get their second lap completely screwed behind a safety car. I manage a decent time, and between that and the problems for others, I squeak through round two in the very last spot.

I refuse to get out of the car again as they fuss about fixing and tweaking. But as I glance around, I catch sight of Nick. He's at the very back of the garage, leaning on some piece of equipment even I don't recognize. He's got his arms folded over his broad chest. His ankles crossed. His aviator shades on. But I know he's looking right at me. I can feel it.

I stare back, and a calming sensation falls over me. As the crew starts to move away from my car and I'm about to make my first round three of qualifying in my F1 career, the left corner of Nick's sexy mouth quirks and he mouths a word.

"*Suerte.*"

It means good luck in Spanish, and he's said it to me before. When we were in our little arrangement and he worked for Frankie, he would text it to me before every single one of my races.

My first lap is shaky. I have a moment of pure panic when I lock up on a turn, and I'm sure I'll hit the barrier. Hit it, go through it, and burst into flames. Again. Thankfully, I stay on the track, but the adrenaline in my body feels like fire coursing through my veins. My hand begins to ache a little. I fight through it.

"How'd I do?" I ask as I enter the pit lane.

"Currently, tenth," Logan's voice responds.

Fuck. Last.

"Lucia you are in the..." Frankie's voice cuts in and then stops. I hear her mumble something.

"What?" I snap. She's going to say something that pumps me up. Some stupid pep talk on the radio, for everyone to hear.

"You've got time for another lap."

Not what I thought she was going to say. And I relax that I'm not having to endure a verbal pat on the back. A few minutes later, I'm back on the track. My jaw is clamped down so hard it starts to ache, but I don't care. My hand is throbbing because I'm tense, but again, don't care. I'm flying on this lap and my turns are tight. I hit the last straight away and gun it.

"P-Five Louie! P-freaking-five!" Frankie screams into my ear.

I smile so wide it hurts. "Freaking awesome! Thank you, everyone. Thanks for giving me breathing space."

I do not want to make a big deal out of this. I mean, it is a bit of a big deal because the last race was so God-awful, but still. It's not a pole position. It's not even top three. "Where is Billy?"

"P2," Logan says.

"Go, Billy! Great job!" I reply. I am completely thrilled for Billy, no joke. And for Mirabella. If we win the team prize - the Constructors — it's just as important, maybe even more so, as a driving championship. Because our team took a financial hit this year getting rid of my dad's partner, who, turns out was a scumbag. If we win the Constructors, it's much-needed money and confidence for the team and will give my dad some breathing room. He's thrown all his money into the team to avoid another partner.

I jump out of the car garage, and everyone claps. I fight to stop smiling so big when I yank off my helmet. Nick is where I last saw him. Same casual pose. Aviators on even though he's nowhere near direct sun. He nods at me with his panty-wetting smile on his face. I lose the battle of taming my grin, and my face blows up with it. Frankie is suddenly in front of me, her arm in the air for a high-five.

"Way to go Louie!"

Billy walks over and slings an arm around my shoulders. "You're finding that footing, Castera. It's an honor to see."

"Thanks, bro," I quip, as I've started doing since he and Frankie became official.

"Let's hop on over to the press, shall we?"

Billy and I separate at the press gallery because he's in second, and there is way more interest in him, as there should be. Sterling Samuels is on pole, the French driver for the American team is in third, and Spencer Samuels is fourth. So I'm right behind him, making my rounds through the reporters.

"Lucia! Solid finish today!" A reporter says when I approach.

"Thanks. Yeah. It felt good out there," I reply smiling. "I guess I like dry and hot conditions."

"Don't girls like it hot and wet?" someone yells out.

"What?" I say because my brain is taking too long to process what was said and by who.

The reporters are not in the private area. They're lined up near the stands, and there are fans all along the fence a few feet away. The male voice came from the crowd. And if I could see him, I would obliterate him with just my stare. The reporter realizes what was said and blinks and coughs. Our gazes connect, and I can see real sympathy in his eyes. An unspoken agreement to ignore the incident entirely passes between us.

"Sorry! It's hard to hear," I say and step closer to the reporter.

"I wanted to ask you what felt different in the car now as opposed to the last race?" He asks, moving on like a professional. Bless him.

I answer a couple more questions from him, and then I move to the reporter with some online site. "Hey Lucia. Middle of the heat when it comes to the top ten. Not bad."

"Thanks." For some reason I'm tense. I don't know why. Maybe it's because when this guy smiles at me, it doesn't reach his eyes.

"Do you think your hair has anything to do with it?" He questions and shoves his mic in my face.

"My hair?"

"Yeah, you've spent your career wearing it pulled back in a braid, and the last couple of days you've had it in a looser style," he points out like this is a normal conversation to have with a professional athlete. Hairstyles. Is he fucking joking? "But it seems the looser the hair, the better the performance. Would you agree?"

"I.. no. I don't even think about my hair, ever," I reply, and it takes everything in me not to flip him the bird and stomp off. I've seen male drivers tell a reporter to their face that their questions were flaming piles of garbage, and the internet cheered them. Fans called them heroes. I know that if I were to do it, I'd be the bitch. The cranky little girl who can't take a joke. So I put up with this shit and try to guide him back into the appropriate zone. "I have so much more to concentrate on. Like the turns. This course is very narrow and unforgiving. The margin for error, as Antonio found out, is slim to none."

"Do you feel that his crash today did you a favor?" The reporter asks. "I mean, your time wasn't the best, but because others behind him didn't get to finish, you made it through to the next round."

He smiles that cold smile he has once again.

"I'd say that while I didn't have the best time in that round, there's no reason for me to think that had the others gotten to finish their lap, their time would have been any better than mine," I reply. "It's conjecture. I don't do conjecture. A couple of them were on soft tires like me, so that could have impacted their time as it did mine."

Out of my peripheral vision, I notice Spencer is waiting patiently to talk to the guy, so I glance over at him and smile. "I'll let you move on to our fourth fastest."

"One more question, Lucia," he says. "What are you wearing race day?"

"What am I wearing?" Fuck this guy.

"Yeah. Any particular label? A dress maybe?" He pushes.

"Gee... let me think..." I punch my brow like he just asked me to solve an algebra question. I turn to Spencer. "Spence, what are you wearing tomorrow?"

"Oh wow, thanks for asking!" He says with mock enthusiasm. "I've never been asked that question before!"

"I wonder why?" I reply.

"Perhaps it's because I have testicles?" Spencer says and rubs his chin like he's really pondering that idea.

"Perhaps!" I agree with a grin. I turn back to the misogynistic reporter who has lost his smile completely. He's turning red because everyone around him is snickering. "I think you should ask Sterling what he's wearing. Last season I think he wore both Versace and Channel to see races."

"And Vuitton. He's a huge Vuitton slut," Spencer interjects about his brother. "Funny though, I don't think anyone has ever asked him about his clothes. Have you?"

Spencer turns to the reporter. He clears his throat awkwardly. "Let's talk about your qualifying, Spencer."

I walk away and promise myself I'll buy Spencer a beer later. Nick is standing a few feet back and falls in line with me as I make my way to the paddock. Now I have the post-qualifying debrief with the engineers and Frankie.

"Little Samuels has your back, huh?"

I look at Nick, and I wish for the first time he wasn't wearing sunglasses. I want to see his eyes because I'm not sure how to take that comment. "He's a rookie too, so I guess we're sticking together," I reply. "I appreciate his support."

"He's a real team player, that little Samuels. Unlike his brother," Nick notes.

"The Little Samuels thing... it sounds like a dig," I say because maybe he doesn't realize.

"He's the younger brother."

"I'm the younger sister. Do you call me Little Castera?"

He holds open the door to our Paddock, and I walk through it. "I don't," Nick replies. "Because nothing about you is little."

"I'm five-four and one hundred and five pounds," I raise an eyebrow. "He's five-eleven and a hundred and sixty-five pounds. And I'm not small?"

Nick doesn't respond, and it annoys me. I know what he's

insinuating, and considering Spencer has been nothing but nice to me and gone out of his way to support me when other drivers, except Billy, watch me get hung out to dry with these stupid questions and rude fans, I want to defend him.

"Well, you know I hate debates," I tell him as we climb the stairs to the second-floor conference room where the debrief always takes place. "So maybe I should find out if your small theory has any merit."

I look over my shoulder in time to catch him almost tripping on the stairs. I hit the landing with the grace of a gazelle and scurry my way to the conference room, closing the door before he can catch up, which is fine. He always waits outside for these meetings. And I want him to stew in what I just said.

I shouldn't, but I do.

TWELVE

YOU'RE GOING TO SLEEP LIKE A BABY

Nick

I'M in a bad mood because Saffron has texted me thirteen times today. Her people got her a new bodyguard. A woman. And of course, none of her sex kitten shit is working on her, so she's still begging for me to come back. I want to send her a text that says, "Spoiler alert. I didn't fall for your shit either, which is why you slapped me." But I just ignore her instead. If she keeps this up, I will call her manager and threaten a lawsuit. That should get her to stop. Maybe. My God, the woman is relentless. There's a knock on my door. Well, the door that joins my suite to Lucia's.

"Always open!" I call out.

It irks me that she has started knocking since we had sex. It feels like it's part of an emotional wall she's building. I don't hate it as much as I hate her budding friendship with Spencer Samuels though. But that's a whole other thing I don't want to fully unpack.

I expect her to be in her pajamas or a tracksuit or something with her hair up or braided. But Lucia is dressed up. She's wearing some cute pants that show off her tiny waist and curvy butt and a shirt that ends right below her tits so her toned, tanned belly is on display too. That tattoo of the flowers on her side is mostly visible.

"I'm having some people over. You are welcome to join," she says. "We're watching Top Gun Maverick. Spencer hasn't seen it. He's got to be the last guy on the planet who hasn't."

"You're having Spencer over? In your room?"

"You know if an overprotective parent and a jealous boyfriend had a baby, it would be you," Lucia announces. Her dark eyes grow serious. "Join or don't. Your choice. This isn't me asking permission or engaging in any kind of debate over my social life."

"I am not here to be your parent or boyfriend," I reply. "You said people. So Spencer and..? And before you double down on some sarcastic comment, I am not asking to be invasive. I'm asking because it's my job. As your bodyguard."

"Clara. And maybe Frankie. She is undecided. Billy goes down on her in the hotel swimming pool the night before a race," Lucia tells me. "Says it brings him luck."

"Okay, you are aware of the term TMI?"

She smiles. "Anyway, offer is extended. Are you going to join?"

The idea of watching her hanging out with Spencer makes the chicken Alfredo I ate twenty minutes ago turn to acid in my gut. "Nope. I'll be in here."

"I'll keep the door cracked then," Lucia suggests.

"Are you worried about Clara or Spencer murdering you?" I ask. She frowns like I'm an idiot for even suggesting it. I am. "Then the door can stay closed. That movie is loud as shit, and I don't want to be bothered by it."

"Okay grumpy pants," she mutters and goes back to her room, gently but firmly closing the door behind her.

I hear them though. Laughing and talking for the next two hours. They're louder than the jet planes in the movie for fuck's sake. And by the time the room gets silent, I'm in an even worse mood than before. I really am a jealous bitch. I wasn't like this when we had our arrangement for two years. Never once did I worry about who she talked to or hung out with. But that's because we had an agreement not to fuck other people. Now we have... nothing.

I go through my normal bedtime routine. Wash my face, brush my teeth, change into a pair of pajama bottoms made out of black cashmere but that feel like the softest t-shirt material on the planet. I don't crawl into bed though. It's just shy of eleven, and her room is completely quiet now. I actually have my ear against the door that joins us like a lunatic. I take a deep breath and turn the handle.

The lights in her living room area are all off. The door to the bedroom is cracked just a little bit, and a sliver of light filters out, slicing a path across the couch. On the coffee table are open and likely empty bags of popcorn, rice crackers, and veggie chips as well as some empty glasses and soda cans.

'Lucia?" I call out.

The door opens, and she appears. She's in a bathrobe, but her hair is still loose and curly around her shoulders, and her make-up is still on. "Yeah?"

"Just making sure you're all good for the night. I'm turning in," I tell her.

She smiles, but it's not a nice one. Not like she normally smiles at me. It's kind of... sarcastic? No... I think I mean cold. Well, not exactly but... something is off. And I don't like it.

"You're not just channeling your inner jealous boyfriend slash protective parent and making sure there isn't a guy hiding in my suite?" She asks and holds the door open wider. "Feel free to check under the bed and in my closet, Daddy."

My dick wakes up at that last word. I mentally tell it to sit down and shut up. She's taunting me. Making fun. I shouldn't like this. I frown. "I'll see you in the morning. Usual seven wakeup call?"

She nods, and I start to turn away to head back to my room but she adds, "Spencer agrees."

"With what?" I stop walking, but I don't turn back to look at her. I'm not sure I want to be looking into her beautiful eyes while having a conversation about Spencer.

"With Billy," Lucia replies. "About having sex the night before a race. He says it not only helps him sleep better, but it also loosens him up for the race. He says just getting head works but that masturbation doesn't."

I feel like I'm turning to stone with every word that tumbles from her mouth. Because I can't help but think she's telling me this because she's going to have sex with Spencer. Or has had sex. Did Clara leave at the same time he did? I have no idea. I was trying not to eavesdrop. I should have been eavesdropping. I should have just accepted her invitation and been there watching him the whole damn time. I'm a total idiot.

"Hello?" She says and her voice is closer so I turn around and find her in the living room a couple of feet away. The room is still mostly dark except for the light from the bedroom. "Did you hear me?"

"I wish I didn't," I tell her.

"Why?"

"Because it sounds like you're telling me you intend to fuck Spencer. Or give him head. Or that maybe you already have?" I replied and let out a huff of air so fast and deep it almost sounds like a growl. Almost. "How are you going to sleep tonight? Well?"

I'm asking without asking, and she knows it.

She doesn't answer right away, and the tension in my chest

amps up higher and higher until I think I'm going to explode. That's when she finally does something. She undoes the belt on her robe, and with my eyes glued to her every move, she drops the robe to the floor, exposing her perfect naked body.

"I don't know how I'm going to sleep," she replies. "I guess that's up to you."

There are a ton of emotions I could feel right now. Relief. Trepidation. Confusion. But they're all eclipsed by lust. I cross the short distance between us and drop to my knees. The hair on the front of her pussy brushes my nose as my tongue slides out and licks her folds. Her hands grab my head. "Nick..."

I eat her out like she's my last meal. And when her knees buckle as she comes I catch her, lay her out on the floor, and fuck her so hard she has to reach behind her head and brace her hands on the wall to keep from sliding across the carpet and getting rug burn. But she encourages me the entire time with words like "more' and 'harder' and 'don't hold back'.

I come with a guttural wail and Lucia panting my name like it's a Tibetan chant as she comes for a second time. I drop down on top of her and kiss her neck, her ear, her temple, and finally, as she turns her head, her lips. The kiss is languid and gentle and the complete opposite of what we just did. Her eyelids are heavy and her smile is satisfied, but lazy. "I'm going to sleep like a baby."

"Good," I say and pull out of her. I get to my knee and scoop her up and carry her to her bed. She doesn't object.

The covers are already pulled back, so I drop her gently on the mattress and pull them up. "Should I sleep naked? What if my stupid stalker breaks in?"

"You can fight crime naked," I smile. "You can do anything, Lucia Castera."

Her eyes flutter open, and she's got this look in them I don't think I've seen before. Like she's basking in my compliment.

She smiles and lifts her arm, her fingers reaching out to me. "I think you should probably stay. Because I'm too tired to get dressed, and I don't want to fight crime naked. You can."

I smile. I shouldn't stay. I don't know what we're doing here. It was supposed to be a one-off walk down memory lane. Not twice. This isn't a relationship or even an arrangement like before. And I know that neither of us like situations that don't have rules and guidelines to follow.

But yet, I find myself crawling into bed and pulling her back into my chest, her head on my forearm, as I fall asleep inhaling the vanilla scent of her shampoo. This feels so right it's scary. How come she doesn't feel it too?

THIRTEEN

GIVE THE OLD LADY MY LOVE

Lucia

"LUCIA CASTERA! P9!" Frankie is screaming so loud I think my eardrums might rupture. "P9 and fastest lap. Fastest lap! You are officially the highest-scoring woman in Formula One history!"

I fight a mix of happy and sad tears. Because even though it's record-setting, even though my name could remain in the history books for this achievement forever, it's still only P9. I'm my own worst enemy and critic. "Oh my God! Thank you everyone! You guys made the pit stops so quick and I just... thank you!"

"*Louloutte*! You freaking made history today, and we are so proud of you!" Dad's voice comes over the radio, and well fuck. Now I definitely can't stop the tears. I fight like hell and only a couple spill out. Hopefully they dry before I have to take off my helmet.

"Thank you, Daddy!' Shit. That slipped out, and it shouldn't have. He won't mind, and of course, Frankie won't even think about it. But the media will pick up on it, and so will the haters. Daddy is so much weaker sounding than Dad. No male driver has ever called their parent daddy on the radio. Ugh. Haters will never let that go. "I couldn't do it without your support, boss man."

I doubt that will fix anything for the internet trolls, but at least I tried. I force myself to let it go and try to enjoy the moment. I fucking did it. Points! Only the top ten drivers at the end of each race get points, and I am officially one of them.

I steer the car back to the garage. Not only my first F1 points but the most of any female ever. There have been other females who have obtained a spot in a Formula One race, but only one ever scored points. In the seventies, an Italian driver named Lella Lombardi scored half a point in a race that got terminated early. There have been very few females since and no scored points. Until me.

I pull out the steering wheel after I come to a stop, and as I get out of the car and pull off my helmet, I'm grinning. The entire crew mobs me. Even Billy is there hugging me. Frankie scoops me up and screams in my ear again. And then Dad is there, and I have to clench my jaw to keep from crying. "High five," I beg him. "Hug me later. Please."

If he hugs me now, it's puddles-ville. I will be a sobbing mess. He hesitates but nods and gives me a big high-five. I head off to get weighed. And when I turn around, Nick is behind me. Shades on, poker face in place. He follows me silently to the press line and stands wordlessly behind me while I answer questions. The universe has decided to keep shining its light on me because the questions are entirely positive. It's a fucking miracle. Most reporters even congratulate me. They get it. Finally!

After it all, I make my way back to the paddock, which takes twice as long as it should because everyone — and I mean everyone — stops to congratulate me. I am grinning so long and hard that my cheeks ache. I finally make it into my private room, Nick steps in first. I step in after him and close the door.

And then I squeal and jump up and onto him like a spider monkey. He laughs deeply. His joy brings me even more joy. He buries his gorgeous face in my neck as he wraps his arms around my back. "You fucking did it, love."

I hate nicknames like baby and love and darling. They annoy me worse than mohair underwear, but right now, in this moment, it feels good. "It's only P9 but yeah. I got points!"

He untangles himself from me in one quick, gentle but swift motion, and as I land on my feet, I feel the weight of his stare. "Don't do that. You can talk it down to the press if you feel you have to, but not to me. This is fucking fantastic, Lucia. Feel it. Drink it in! You've earned every goddamn ounce of joy."

I stare at him until I can no longer see him because tears are blurring my vision. "I did. I earned it. AND IT FEELS INCREDIBLE!"

He belly laughs, which is somehow buckets of hot, and scoops me up hugging me tightly against him and lifting me right off my feet. I love how it feels to be manhandled by him. Nick isn't overly bulky, but he is all muscle and six foot two. He's imposing. And he knows exactly how to make me feel even tinier than I am. And it's amazing.

I want to kiss him. And I pull back to do it. His face grows serious, and he loses his smile and leans into me. And then my dad swings open the door, without a single knock or warning. Nick pushes me off him so quickly I would be on my ass if my reflexes weren't so good.

I smile at my dad, ignoring the fact his eyes are as big as dinner plates, and hold out my arms. "Here for that hug?"

"*Oui!*" He says and pulls me into him. "I see someone else got one first."

"I'll be outside if you need me," Nick says and heads out the door, closing it behind him.

"You were a force out there, Lucia," Dad says and cups my face in his hands. "The first female to ever score the fastest lap and two points. My girl!"

I start to well up again. Oh God, I loathe emotions. I have such a hard time managing them. I wish I didn't. I think it's the part I hate most about being on the spectrum. I pull away from him and sniff. "Still want me to retire?"

"Yes," he says without an ounce of hesitation. I'm devastated. "Lucia, I will always want you to remain the safest possible, and this sport is perpetually dangerous... I mean we both know. But I also accept that you are not going to retire. And I support you one hundred percent even if I have to live in constant fear of losing you. I support you, *louloutte*. With my whole, terrified heart."

I want to argue with him. I want him to stop being scared. I want him to have no doubt whatsoever. But I know that's a losing battle. "If I hadn't had that stupid crash, you wouldn't be like this."

I wish I could just sew my mouth shut sometimes. I'm going to ruin this perfectly perfect moment. And I can't stop myself.

"No. I worried before, plenty." Dad moves closer to me again and holds both my shoulders. His eyes start to fill with tears. "And that comment about the new baby replacing you. In case that wasn't a joke, please know that you are irreplaceable. From the second you were born, you took ownership of a piece of my heart that no one can touch. Or take. Or overtake."

"I don't want to cry again, Dad!" I say as my eyes water. "Please just be happy about this race."

"I am!" He promises and smiles. "My daughter is in the history books."

"Damn right!"

"And romantically involved with her bodyguard!" He declares with the same level of enthusiasm.

I grow still and stare at him. He loses his smile and arches one of his big salt-n-pepper eyebrows as he folds his arms and waits for a response. I open my mouth to lie, but I suck at lying. "It's not a new thing. We were involved when he was guarding Frankie."

"Yeah. I know, but I thought it was over," he replies as I move to grab a drink out of my mini-fridge and offer him one. He shakes his head.

"It was over. But now he's back, so it's... I mean it's not a thing again," I reply and twist the cap off my Evian. "It's not what it was, but it's not... nothing."

"Very informative," Dad snarks.

I roll my eyes. "And it's not romantic. Don't use that word. We've never been romantically involved."

"Really?" He looks baffled and cocks his head. "Then what would you call it?"

"We're... carnally involved." Okay, so that's not the right thing to say to your only living parent. Or any parent. Especially if you are not trying to die of embarrassment or make them die from it.

Dad's eyes get wide again, and his cheeks start to burn. So do mine, and I take a sip of my water and almost choke. When I recover I say, "Look, let's just call this an off-limits topic and move on."

"Sounds like a good plan," Dad agrees. "I have to catch a flight back to Spain. We have a doctor's appointment in the morning. Did you know the critter is the size of a pineapple now?"

"Critter?"

"Yeah. Adelaide calls it a nugget, but that reminds me of

McDonald's, and I am not going to nickname my baby something from a fast-food chain," Dad declares.

I laugh. "Well we want the fast part, right?"

"No. This kid can be slow. You're the only racer I'm allowing in this family," he replies, and I try not to start another argument. "Anyway, pineapple. Can you believe it? I had no idea what fruit size either you or your sister were at any point, but nowadays it's common knowledge apparently. This new age parenting thing is quite the learning curve."

"Uh-huh," I smile and try not to laugh. "Well if you can handle a twenty-nine-year-old wife, you can handle this."

He glares, but it doesn't last. His eyes are twinkling a second later. "She's thirty now."

"Right!" I smack my forehead with my palm. "Give the old lady my love. No joke."

"I know, and I will." He kisses my forehead. "Love you my girl."

"Love you Daddy. I'm really happy you were here for this."

"*Moi aussi*." He blows me an air kiss and opens the door. Nick is in the hall. I can see him. He looks like he just committed some kind of heinous crime. I almost laugh.

Dad claps his shoulder as he passes. "See you both in *Donostia* on the break. *A bientot!*

He leaves and Nick walks back into my suite and closes the door. "So? Is he going to fire me?"

"Nope," I say and give him a reassuring grin as I start to change out of my driving gear.

As soon as my suit, which was half off anyway, gets pushed to my ankles and I step out of it and reach for my shirt to pull over my head, Nick starts for the door again.

"You don't have to leave. I mean, you've seen it all before."

"Yeah but..." Nick runs a hand through that thick, sexy mass of brown hair that I adore. "I just feel like maybe we should set up boundaries."

I'm feeling this surge of joy, still, and it makes me want to take risks, so I do. I stare him straight in the eye. "Look, I miss our arrangement. I know that our current situation can make it a little more... complicated. But you and I are very rational people, and we can make it work. If you want to."

He doesn't look thrilled. That said, he doesn't look repulsed by the idea either. Or like he'd rather run into traffic, so... maybe that's a good sign? He runs his fingers over his jaw. And as he thinks, I do what I do — backtrack.

"I mean it's not mandatory," I tell him and hold the shirt I just pulled over my head in front of my fire retardant sports bra. "I can stay in my lane. I won't harass you again for sex."

I start to walk to the bathroom. It's small and annoying to change in, but I'd rather bump my elbows on the wall in there than stand here feeling like I just overstepped. He hooks my elbow as I walk by, and the next thing I know, we're kissing. He's got his tongue pressing against my lips, looking for entrance, which I gladly give him. His hands move from my elbow to my face, and he holds my mouth to his until he's good and done.

"There's no lane, Lucia," he announces. "We're carpooling."

"What?" I laugh at his lame attempt at an analogy.

He smirks. "You and me. We're in the same lane. On the same page. All that stupid shit. I miss our old arrangement too. So let's just agree to reinstate it for a while."

For a while... something about that feels off. He's saying we have an expiration date. We always have had one, I guess. That was always implied, and I thought we'd reached it. But now... that I can get a better grip on my emotions and the trauma of the accident has passed... I guess we aren't done. I smile up at him. "Okay. Good. I'm glad."

He drops down onto the small sofa, throws his arms across the back, and crosses his leg, ankle on the knee. "Now. Let me watch you change."

I grin. Today just keeps getting better and better.

FOURTEEN
CALL ME YOUR HIGHNESS

Nick

I WAKE UP, and she's still sleeping. She's curled up next to me. Her head off the pillow, chin angled down, and her arms tucked in near her chest like a T-Rex. Her hair is wild, branched out in corkscrew curls behind her. I smile down at her. I could get used to this. No, scratch that. I am used to this.

It's been four days since we left the last race and came here to her hometown in Spain. We've spent every night in the same bed. The days are spent working out, walking the beach, and eating the incredible pintxos the town is world famous for. She's been upbeat and carefree. Well, as carefree as Lucia gets. So many people call her uptight. I've watched it over the years, but she isn't. It's how she functions. She runs at a higher frequency than most, and I get it. I respect it.

I slip out from under the sheets, grab my sweats and pull them on, and then I sneak out into the living room and make two coffees. Lucia never sleeps late, so I know she'll be up before it gets cold. I take mine, open the doors to the balcony, and step outside. It's chilly, but the sky is blue. San Sebastián, or *Donostia* as it's called in the native language of Basque, is in northern Spain, so, not hot in March, but still stunning. I'm not sure what's on the agenda today. When in 'break' mode Lucia doesn't like to talk schedules. Mentally, I know she has one. She always has one, but she doesn't like to share it ahead of time. It can make guarding her tricky, and Mick used to bitch about it all the time, but I don't mind it.

Luckily, things have been very quiet since the incident that got Mick fired. Changing hotels and not staying where the rest of the team stays, seems to have worked. Now I think it's fairly certain if you're a Lucia Castera fan, you don't know where she is during the break, but I've asked her not to post on social media. She's fine with that. She rarely posts anything other than official snaps from the Mirabella PR team. Unlike Frankie, who was a seven-figure Influencer before being pressured to take over the racing team for her dad, Lucia isn't a fan of social media. Frankie still has a side-hustle shoe company she launched last year, so she's still on Instagram and Tik Tok daily.

I sip my coffee and stare out at the beach in front of me. There are a few dogs and their owners, but that's it at quarter to nine in the morning on a random Thursday. I listen to the waves lap the shore and watch the dogs play until it's so cold my nipples could cut glass. Then I head back inside and close the doors.

Lucia is wandering out of the bedroom in my long-sleeved Henley, which gives off the cutest little black dress vibes on her. She beelines straight for the coffee waiting for her. "Angel. That should be your middle name."

"I'll let my mom know she failed when she picked Thomas," I reply, and she looks up at me, the sleepy expression on her face slipping and being replaced with a look of awe.

"Your middle name is Thomas?" She questions.

"One of them," I reply. "Nicholas Thomas Winston Darcy. The third. And Fuck you if you make a joke."

She starts to grin and then laugh as she drops some Vanilla oat milk I left out on the counter into her coffee. "What the hell are you, royalty?"

"Only on my father's side," I reply and her smile falls. "My dad is like forty-first in line for the throne. He was the second cousin of the queen. And technically an Earl. I mean, it's all just garbage. He's not going to ever... anyway. My mom is French, which is where I mostly grew up after they divorced before I went to boarding school in Canada because I was a little shit neither parent had the patience to manage, and why am I rambling on with all this?"

She looks utterly absorbed though. She hasn't bothered to pick up her spoon and stir that milk into her coffee. She's staring, unblinking, at me. "How did I not know any of this? I mean, I knew you were French because you speak it perfectly, but you have an American accent, so I thought that you were North American."

"It's a Canadian accent. Well, maybe a bit American because I went to college there on a football... aka soccer... scholarship," I explain. "So what's the plan today?"

She finally starts to stir her coffee. "I can't believe I didn't know *any* of this. You know everything about me."

"It's the job." *And I love you.* I take a long sip of my coffee to prevent that second part from slipping out. "Also, I can speak with a British accent, love. If I spend too much time with my brother and my blokes from London, or I get a wee bit too sloshed, I slip into it without even a thought."

I say that all in the posh London accent that I started my life with since we lived in Kensington until my mom caught my dad with his secretary bent over his desk when I was nine. Everything about Lucia's face lights up like a Christmas tree. "You sound hotter than Prince Harry."

"You think Prince Harry is hot?" I make a face like my coffee is manure. "That's a relative of mine. Gross."

She laughs. Lucia's laugh is too loud, too high, and always out of control. It's like it takes her by surprise every single time. And I find it beyond endearing. She slaps a hand over her mouth and leaves her coffee on the counter as she walks over to me. She reaches up high, because of our height difference, and wraps arms around my neck. "I have been fucking someone in line to the throne. Are you an Earl too?"

"No. I declined a title. So did my brother."

"Why?" She looks like I just told her I believe the earth is flat or something.

"Because it's all malarkey," I tell her in a British accent again.

"Maybe, but it's hot as hell," she kisses me slowly on the lips, and I immediately want to deepen it, but my coffee breath stops me. And before I can ask her to please hold while I brush my teeth, she is letting go of my neck and letting her hands slide down my bare chest. And she's sinking to the floor. She pinches my nipples, and a current of lust shoots its way down into my sweats. She palms my budding erection as her knees hit the carpet. "You asked me what my plans are for the day. Well, I'm gonna start by blowing a fucking potential King."

"I'm not..." She's pulled my sweats down my thigh and is licking the tip of my cock like she's tasting an ice cream cone. "Fuck it. Call me your Highness."

She giggles. "I want you to come down my throat, your highness."

Holy shit, this woman is everything.

. . .

FORTY-FIVE MINUTES LATER, we're stepping out of our joint shower and she's rushing into the bedroom to grab her phone off the nightside table because it's buzzing. "I know. I'm almost ready. Come up!"

She hangs up. I wrap a towel around my waist and watch her as she flies around the room like a Tasmanian devil throwing on clothes. "I am going for a spa day with Frankie. And I'm late. She's downstairs."

"Frankie and Billy are in town?' I ask as I walk over to my suitcase. I technically have the room beside her, but I don't even pretend to stay there anymore. She doesn't seem to mind. "I thought they were going to Paris for the break?"

"They changed their minds," Lucia says. "Billy wanted to surf, and Frankie wanted to spend time with Adelaide, who wanted her advice on the color scheme for the nursery. Both the one here in the beach apartment and the one in their new house in London. She brought like a whole design board for Frankie to look at."

"Oh. Okay," I tug on my underwear and black jeans.

"You don't have to come," she says. "Jack is coming. We'll be fine with just him in the spa. They have their own security too and have agreed to clear rooms for us."

"Okay..." I still don't know Jack all that well, so I'm not totally on board with this. But standing around waiting for her and Frankie to finish with their mud baths and salt scrubs and whatever else is a long, boring day. I've done it before. And I will do it again, if I have to. "I don't know."

"Nick," Lucia pauses and looks at me with soft brown eyes and a softer smile. "Your Highness. I swear I won't go anywhere else, and you can even meet us there when we're done and walk back with us."

"How about I walk you there and back?" I counter.

"Cool. And then go see my dad," she announces as there's a

knock on the door. I rush to grab my shirt and pull it over my head. Bash may have caught us in a less-than-professional moment, but I don't need anyone else figuring it out. Lucia hasn't mentioned it, that I know of, to anyone, even Frankie. And I feel like maybe it's better that way.

"See your dad?" I repeat as I follow her out of the living room and subtly push open the door to my suite. That way Frankie and Jack will think I've just come from there.

"Yeah," Lucia says like it's no big deal. "He wants a debrief or something. He texted me earlier and asked that you swing by."

"And you're just telling me this now?" I question.

She pulls open her hotel room door, and Frankie's smiling face is right there on the other side. Jack is behind her. She enters and kisses Lucia on both cheeks and then walks over to do the same to me. Jack follows like a ghost behind, with nothing more than a nod to me.

"You two are getting a late start," Frankie says and breezes farther into the suite as the door closes behind Jack.

I run a hand through my wet hair, pushing it back off my forehead. "Yeah, well, someone didn't tell me her plans until a couple of seconds ago. I'm gonna go style my hair," I reply and head toward Lucia's bathroom. And then I catch myself. Fuck. My shit is all in her room.

I turn and walk into my own, empty room. Thank God for five-star hotel amenities. They have a little tube of hair gel and a tiny thing of hair spray I can work with. But my new problem is my shoes, socks, jacket, and phone are all in Lucia's bedroom.

"Should we just meet you in the lobby?" Lucia calls out.

I'm about to say yes when Frankie calls out instead. "Or, you know, you could just come in here and get ready while we talk since your stuff is in here."

"Shit," I whisper and take a deep breath and head back into Lucia's hotel.

Frankie is grinning. "Thought so. And hey, no judgment. I'm happy for you two."

"Jealous we're having unattached sex?" Lucia asks with a wink as she stands in front of the mirror above the coffee bar applying mascara. "Should Billy be worried? Bored of the old relationship sex already?"

"No," Frankie says firmly. "And is that what you're calling it this round? I thought it was fuck buddy friends?"

"It was. It is." Lucia replies quickly. "Same difference. Except the whole he has to keep the stalkers away from me instead of you."

"Uh-huh," Frankie catches my eye. "That's the only difference this time. Okay then."

She sounds like a mother who has just listened to her child explain why closet monsters really exist. She's not buying a single word out of Lucia's mouth. But she should. Her sister is black and white and doesn't say what she doesn't mean. I hate that that's a fact right now, but it is. I shrug at Frankie and head into Lucia's bedroom to finish getting ready.

Five minutes later, we're walking out the lobby doors, Frankie and Lucia side-by-side and Jack and I a little bit behind them. We both put on our shades and stay silent as the girls talk, and we scan the passers-by. This is technically their hometown, and locals rarely bother them, but I stay hyper-vigilant because of this unknown threat. I'm beginning to let myself hope it was just some super-informed troll and will be harmless.

The spa is located a five-minute walk from the hotel, right on the water. I pause outside the doors and turn to Jack. "Message me when they're in on their last treatment. I'll head back."

"Sure thing." He nods but his expression is borderline hard. He doesn't approve of the fact I'm sleeping with my client. I don't owe him an explanation, and his opinion shouldn't matter, but for some reason, I care.

I decide I'll take him for a drink or something before we get back to the race schedule and try to explain this whole thing with Lucia. Of course, I have to figure it out myself first. And in the meantime, I need to get to Bash. He holds open the door for Frankie and Lucia, and they wave good-bye to me. Lucia adds a cheeky. "See you later, your highness."

And I have to turn away so no one catches my smile. That girl... Jesus.

FIFTEEN

THAT DOESN'T SELL PAPERS

Nick

I WALK ALONG THE SEAWALL, watching the waves crash, and stop in old town to get a yogurt bowl and another coffee at a small shop on one of the narrow cobblestone streets. As I eat, I call Bash to see when and where he wants to meet. He answers on the first ring, and he sounds normal as we make small talk, but my gut says it isn't.

"Come by the house in, say, about an hour?" Bash offers.

"The house?" I repeat.

"Yeah. Has Lucia never taken you here?" Bash asks, and before I can say anything, he answers himself. "I suppose she wouldn't. It's not a place she likes to be. Okay, I'll text you the address."

He hangs up, and I'm still trying to figure out if he means the house I think he means. The one that he hasn't lived in since his first wife died of cancer when the girls were barely teens. Sure enough, when the address comes in, I know that's the exact house he's talking about. Frankie used to have me drive by it almost every time we were in town, but we never stayed there or even went inside. Lucia never even acted like she remembered it existed and frankly, neither did Bash, so this is a plot twist I didn't see coming.

I waste an hour sipping my coffee slower than required and then walk back to the hotel. The sun is fighting the spring clouds and winning, so more people are on the seawall and with their dogs on the beach. I can even take off my jacket as I approach the hotel and give the valet the tag for the Range Rover rental.

The house that Lucia spent a good chunk of her early child-hood in is located past the popular tourist beach, past the more residential beach, and halfway up the mountain on a narrow, winding road. The house is traditional Basque architecture. White stucco walls, dark red trim. And it's actually not as big as I would have expected for the money Bash was raking in when he bought it. He purchased it at the height of his racing career, when his wife, Mirabella, got pregnant with Frankie. She was Italian. He was from just across the border in France, and they were both fluent in Spanish and loved the ocean, so this seemed like a good spot to put down roots.

The front door is ajar as I walk up to it, so I push it open and call out Bash's name. The house smells a little bit of dust, and I fight the urge to sneeze. It's a museum, I realize as I go further inside, down the hall, where an antique credenza is located with about twelve framed photos of various sizes across the top. All family photos. I pause to look at baby Lucia. She was a cutie, all apple cheeks and wild hair. I can't help but smile at the photo in a silver frame of her and Frankie sitting on the beach. Frankie is in a pink and yellow two-piece with ruffles sitting on a bright pink towel. She's staring right at the camera with a big smile. Lucia is behind her in a simple navy tank, her arms wide, covered in sand, her hair curling every which way, and cut short.

Her mouth is open like she's screaming, but happy, like a squeal of joy judging by the twinkle in her eyes. She's holding a red plastic sand shovel in one hand and a snorkel in the other. But the oddest part of the photo is she was in full socks and sneakers.

"She was unique, even as a child," Bash's voice fills the long, wide hall, and I turn to make eye contact. "When she was really little, she hated the beach. If sand touched her, she would lose her mind. But she grew out of that, except for her feet. She didn't like sand on her feet, so she wore her shoes and socks. Even in the water. I can't tell you how often we had to replace tennis shoes for her."

"What about water socks?"

Bash shakes his head, a small smile on his lips because even though he's complaining, he really isn't. "Nope. Had to be canvas tennis shoes. And don't even get me started on her ridiculous tan line from those little socks."

He chuckles and I join him. Does he know? Or, like Lucia, is he oblivious to the fact that she's on the spectrum? I have never asked him, and I learned with Lucia, not to assume. "My brother had this massive issue with the consistency of berries as a kid. He just couldn't handle them at all, in any form. And I think he still doesn't eat them."

Bash nods. "Lucia ate anything, thank God. Frankie too."

He walks closer and pulls me into a man-hug, which is normal. Bash is very affectionate and has treated me more like a friend than an employee for years now. But still... I feel like there's a shift somehow, even though he isn't acting like it, because of what he walked in on at the last race. He turns and starts back down the hall and motions for me to join him.

We pass a bathroom and a closed door that's probably a closet before the hall ends at a huge living room with two sets of glass doors that open onto a terrace. The view of the beach below and the ocean is unobstructed and stunning. I can't believe they just let this place sit empty all the time.

"So, I didn't want to worry Lucia, but," Bash scrubs his chin and frowns before speaking again. "Someone was here last night."

Shit. "They broke in?"

Bash shakes his head and continues through the living room. It's furnished, but the furniture is covered in plastic tarps. He turns left past the fireplace and into a smaller wood-paneled room, which contains only a desk in the middle and a shelf on the back wall that has an internet box on it, the green light blinking. There's an open laptop on the desk, and he walks over to it as he gives me more details. "We're never here, as you know. I do have a cleaning company come in once a month, and there's a gardener. And we installed cameras inside and out."

"And the cameras tripped last night?" I ask, and Bash nods. He moves his hand to the mousepad on the computer. As I come around the desk, I see it's open to footage already. Bash just has to press play.

"I got the alert on my phone last night. Sometimes, I mean always so far, it's just been an animal that trips it late at night," Bash explains. "So I didn't look at it right away. When I replayed the footage about twenty minutes after I got the alert, I saw this."

He hits play, and there's a figure climbing over the short terrace wall. This means he came up the hill, because there's nothing in front of that terrace but a sharp, slopping hill covered in brush. He's got his hood up and his head down so the camera can't pick up his face. He's also wearing joggers and a backpack. Infuriatingly, the cameras are black and white and because it's so dark, I can't make out any specific details of him or his clothing. Except for the Nike check on his shoes.

He hops the wall and stands on the terrace for a minute. As

is typical with homes in the area, the double doors and all the windows have wooden shutters that aren't ornamental, and they're all closed tight on the house. He creeps around the patio for a minute, trying to pull one of the shutters open on the doors. When that doesn't work, he pulls off his backpack, takes something out of it, and places it on the terrace in front of the door. It's a... box?

Ice-cold fear starts coursing through my veins. All I can think is bomb. The guy startles visibly on the camera and then throws his backpack over his shoulder and jumps over the terrace wall again and out of camera range.

"Where's the package?" I ask immediately. "Is it in the house? Did you call the cops? Did you move it yourself?"

"I called the police last night and met them here," Bash said. "They investigated the box, which wasn't sealed. It contained a picture of Lucia and a... a bra."

"What the actual fuck," I hiss.

Bash grimaces. "The picture was of her, but it was photoshopped. It was the promo shot we use of her in her race gear, which like Billy who is beside her in the picture, is undone, the top part hanging at her waist. She's wearing the standard Mirabella shirt underneath, also like Billy. Or at least she is in the real shot. This person has photoshopped a different torso on Lucia. One with huge tits in a mesh red lace bra and a belly ring.

"The note?" I say turning the picture over so I don't have to look at it with her dad. Or at all.

He hands me the paper. It's simple printer paper.

You should hang up the race suit and become an internet whore like your sister.

If I could, I would tear this thing into shreds, but I can't. I put it face down on the desk, like the picture. "And the police?"

"They aren't equipped for a huge manhunt," Bash grumbles. "And they don't think this is serious, despite the previous issues."

"Not shocking, although frustrating," I reply and force myself to remain calm. "Okay. But they took a report? Because when we finally catch this asshole, we will need it for prosecution. Because I *will* find this fucker."

Bash grabs my shoulder and squeezes it. I try to smile at him, but it likely looks as false as it feels. The smile Bash gives back to me is just as forced. "How has she been so far on the break?"

"Good," I reply. "The buzz from scoring points is sticking with her, but she's gonna spiral when I tell her about this. And I have to tell her. I promised her no lies."

"Understood," Bash sighs. "Even though I was hoping you wouldn't say that."

"Yeah. Sorry."

His eyes are very similar to his daughter's. So are his grit and determination. And his bluntness. "How long have you two been together?"

Ugh. I should have known this was coming, and he has every right to be concerned. I rub the back of my neck. "For a while when I was working with Frankie. And then we weren't. And now we are again."

He nods. Bash is a traditional guy. He married Mirabella after a whirlwind romance when he was young and by all accounts was faithful throughout the marriage, even as he won championships and women threw themselves at him. I've seen it happen to Billy and Sterling and all the guys in this sport. And after she died, Lucia says if her father dated, he kept it very private. She had no clue, and Frankie says that Adelaide was the first real girlfriend her father had since her mother. And he married her. So this whole 'I'm just your daughter's bed buddy' is going to be impossible for him to grasp. And not exactly something I would want to explain.

"Can you be her boyfriend and her bodyguard?" He wants to know.

"Yes. But I'm not her boyfriend," I reply. His eyes land on mine, and I have to look away. I can't watch him process what I'm not telling him. Holy shit, this has to be the most awkward moment of my life.

"So you *are* dating that singer?" Bash says and he sounds annoyed. "And Lucia is fine with being the other woman? And you're the type of guy that would let my daughter be the other woman?"

Whoa. What?

I look at him again. His expression is fierce, as it should be if what he's saying were true. I lift both my hands in confusion. "What singer? I'm not dating anyone. In the last three years, I've only ever been involved with your daughter, regardless of labels, and I only want to be involved with Lucia. What are you talking about?"

He pulls out his phone and I wait the inordinate amount of time it takes for him to punch in something on his keyboard. Bash is the most technologically inept person I have ever met. My grandmother can work a cellphone better than him. Finally, he pulls something up on Google and points his screen toward me. "Adelaide showed me this, this morning. It's Page Six."

Of course his wife reads tabloids. I look at the headline.

Saffron Kent's bodyguard does cavity search the same night she was at club with her ex Axl.

The photo is taken outside her house on the last night I worked for Saffron. When she tried to kiss me. And of course it's snapped in that perfect moment where our lips connect. It looks like some kind of actual romantic moment. No photo of me pushing her away or the slap that followed. Of course not.

That doesn't sell papers. They want this to be something. Romantic triangles sell.

"This is not real. What's real is she tried to kiss me, I pushed her off, she slapped me, and I quit. Well, she fired me for not kissing her back," I swear under my breath. "And you called. And for the record, I would have left Saffron to protect Lucia even if Saffron wasn't problematic. I'm the best at what I do, and I wouldn't want Lucia protected by anyone else."

He studies me because he wants to believe me, but he's not sure if he should. He tucks his phone back into the pocket of his blazer. "So you're not involved with the singer?"

"Never was. No."

"And you're not Lucia's boyfriend, but you have feelings for her?"

"All the feelings, if you want me to be brutally honest," I reply because I know he won't tell her. "I love Lucia. I have for a very long time. But your daughter doesn't... isn't in a place to love me back. And maybe she never will be, but I'm here for as long as she needs and wants me. And I can keep her safe from this psycho better than anyone."

"I don't doubt that last part. It's why you were my first call," he tells me. "However, I do doubt the other parts of your little soliloquy. Lucia has feelings for you. Everything about her shifted once you walked back into her life. She's coping with the crash and the pressure of this season much better, and I know it's because you're here. And she may not know how to show those feelings the way other people do, but she has them. And I hope you'll give her a chance to figure out a way to show them. Because I like you, and I like the idea of you with her."

"Thank you," I say. This is still awkward, but it's a comfortable awkward if that makes sense. "I hope you're right. And I have all the time in the world to wait."

He nods. "So.. you're going to tell her about this?"

"Yeah, I mean, we've learned a lot about this asshole now," I say to Bash, thankful to be talking about something other than my personal relationship with his daughter. "He knows someone on the team well. Or someone close to your family. Because the address of this house is hard to come by. But he doesn't know immediate family well because everyone who does knows that none of you stay here. He thought she would be here."

Bash nods. I reach out and squeeze his shoulder. "I'm going to put together a profile with everything I think I know about this guy and send it to police along with screencaps from this footage. And I will study the hell out of it for any more clues to his identity. I have a friend who can clean up video footage. If he can clean this up, we might be able to make out more of his face."

"I brought this thumb for you to load the footage on," Bash pulls a thumb drive out of his pocket, and I take it and move to the computer.

I quickly download all of the footage and pull out my phone to take photos of the note and the picture. "Put this in a safe. I assume you've got one?"

"Of course."

"Also, I'd get motion detection spotlights put on the outside of the house," I add, and he frowns.

"We had them. Neighbor complained and we took them down." Bash grumbles.

"Fuck the neighbors. Put them back. At least until this thing is solved," I tuck the thumb drive into the pocket of my leather jacket. "I should get going."

Bash nods and we walk through the house to the front door again. He pauses on the threshold as I step through it. "You know, I should just sell this place but... well, I hold out hope one of the girls will want it when they start their own family."

"Maybe they will."

Bash shrugs, and he seems very unconvinced. "Keep in touch about all this, and I'll see you in Madrid at the next race."

I nod and head out.

I try not to get ahead of myself with all the bombs Bash unintentionally dropped on me. The stuff about Saffron and me in the news. I get behind the wheel of my SUV and make my way down the winding hill to the ocean and the hotel.

SIXTEEN
FULFILL PART OF THE FANTASY

Lucia

"I THINK I used the words 'do not freak out'," Nick says sharply as he stands in the middle of my hotel suite and watches me as I pack my bags like it's a timed event.

"I know what you said," I reply as I shove my pajamas into my suitcase. "And you even used the word please. Bonus points for politeness."

"Lucia, why are you packing like the hotel room is on fire if you aren't freaking out?" Nick asks.

I turn and look at him. His brow is furrowed. His impossibly blue eyes are laser-focused on me. His mouth — that magical, talented, dirty little demon of a mouth — is in a flat, hard line. He's not angry but he's thinking about getting angry. I can't blame him. I have talked about this with Carmyn. I have a tendency not to express myself very well when I'm upset. Or express myself at all.

I stop moving and even drop the pile of workout gear I'm holding onto the floor. I walk over and stand directly in front of him, put my hands on my hips, and try to dig the words out of the tornado of emotions clouding my brain at the moment. "I'm not scared. I'm mad. I'm…offended? I don't like that he went to my mom's… to that house. It's sacred."

"I understand that feeling," he tells me. I appreciate that Nick doesn't talk to me like I'm insane. Sometimes, even Frankie looks at me when I'm in the depths of some big emotions like she thinks I'm losing it. Nick never has. "But I don't understand why we have to leave."

"We aren't leaving San Sebastián," I tell him. "We're moving into the house."

"What?"

"If that fucker comes back, I want to be there," I say. "It's our best shot at catching him, right?"

"No," Nick says. "He likely won't come back. And keeping you away from him is my priority."

"Then it's another reason to go stay at the house," I argue, hands on hips. "Because if he's not going to go back there, it's the safest place."

Nick opens his mouth but says nothing for a long minute. Then he sighs. "You've never stayed there since your mom died. Do you think now is the time to do it? When you're upset?"

"There isn't ever going to be a good time," I reply because I've come to realize that over the last several years. And the only thing that hurts more than the idea of being there again is the idea that my dad might sell it because none of us ever use it. "I'll text Dad and tell him we're going so he doesn't freak out when the cameras go off."

"If you're sure…"

"I am." I am so *not* sure, but I don't know what else to do. And I feel like I need to be there.

So we finish packing, and Nick drives us to the house. It's a few moments before sunset as we park in the driveway. I hop out of the SUV and take a deep breath. The air is chilly and salty even up here with the ocean so far down. I walk around the car and take his hand. "Leave the bags for a minute. We can't miss this."

I tug him forward. As he locks the SUV, I unlock the front door, and without flipping on a light, I guide him through the darkened house to the back patio. The terrace where this asshole left his rude little message. The sun is kissing the ocean's horizon. It's a fiery orange ball. The sky above it is a kaleidoscope of oranges, pinks and purples. The ocean ripples and shimmers in front of it. I pull my phone out and snap a photo. And then I impulsively turn the camera around and pull Nick closer.

"What are we doing?" He asks, his voice an ocean of trepidation.

"A selfie," I reply. "Don't worry. I won't plaster it all over the internet."

I snuggle into his chest as he leans against the stone wall of the terrace and throws an arm around my neck, hugging me. We both smile, the sky a neon rainbow behind us. The picture is perfect, and it hits me, I don't have a single shot with Nick. I mean I could go on the internet and find a hundred shots of us together, but none that I took.

He kisses the top of my head as I admire the picture. "For the record, you can plaster this on social media and I won't mind. Hell, you can make it into a t-shirt and wear it on the daily."

I laugh. "Please. Could you imagine the media's reaction to that? Lucia Castera obsessed with her bodyguard. But of course if a male driver dates anyone, it's seen as sweet, but me. No that would just be 'she's distracted'. She's unfocused. Women can't be in love and good at their job at the same time!"

"What did you just say?"

I replay my rant in my head and every muscle in my body tenses. I just said I love him. Well, in a roundabout sort of way, but I did. I said that. Oh shit. How do I control, alt, delete that? I point to the sunset which is fading fast. "Enjoy the view. I'm just ranting."

He hesitates but turns to the incredible view. I step back and retreat into the house. It looks exactly like it did the last time I lived here. It was the year my mother died. I was thirteen. I woke up one morning in this house, in my bed, without knowing it would be the last time. When she died that day, Dad immediately moved us all into a hotel. He said we needed to take a break. And so we a break. Fourteen years of break and counting. I walk through the house slowly, turning on every light in every room as I pass.

Eventually, Nick is behind me, carrying our luggage up the stairs. "What did your dad say about us being here?"

"He was surprised but isn't objecting," I reply and stop in the long, wide hallway.

Memories rush over me, like a wave. Frankie's room is to the left. Next to that is my mom's studio. To the right is the bathroom we shared and then my room. At the end of the hall is my parents' master suite. I don't know where to go. We can't sleep in my childhood bedroom, even though I had a double bed. I don't want to sleep in Frankie's room or my parents' room.

I decide to head into my mother's studio. Nick follows. I flip on the light and the room erupts in stars. My mother had all the overhead lights changed to this star-shaped pendant lamp made of brass with little holes in it everywhere that cast pinhole light all over the room. It looks like stars. She also had a regular standing light in the corner near her pottery wheel. My mom made pottery as a hobby. The starry light and the shelves holding a whole bunch of her different pottery creations instantly make me smile.

Nick stops beside me after leaving the luggage in the hall. I reach out and take his hand in mine. It feels good. "We can sleep on that."

I motion with my chin to the oversized Moroccan day bed in the corner by the window. His handsome face morphs into a glare of skepticism, but I ignore that and march back out into the hall. "I'll find bedding."

I grab some sheets from the linen closet that hasn't been used in years but doesn't smell musty or anything. Dad probably has the cleaners wash the linens too even though we never stay here. I walk back into the room, and Nick has moved our suitcases to the corner and is looking at the pottery on the shelves. He's quite the specimen standing there in the twinkling light, in his standard black everything. His features look more chiseled than normal in the dim lighting. His eyes lighter than normal. "Where did you get those eyes?"

He turns and smiles. "My grandmother on my mother's side. My mother has blue eyes too but not this blue. "

"They're ridiculously attractive," I inform him. "You must have been such a heartbreaker in school."

"I didn't date much," Nick says as he walks over to help me make the bed. "I was bouncing back and forth between my parents' homes and then when I got sent across the pond, I just wanted to focus on athletics."

"Yeah, so heartbreaker," I smile as he glances up at me and shoves a pillow in a pillowcase. "Your lack of interest was probably heartbreaking for so many girls who had crushes on you."

"Don't I have to have done something to cause heartbreak?"

I shake my head and tuck the fitted sheet under the mattress on the left side. "Nah. There's passive heartbreak too. Where you don't even realize you've done it. I would have had passive heartbreak if you'd ignored me when I first started crushing on you."

I finish with the fitted sheet and stand back up from my bent position only to find him right behind me, hovering so close I have to grab his arms above the elbow so I don't tip over. He wraps a hand around my waist to help steady me, our torsos flush. "I had active heartbreak when you ended things after the crash."

No. Nope. I do not want to discuss this! My brain would be stomping its feet inside my skull right now if it had feet. I let go of his arms and place my hands on his chest to push away, but he won't loosen his grip on my waist.

"Look, that was an emotionally volatile time for a normal person. And I'm not normal. So I overreacted. If you want an official apology, I will give one. I *am* sorry."

I feel a pinch in my chest. Should I have said this sooner? Did I really hurt him that badly? We were supposed to be casual. Nick pushes my hair back, away from my face, and as his fingertips glance across my cheek, I shiver. He's so gentle for a guy who comes across as so imposing and almost menacing when he's working. "I don't need an apology. I owe you one. I shouldn't have pushed you on something so personal and none of my business," Nick says quietly. "One in forty-four children are on the spectrum, Lucia. The difference is most know about it from a young age, thanks to adequate testing and informed doctors nowadays. They don't have to be blindsided, in their late twenties, by a bumbling doctor. Weeks after almost losing their life. And I should have known it wasn't the time to psycho-analyze you further. I was a jackass. I really was."

He looks... guilty. His eyes move away from mine, and his shoulders hitch up a notch like he's tense. I reach up and cup the side of his face, forcing him to look at me. "Hey. I forgive you. I know you were just trying to help me."

"Still..." His chest raises and falls in a heavy sigh. "I have been thinking about it a lot, and I was the one who handled that whole time after your crash wrong. Not you."

"We can sit here and slice up the blame like it's an apple pie, or we can have sex," I announce and grin. "Your call."

He grins back, and the stubble on his jaw tickles my palm since I'm still holding it against his cheek. I use that hand to pull him closer and kiss him long and hard. My tongue sweeps into his mouth and he yanks my body flush to his. As soon as we break apart, he is tugging my shirt up, out of my pants. "Are you sure you're okay with this?"

He means the location, not the sex part. Even in the dense fog of lust, he's thinking about my feelings. I think Nick thinks about them more than I do. And he definitely understands my emotions better than I do. I adore that as much as I need it. "Teenage me always planned on sneaking a boy back here and losing my virginity in this house one day when I met the right guy and my parents were away. That ship has sailed, but at least I can, you know, fulfill part of the fantasy."

Nick's lips kiss their way down toward my collarbone. His fingers are roaming under my shirt, up toward the clasp on my bra. I whisper, fighting a giggle. "We have to be quick and quiet. I don't want to get caught by my parents."

"Are we pretending we're teenagers then?" He whispers and there's a chuckle after it.

"Yeah," I whisper back running my hands down his abs to his belt. "Except the sex is going to be adult as fuck."

He laughs and I shush him. "We'll get caught."

"Honey, if we're having adult sex," Nick replies as my bra comes undone under his deft fingers. "You're going to be screaming my name so loud Bash might hear you in his apartment across town."

I laugh, and then he picks me up and tosses me onto the freshly made day bed.

SEVENTEEN
YOU'RE PROBABLY MY BEST FRIEND

Lucia

I WAKE UP, after a quick post-orgasm cat nap, my stomach growling like an ornery bear. I stretch and yawn, and Nick's hands slide over my bare belly as he pulls me closer. I have always loved how perfectly I fit against him. I feel like a missing puzzle piece that's found its place.

"I need to eat something, or I will get hangry," I warn him with a smile on my lips.

He groans, kisses my shoulder, and lets me go. I have to climb over him to get out of the day bed. It's not graceful, especially naked but at least he keeps his eyes closed so he doesn't witness it. I pull on some undies and grab his shirt. "Hey!"

"You've got others," I mutter and he laughs. "So, nap?"

Now his eyes are open — wide. "Pizza during the season? Who are you and what have you done with Lucia?"

I grin. "I had no real breakfast and watercress and pickled radish salad at the spa. I deserve carbs."

"I don't disagree." He replies and sits up, pulling his phone from the discarded jeans on the floor. "Diavalo?"

He knows me so well. "Extra-large."

He looks shocked again, and I smile.

"Well, if we're throwing caution to the wind, I'm getting a provolone starter."

I fake gasp. But I'm kind of jealous. It's this bowl of melted cheese with spices and chopped marinated tomatoes on top, and they give you buttery, toasted sourdough bread points to dip into it. And although I can manage a cheat day with pizza, I can't add that to it. I listen as he places the order in perfect Spanish, and as always, I'm floored by his ability to speak so many languages.

"What did you take in college?' I ask him, because I have no idea.

"Criminology with a minor in linguistics," he replies and stands up. The bed sheet drops, and he's gloriously naked.

I don't even pretend not to take in every long, thick inch of him. Even soft, he's a masterpiece. And all his smooth, tan skin pulled over well-developed muscle is every woman's fantasy. "You could have skipped school and been a model or something. Look at you."

He huffs out a silent laugh. "Thanks, but you're biased."

"Why? Because you work for me?"

"No. Because you have feelings for me," he says as he bends down and starts to tug on his black pants.

I open my mouth instantly to form a rebuttal, and those flawless blue eyes of his flick up to find me like that. Mouth agape and nothing coming out of it. He shoots me the softest smile I've ever seen on his rugged face. "Let's just forget I said that."

"Let's," I agree and start for the open door. "I'm going to get us plates and stuff. I'll set it up on the terrace. I hope your cool with tap water because we've got nothing else."

"I can make do," he replies as I bound out of the room and down the stairs.

With every step, I talk myself out of freaking out. He's right. That's what has my brain overheating like an old Chevy truck. I have feelings for him. I always have. Big, dumb, overwhelming, and absolutely terrifying feelings.

I set rules for myself so I could succeed in my career. No serious relationships. No time-consuming friendships, which, to be honest, isn't much of an issue because I've never been big on friends. Or they've never been big on me. And men have been mostly the same. I mean, yeah, they are always ready for a good roll in the hay but not always into committing to someone who spends half the year jumping around the globe. It's not that I couldn't have a boyfriend. I can. Same with friends, I guess, but it is a lot of work for me. I haven't found someone who takes me as I am. And who I find easy to understand. My only real friends are Frankie and her best friend Jennie, and now I think I'd consider Clara a friend. Spencer too, sort of. And Billy.

I reach the large kitchen and start opening the cupboards. All the dishes are my mom's creations. I pull them down with extra care and take a second to admire them. I don't feel as emotional as I thought I would about them. Or any part of this place. And it feels right being here with Nick.

The pizza arrives as I'm setting up the table on the terrace. Nick already wiped it down, because it was dirty from sitting unattended in the element for years, and he lit candles he found in a drawer in the dining room. My mother adored ambient light like candles and smaller sconces on the walls over big overhead lights. Or pot lights. Oh, how she hated pot lights. I'm smiling as Nick brings the pizza in.

"What?" He asks.

I shake my head. "Just thinking about my mom."

He puts the giant pizza box on the table in the center and a smaller box with his provolone cheese deliciousness directly on the plate in front of him as he sits down. My mouth is watering looking at the savory, delicious cheese dish. He dips one of the toasted bread points into it and holds it up. His eyes lock on mine. "One bite won't kill you."

"You are the worst temptation," I say, and I mean it in so many different ways. But I can't screw up my diet. I know that it probably won't kill me, but I also know if I start, I won't stop. And even one bite will make me feel guilty. "I obsess about everything, including my fitness and nutrition during the season, you know that."

"I can go eat it inside," Nick offers but I shake my head.

"I enjoy watching you enjoy it," I reply opening the box with the pizza. "Besides, I have this bad boy to devour."

Nick chuckles and eats his cheese-covered toast point. He starts to dip another one in. "I'm proud of how well you're handling this. All of this, actually. Not just being in the house, but the season, the media scrutiny, and the stuff with this mysterious asshole."

"I'm not handling it well at all," I reply, feeling like I can let my guard down with him. He always makes me feel so safe. In every situation. "I want to rage cry at least once a day. This is harder than I thought it would be, racing at this level so soon after that crash. Sometimes I wonder if I should have stayed in F2 another season."

"I understand the doubt," Nick replies as he stops to pour water from the jug I filled into the glasses in front of both of us. "But you don't play it safe Lucia, and you would have been more miserable if you had tried to do that."

I think about it, and maybe he's right. I watch him as I chew on the crust of my first slice of Diavalo. He's so much more than

I give him credit for, and I think that's why I am so scared of letting myself care about him. He's polished and refined like a fine gem, and I'm this... rough-edged rock. And I'll never be able to smooth out those edges. They're part of my DNA.

"Hey," Nick's voice is soft and gentle. "What is planting itself in that big beautiful brain of yours? It doesn't seem good, judging by the look on your face."

"No. It's not bad," I swallow a chunk of crust and reach for my water glass. The wind is swirling around us, warm and soft. I can smell the salt from the sea below, and I inhale deeply to ground myself. "I was just thinking about how different we are."

"We've had very different life experiences," Nick surmises calmly and reaches for his own slice of pizza now that he's done with his appetizer. "But we fit."

He's saying what I know to be true, so the fact that it sends a ripple of panic through me is ridiculous. But it does. A fierce, undeniable ripple. "I see that look, Lucia. I'm not asking anything of you. Deep breaths. I know the box you need to keep me in, and I'm in it. I promise."

My lungs start to be able to expand again. "The reason we fit... we work is because we know what this is and what it isn't. I am not suited for a deep commitment or a long-term one. It's just not who I can be."

"I'm not disagreeing with you, but I would like to know what makes you think that," Nick says. His voice is as even as it always is. It's reassuring even though I know that he is asking me this because he doesn't understand it. And when people don't understand me, it usually feels like an insult or a personal attack, but I don't feel that right now.

So I decided to wade right into the emotional deep end of this very touchy conversation. My toes wiggle against the terracotta floor. It's cool and smooth against my bare skin and grounds me. "I told my psychologist about what you said. And she agreed and was shocked I had no idea. That no one had diagnosed me before."

"Okay," Nick says and reaches for another piece of pizza. I'm really grateful he isn't just sitting there staring at me. This is a heavy topic for me, and I would feel like a freak if he wasn't acting normally.

"And that's when I remembered the tests," I tell him and pick up another piece of pizza for myself, but I drop it onto my plate instead of lifting it to my mouth. "When I was, like, twelve, and Frankie and I were finally at that boarding school. I remember my parents showed up one weekend unexpectedly. We were so excited about the unscheduled time with them. Dad said he was going to take Frankie shopping on Saturday and I was going to go do something with Mom, and then we would switch for Sunday. It was exciting that we were each getting one-on-one time with them."

He lifts those pale eyes to me and waits for me to continue the story, but I have a feeling he knows where this is going. I tell it anyway. "So I get up Saturday, and Mom and I watch Dad and Frankie drive off, and then we walk into town from the school. We grab breakfast, and that's when she tells me that the school asked that I get some special testing. I freaked out, of course. I was doing okay in all my classes. I mean, not stellar, but I was getting by. My history teacher had it out for me, though. I asked if it was him that requested this. He was always telling me I talked too much. And Mom assured me that it wasn't him specifically. She kept telling me there was nothing wrong with me, but that these tests would help determine if I needed advanced classes or other things."

Nick nodded. "ASD can't be diagnosed by tests. It's not a learning disability, Lucia."

"Yeah, I know. I've done all the research now," I reply sharply. Too sharply. I pause and give him a small guilty smile.

He winks at me with his easy grin. I relax a little. He really does get me. "But it turns out it was a couple of comprehension tests, and they were all emotional aptitude type questions, and then it was about two hours with a shrink."

Nick swallows the last of another slice and wipes his hands in his napkin. "So..? Did they tell you anything after that?"

I shake my head. "No. Mom said she would tell me everything, but they wouldn't hear from the shrink for a couple weeks. Dad had to get back to the race schedule, and she said we would discuss when the season was over and not to worry."

"You worried."

I laugh. "I obsessed. I bugged Frankie about it, begging her to ask them to give her more info about it. They wouldn't. And so I cornered every teacher over the rest of the semester, and each one either acted like they had no idea what I was talking about or simply refused to discuss matters I should be discussing with my parents. I even cornered the dean of the school and swore at him when he didn't tell me anything."

"And then?"

I lift the piece of pizza on my plate but drop it back a second later. I no longer have much of an appetite. "And then, I stopped obsessing because Dad showed up at school and told us Mom was in the hospital and we needed to come home. And that became our whole world. My mom fighting cancer and losing."

"And no one ever brought up the tests again?" Nick looks sad.

I shake my head. A lump is rapidly growing in my throat, and so I barely manage to get out my confession. "I didn't want to bring it up again... in case it was something bad. I didn't want my mom's last thoughts about me to be disappointment or concern."

I can't see him anymore. My vision is blurred with tears. So I stand up to leave the table. But suddenly he's there, arms around me, pulling me into him. I bristle and brace myself against his chest, trying to push away. "Nick. I don't want to cry."

"But you're going to," Nick replies simply. "So I'm going to comfort you. And guess what Lucia? You get to cry. It's valid. Your emotions are always valid."

I cry silently, biting my bottom lip and letting the tears fall onto his shirt, he rubs my back, the way my mom used to when she wrapped me in a towel after I came rushing out of the ocean on a particularly cold day. That memory brings a new flood of tears to my eyes. Nick remains silent and calm through it all. When I'm finally able to get a grip, I feel embarrassed and pull away, turning to look at the dark mass of ocean below the terrace railing I lean on.

"Don't get all shy and embarrassed," Nick says as he steps up behind me, leaning against my back with his front as he puts his hands on either side of me on the terrace ledge. "Above all else, I'm your friend. And you can be raw and real in front of friends."

"You're probably my best friend," I whisper into the darkness. I feel him press his lips to the top of my head before dropping his chin to rest there, because I fit into him just right.

"You are definitely mine," he whispers back. "And for the record, I don't think Bash and your mother ever got those test results."

"Why would you say that?" I ask, and something warm and bright starts to spark inside me at the possibility. Hope. It's hope that my parents didn't find out I was autistic and hid it out of fear or shame which is what has been spinning around my head for months since I found out.

"Because he is not someone who would be ashamed of you. For any reason," Nick replies. "And your mother sounds like she was the same way. I think that it's likely that in the chaos of her illness and death, it just never got followed up on. Think about it, Lucia. It makes sense."

The idea feels possible. More than possible, it feels valid. I exhale a long slow breath, and the shame I felt drifts off with it. "I need to know for sure."

"Then ask him," Nick replies like it's that simple. Maybe it is?

I feel exhausted suddenly, and my body sags against his. He supports my weight and guides me over to the table and chairs again. He sits down where I was sitting earlier, pulling me down with him. I'm sitting on his lap, and he reaches around me and lifts the untouched slice on my plate. "Finish this. You only had one slice, and that's not nearly enough indulgence on a cheat night."

I smile and take a big bite of the piece as he holds it in front of my mouth. This man is being a gem again, and I couldn't be more grateful.

EIGHTEEN
FANCY MEETING YOU HERE

Nick

THERE IS a multitude of reasons why I hate flying commercial. I know how very spoiled that sounds. But seriously, private is where it's at. There are no long security lines. There's no wandering around public lounges with masses of strangers. But Mirabella Racing needs to cut expenses this year since they're down one major business partner. I'm not about to complain. A downgrade for the Casteras means first class on a commercial jet, not economy. But still, it's the lounge and the airport itself that I dread. Because anyone can approach Lucia or Frankie, and anyone does. We've flown from San Sebastian to Madrid, and now are waiting for our flight to London here, and they've been stopped for selfies or autographs nine times already. In fact, one of the security guards asks for a pic with the two of them. Of course, they don't mind, and they shouldn't. But as the bodyguard, it's a bit of a nightmare.

"How was the rest of your week?" Jack asks me as we stand

side-by-side with our eyes focused on our clients, who are chatting with a fan.

"Uneventful," I reply.

"I assume you mean on the stalker front?" Jack questions.

I take a half-second to stare at him. He doesn't move his eyes from Frankie, but I can tell by the sharp downward turn to his mouth that he's referring to my private relationship with Lucia. And one part of me doesn't totally want to kick him in the teeth for his judgement.

"We were in a..." can't call it a relationship, I remind myself. "We were involved before I started working for her. And because it's casual, I can stay focused. Please feel free to tell Bash about anything you think is lacking in my performance as her protection. I encourage that. I would never want to fail her."

"I didn't say you were failing her," Jack replies.

We start to walk as Frankie and Lucia say good-bye to their fan and continue through the airport. Billy isn't with us. He and Clara are taking a later flight. She's under the weather, and he insisted she sees a doctor before they head over to the UK for the next race.

"Then please let me know what you *are* saying," I prompt my co-worker. "I want to be clear about your concerns."

His professional demeanor, which has been spot-on since I started back with the Casteras, slips a little, and he looks up at me with a hard stare. "Dude, you're better trained than I am. You know that even the sister of a client is off-limits. This is going to create a problem. I bet it already did, and that's why you left in the first place. It's unprofessional even if Bash seems peachy about it."

"Yeah. Well, he is. And I am too. And Lucia is for now, so I think that until you see me fuck up — which you won't — you should focus on your job," I reply flatly, and the conversation ends as we approach the private elevator to the first class lounge.

We have about an hour and a half to kill before the flight to Heathrow.

I step forward as the elevator doors open. No one is in it, so I hold the door while Frankie and Lucia step inside. Jack follows and I join, hitting the closed button. The elevator goes straight up to the lounge and nowhere else. We get out, and I take the front while Jack takes the back. We make it into the lounge without being approached by fans. Lucia walks up beside me and smiles up at me. She looks absolutely edible today. She's got her hair loose and wild, and she's wearing a pair of flowy pants and a half top, both made of the same soft-kitten gray cashmere. She's never one for much make-up, but her full lips are this perfect shade of rose. I almost didn't let her out of the house when I saw her because all I wanted to do was mess up that lip gloss and run my hands over every inch of that soft fabric covering her.

"I'm gonna catch some Zs in one of those private relaxation pods," Frankie tells us, pointing to the long hall where there are private spaces.

"Oh, you mean the pods where Billy crawled up under your dress and gave you an earth-shattering orgasm once?" Lucia asks casually, like that isn't private information.

Frankie doesn't even blink at her sister's TMI share. "Different airport, but yep."

She trots off and Jack follows, acting like he didn't just hear something that I'm sure has his brain melting. I have no idea who he worked for prior, but I'm sure they weren't as bold as the Casteras. I'll have to look into that, though. Always good to know the history of your teammate. Lucia looks up at me, and bats those naturally thick lashes. "Wanna let me give you head in one of those pods? I bet your dick will look great with a ring of this lipstick around it."

"How you continually leave me gobsmacked after all this

time is a real gift, Lucia," I whisper back and can't help but smile. "And thank you, but no. I'm in work mode and have to stay there until we're settled in the hotel."

She pouts, pushing out that full bottom lip that could be touching my cock right now if I wasn't such a good boy. I set a hand on her shoulder and lean closer so I can lower my voice but she will still hear. "When we get to that hotel, I'm going to lock the door, drop my pants and feed you my cock like it's a fucking ice cream cone, so reapply that gloss before landing. Alright, love?"

Oops. The *love* thing might have been a little too much for her to handle. She stiffens a little under my hand, but then she grins and nods, happily. I drop my hand from her shoulder and clear my throat. "I'll get us some drinks. You have a seat over there."

She obediently wanders right to one of the two leather bucket chairs I pointed at and drops down into it. I turn and make my way over to the bar. I order an Orange Fanta for me and a Coke Zero for Lucia. As the bartender gets our drinks, a voice hits my ears, and my heart fills with dread while my brain fills with disbelief.

"Nicky! Fancy meeting you here."

I track the unwanted sound, and there she is. Saffron is sitting at the other end of the long bar. A crystal glass filled with clear liquid is in front of her. She waves with a bright smile on her face. I nod, and her smile drops. "Oh, come on, Nick. Please don't be like that."

"Like what?"

"Cold. Mean," she pouts and jumps off her bar stool.

Of course she's going to come over. Because it's the last thing in this world I want right now. Or ever. The bartender serves the drinks, but I don't pick them up. I have to deal with this first.

Saffron stops in front of me. I scan the nook where the bar is located. There are two men in suits sitting a couple seats over from Saffron. Another guy in a pair of black jeans and a white t-shirt under a black blazer is sitting in a club chair against the wall behind Saffron's seat. His eyes are glued to her. That's the new me. Guess the woman they hired for her didn't work out.

"I owe you an apology," Saffron announces. She straightens her shoulders, juts out her chin and lifts her eyes to lock on mine. "I'm so sorry that I treated you so poorly when you were my employee. I was going through a rough time, and I tried to suck you into that. It was wrong."

"Thanks," I say, a little bit surprised that she seems to mean it. "Water under the bridge."

"Okay. Good." Saffron sighs and looks down at the drink in her hand. It's fizzing and clear, and normally I would think it was a gin and tonic but it's not the right type of glass for it. She looks back up at me. "I lost a good one when I lost you. I have smartened up, but I guess you won't reconsider."

"I can't," I reply. "I am already working for someone else."

"I heard," Saffron nods. "Back on the race car thing. The girl who used to be an influencer who runs that Spanish team with the hot Aussie driver."

I smile. "Yeah I used to protect her. Now I protect her sister."

Saffron blinks. "The girl trying to be an F1 driver?"

Damn. And I almost thought she was actually a good person. "The woman who is an F1 driver. And don't act like you don't know that. You've mentioned her before."

"Yeah. That's what I meant, " Saffron plays with the straw in her drink. "I follow the sport a little. Axl was into it. I have been to races before. I've been asked to sing at the UK Grand Prix next weekend, which is where I'm headed."

"Why were you in Spain?" I ask, because if memory serves

me, she was supposed to be on tour, and she didn't have any stops in Spain.

"I... it was a pit stop," she mutters and looks up at me again. Her eyes are wide and filled with something soft like vulnerability. It's nothing I have ever seen on her face before. "I gave up drinking. I've got... there's some stuff happening you should probably know about."

Something catches my eye behind her. The new security guard is holding up his phone. Is he... taking photos of us. I step around Saffron and walk right up to him. He stands immediately. We're the same height. He's got more weight on him, but I'm not sure it's muscle. I don't think I would have a problem in a physical confrontation with him, and I am more than willing to find out if I have to. "What the fuck did you just do?"

"Why the fuck do you think it was your business?" He snarls back.

"Eddie. Eddie, calm down," Saffron says tugging on the sleeve of his cheap blazer.

"Did you take a photo of me?" I growl.

"You're with my client," he replies, his eyes narrowing in malice. "You don't want your photo taken, don't talk to her."

"I didn't talk to her," I remind him. "She talked to me, and if you sell that shit to a tabloid, I will know and I will break your phone and your legs."

"Nick!" Saffron snaps.

I turn to her. "Where did you find this imbecile?"

"Nick."

Lucia.

I turn and see her standing at the other end of the bar, where our drinks are sweating rings onto the gleaming oak bar top. Her dark eyes are wide and focused directly on me. She doesn't say anything more than my name, but her expression says everything. She's confused and on the brink of freaking out.

"Lucia, this is Saffron Kent. I used to work for her. She's singing the national anthem at the race," I say as I make my way back to her. I grab both drinks off her bar and hand her the Coke. "And that's her bodyguard, who likes to risk his life by taking pictures of people he doesn't know."

Lucia looks up at me. I smile at her. It's real and soft, and although she is still worried and confused, she smiles back. And then she looks past me to Saffron.

"You ever think of hiring someone else, I'd be happy to take him back."

"I'm sure you would," Lucia replies coolly. "But it's not up to you. Or me. Nick decides where Nick wants to be. See you on the weekend, I guess."

Lucia takes my hand, laces our fingers, and pulls me back to where we were sitting before. She remains uncharacteristically silent as we both sit down and sip our drinks. I watch her, trying to figure out what I should say. I don't know if there's anything she wants to hear right now, and that's weird because I'm usually so in tune with what she needs. She is staring at her drink, moving the melting ice around with the straw, taking the occasional sip. Finally, she says, eyes still downward. "Did you have an arrangement with her? Like the one we have?"

"Absolutely not."

"Hmm."

"Lucia," I say her name firmly. "Look at me."

She inhales a long slow breath, but eventually her eyes find mine. People mill about around us by the bar, and at the buffet nearby, but I ignore all of it and focus everything on her. "You are the only client I have ever slept with. The only one I would ever sleep with. Because you have always been more than a client. More than a client's sister. And you hate to hear that, but it's true. And it's why I don't want you to feel anything when you see Saffron wandering about this weekend trying to insert herself into my path. You are special. She isn't. Not to me."

Lucia's eyes pull away from mine, and I turn to see Frankie walking toward us. "Couldn't sleep. Or rest. Or anything. Want to check out the buffet with me?"

Lucia puts her drink on the small table between our chairs and stands up. "Want anything?"

I shake my head. As she passes, Lucia lets her hand graze my shoulder. It's purposeful, and I take it as a good sign that my words sunk in. I sure as hell hope so because I mean them.

I watch Saffron and that dumb ass bodyguard leave the lounge, which I hope means they aren't on our flight. That would be a new level of hell I do not deserve.

NINETEEN
NOT EVEN BEFORE THERE WAS A YOU

Lucia

I JUMP out of the car, and there is absolutely no way I can contain my joy on this one. I stand on the hood and lift both my arms in victory and roar. I fucking roar, unabashedly. The team jumps and claps and whistles. Billy walks over, and as I jump to the pavement, he wraps me in a hug.

"Way to go, hot shot!" He says and lifts me off my feet.

"You're P1 not me," I remind him.

"P3 is amazing, rookie. Do not act like you don't know it," Billy says and drops me to the ground, grinning as widely as I am.

"Look at my Dream Team!" Frankie's voice calls out, and I turn as she nearly jumps on top of me. "I am so proud of you both!"

She high-fives Billy and hugs me. The media has over-scrutinized them ever since they came out with their relationship. So Frankie works really hard to keep it casual while at work. Billy winks at her and walks over to do an interview. I yank off my helmet, and my eyes scan the people milling around. "Where's...?"

I see him. Nick is walking casually toward me. His gait is slow and casual. He walks right up to me and hands me a towel and water. I wipe my face and take a sip of the water, and when my eyes find his again, we're both smiling. He touches my arm and leans down. "Proud of you, Love."

My heart has a little seizure at that pet name again. It's uncomfortable, but I ignore it and smile at him. "Gotta go let them ruin this moment."

"Don't let them."

"Sage advice," I reply and walk to the media.

The questions aren't as stupid as usual, but one jerk asks, "Lucia, I was on a fan page the other day and one of the most asked questions was what do you use in your hair?"

"What?" Is he fucking kidding me right now?

"There are female F1 fans, Lucia," he says with a tone that drips condescension. "And they talk a lot about how curly your hair is and how you manage to avoid helmet hair. Tell them your secret?"

"I'll be sure to do that," I reply with an icy smile. "Just as soon as you ask Billy about his skincare routine. Have you seen how smooth his pores are? Is that toner or some kind of serum? Let me know when you find out!"

I blow him a kiss and give him a wink before I walk away. Spencer falls in step beside me. He knocks my shoulder with his own. "Nice job there, Castera. Fuck them and their misogyny."

I laugh. "Sorry about your qualifying."

Spencer's brakes overheated, and he had to bail out of the first round. He'll start fifteenth for the race tomorrow. Less than ideal on a track where there are few chances to overtake. "They can't all be winners. At least no one asked me about my hair routine."

I laugh again, and Spencer looks last me into the garage. "Clara around?"

"Yeah. She stayed at the hotel today though," I explain. "Food poisoning."

He shudders. "I'll take overheating brakes over that. Tell her I said get well soon."

I nod, and Spencer's eyes move to the garage and back to me as he starts to walk away, continuing to his team's paddock. "And tell your boyfriend I mean no harm because that glare of his says he thinks my intentions are less than pure. And he can most definitely harm me. I ain't even going to pretend that isn't true."

I glance over my shoulder and see Nick. As usual, he has those mirrored aviators on, but yet Spencer accused him of glaring. And he would be right. Nick has this way of emoting 'I will fuck you up' vibes without actually making eye contact with you. "Will do, but he's not my boyfriend. He's my bodyguard.... With benefits."

Spencer laughs and nods. I walk into the garage. Frankie is on her cell, likely with Dad. I walk over to Logan, who is standing in front of a screen, reviewing the race with Cedric, our backup driver. He's been attending a hell of a lot of races. He doesn't have to be at every single one. He's supposed to be on call if we need him. But I guess he's eager and excited to be part of the team.

"Amazing results, Lucia!" Cedric calls out to me as he approaches.

"Thanks!" I reply. "Let's hope I can hold it."

"It's an unforgiving track, but I have faith in you," Cedric tells me. "You're finding your footing! I knew that crash last year wouldn't keep you down long. How is the hand?"

I flex my hand and look down at the pink skin. "Tight, but nothing an ice bath and some stretching won't fix."

"Lucia," Nick says, and I realize he's right beside us now. "We have plans."

"Right," I turn to Cedric and smile. "I should go so that he doesn't try to stare you into oblivion. He likes to do that."

"What?" Nick balks.

Cedric looks confused and maybe a little bit nervous as his stare bounces between me and my bodyguard. I reach in to hug him because it will annoy Nick, and I'm feeling petty right now. Shocked, Cedric hugs me back—lightly—with a pat on the back, and I catch sight of the tiny four-leaf clover on the inside of his wrist. That tattoo didn't bring him any luck last year when he was dropped by Mayflower racing halfway through the season. Luckily, now he has us. He's not racing every weekend, but it's better than having no team at all.

"You guys have fun, wherever you're going," Cedric says and shoves his hands in his pockets as he wanders back to the garage.

I start toward the paddock so I can shower and change before we go to this shower for Dad and Adelaide's baby. It's being hosted by a bunch of models that used to work with Adelaide since her family is not in her life anymore.

We walk in silence until we get into my private room. He shuts the door behind us, and I hear the faint scrape of the lock as he twists it. That's a clear indication that we're out of employee-employer mode and flipping into sex-friends mode. I get wet just thinking about it, but I'm sweaty and gross from the qualifying.

"What was that death stare mumbo jumbo with Cedric?" He asks.

"Spencer mentioned that you were staring at him like you wanted to kill him while we were talking," I explain and start to undress. "Just wanted to give Cedric a heads up so he didn't endure the same possessive garbage."

"I'm your bodyguard," Nick says in that stern daddy voice he gets sometimes which makes me even wetter. "My job is to stare people into oblivion."

"People who are a threat or an unknown variable." I remind him as I step out of my race suit and start yanking off the fire-retardant undershirt. "Spencer Samuels is neither of those things."

"No, he's just a guy who wants in your pants," Nick growls.

Ah. There it is. I don't like jealousy because it implies some kind of ownership in my opinion, and no one owns me. I stand there with my hands on my hips, in nothing but a fire-retardant sports bra and underwear. "First of all, you are completely wrong about that. If he wanted in my pants he would have gotten in years ago. I've been single this entire time, well before you and I had our exclusive arrangement, and he could have made a move then. He never did."

"Did you want him to?" Nick asks, and that question annoys me.

"Who cares?" I ask as a challenge. He's not allowed to care. That's in the fine print of this agreement, and if he starts caring, then this gets all screwed up.

He moves away from the door to stand right in front of me. He takes his shades off the top of his head and tosses them on the small table beside us. How can eyes so light and bright in color seem so dark when he's in a mood? I will always be fascinated by that. And turned on. "You cared whether or not I fucked Saffron."

"I didn't."

He smiles because he knows I'm lying.

And now I'm annoyed he made me lie. Or rather, he made me feel like I had to lie. "I was interested in the answer. I mean, I don't think much of her. It would have irked me that you wanted someone so... not worth your time."

"I don't think Spencer is worth your time."

I lift my eyebrows. "Seriously? The man is a brilliant driver. He's always kind and has little to no ego. He's easy on the eyes. He started an animal rescue charity. What makes him unworthy, Nick?"

Nick's ocean-colored eyes get stormy like the sea in a hurricane. "Did you want to fuck him? Do you want to now?"

I reach out and take his hand and shove it into my underwear. "This only happens for you. Not him. Not ever. Not even before there was a you."

His fingers slip through my folds, slick with desire. The intensity in those eyes of his shifts from anger to lust. Two fingers push up into me and I shudder out a breath and grip his shoulder as he fucks me with his fingers. "I like that you get wet from just talking to me."

"I like it too," I whisper back. "Now make me come. Please."

His mouth crashes down on mine, and we stand there, his fingers working magic until I can barely stand. And then he wraps an arm around my waist and rubs his thumb over my clit, and an orgasm shakes me to my core.

He kisses my neck and my jaw and then my lips again and whispers against them. "Now go get cleaned up so you can go to Adelaide's shower."

I stumble away from him. He lifts his hands to his mouth and licks them clean. I groan because watching him do that makes me want to do anything but clean up. He grins. "Lucia. Now."

"Fine!" I moan and disappear into the bathroom.

TWENTY
PISCES CASTERA IS WORSE

Lucia

THE BABY SHOWER is being hosted at a country manor forty minutes outside of London. On a horse farm, which has me low-level panicking. Nick keeps glancing over at me while he drives. I refuse to sit in the back like Frankie used to do and like I'm sure his former employer Saffron used to do. It feels weirder and weirder the more we see each other naked. I mean, I had no problem with it when he worked for Frankie, but now it's just... off. So while we were on vacation last week, I stopped doing it. He didn't complain or anything, but he explained the reason clients are in the back is it's easier to protect them if something goes south while in transit. So I agreed to sit in the back to and from the track or for work events. But this is a family event, so I'm in the front seat next to him, staring out the windows and drumming my fingers nervously on the center console. I feel his large hand drop over my wiggling fingers.

"What has you worried?"

I glance over at him. He's gorgeous today. I mean he's

gorgeous every day, but today he's wearing a white button-down that's a little tight and a little rumpled, and both things are perfection on him. He's paired it with a grey coat and a pair of perfectly worn jeans and black boots. "You should wear white more often. It makes your dark hair pop and your skin look positively glowing."

He frowns. "The only one who should glow today is Adelaide. The pregnant person."

I ignore that deflection. "Seriously. You always wear black, and you look delicious in other colors. Wanna pull off into that cow field and have sex?"

"Wanna tell me what's got you so antsy?" He asks, and sadly, he keeps driving and doesn't stop to give the cattle a show and me an orgasm.

"I don't like horses. Or models, and this event will be full of both." I hate that I admitted that. It makes me feel weak.

"Let's start with the horses," he says casually. "Why don't you like them?"

"They're like... big. And fucking scary. Like dinosaurs that can kill you at any moment," I blurt out. "If they have horseback riding or something, I'm not going. I refuse. I'll say it's like a clause in my contract that I can't ride wild, massive animals, and you have to back me up, okay?"

"Your dad and Frankie will be there. They will have to back you up because they'll know what your contract says, Lou," He is fighting a smile. I can see it.

"They think my fear is illogical," I admit as I watch the green pastures whiz by. I try counting the cows as we pass, to calm myself. Counting has always soothed me. "Mom signed both Frankie and me up for horseback riding when we were little. I was about seven and Frankie eight. I hated how little I was next to the thing. And then the trainer lifted me onto the horse, and holy shit, it felt... weird. And I didn't like how it moved. I mean have you ever ridden on a living thing? It's weird."

Now he's not even attempting to hide his smile. "I have ridden a horse or two in my lifetime. I don't mind it. And you know that you drive at terrifying speeds in a car that is... that has almost killed you before right? A horse isn't going to burst into flames."

"No, but it can buck you," I reply. I want to drum my fingers again, but he's still got his hand resting on top of them. "I refused to ride, so my mom would sit with me and watch Frankie ride. There were other girls there too. Older ones and this teenage girl was jumping over walls with her horse. Not walls but you know... barriers or whatever. And the horse suddenly didn't want to anymore, and it reared up, and she went flying off the back into the dust and rolled away just before the horse slammed down onto its back, right where she had been lying. If she hadn't moved... My mom took one look at my face and promised I never had to ride again. And I haven't. And I won't. And stop laughing at me."

Nick realizes he's smiling and stops. "I wasn't going to laugh. I'm smiling because you are endearing when you're vulnerable. And I am happy you told me about this fear."

"Because now you have confirmation I'm a weirdo?"

"No, it's human. You can be human with me Lucia. I like that you are," He replies as he turns off the country lane we're on and onto another one. "I hate moths."

"What?"

"I'm fucking terrified of them. If you ever want to see me scream like a little girl, put me in a room with a moth," he announces.

Is he kidding right now? "They're just ugly butterflies."

"I am not a fan of those either. They fly around like little unhinged maniacs, and I swear they dive-bomb me. Freaky little things," Nick has a deadly serious look on his face, and his skin has paled. "An elephant moth once landed on my lapel in France. Carcassonne. It just sat its giant, winged ass on me, and I lost my shit. It was at a cocktail party for my friend's engagement held by a pool at a hotel, and I started flailing, throwing my glass of red all over anyone within a three-foot radius of me. The bride's mother was furious and covered in merlot."

"I hear it's lovely in Carcassonne," I tell him, and now I'm fighting a grin.

"I'll never go back. Ever," he swears. "If they move the French Grand Prix there, you're on your own."

He glances over at me, and I burst out laughing. He swears at me but joins in. By the time we pull up to the manor house which can best be described as a small castle, we both have tears streaming down our faces. A valet walks up from the stone steps of the house and opens my door, and I nearly tumble out. He looks horrified in that dignified way only British people can. "Sorry sir!"

"Umm... I... the party is in the rose garden to the left."

"Are there moths near the garden? Butterflies?" I ask him giggling but with a straight face. "Because if so, I am going to have to politely request we move the party indoors. My body-guard is petrified—"

"Thank you. Ignore her. She's drunk," Nick says to the valet as he hands him the keys and tugs me off toward the garden. He hands me the elaborately wrapped gift I brought, which had been on the back seat. "I'm going to spank you for that later."

"Promises, promises," I wink at him.

He shakes his head at me like he's had enough of my entire existence, but he's smiling widely too, which means he hasn't had enough. I grin back and reach for his hand, lacing our fingers together. "Lucia..."

My name comes out in a low, slow way. In a tone that has lost all its levity.

"What?" I ask innocently. "This isn't a work thing. You're not on the clock. You came as a friend to the family. And as my date."

"Really?"

"Yeah. Why not?" I say with a shrug as we descend the ancient stone steps into the sunken rose garden, which is filled with round tables covered in expensive linens and gleaming china. There's a buffet and a bar at the far end, and that's where most of the guests are gathered.

Just as predicted, every woman there is my age, wafer-thin, and as tall as Nick. Except for Frankie, which is why I see her across the garden immediately, and I head straight for her. Some older men are sitting and standing around by the bar, including my dad. I wave at him, and he smiles brightly and starts to disengage from his buddies.

I drop the gift onto a table behind Frankie and turn to her. "Where's Billy?"

"He got sidelined by a couple of the models that wanted selfies with the race car driver," Frankie says, and her hazel eyes drop to where my hand is still entwined with Nick's. She looks up at me, but leans in to kiss Nick on the cheek. "Hey! How are you?"

"Good," Nick says.

"As long as there are no moths," I mutter.

Nick focuses his stare on Frankie. "Do you know if there are horses to ride? Lucia is dying to ride a horse."

I laugh. Frankie looks at me with her mouth hanging open. "You want to try horseback riding?"

"Nick, why don't you go save Billy from the models?" I suggest.

"Sure thing," he replies easily. "Which way?"

Frankie points off past the rose garden, and sure enough, by an enormous swimming pool, Billy is posing for photos. Nick squeezes my hand and walks away as Dad joins us. "My babies. It means so much that you're here."

He kisses Frankie's cheek then mine. "Wouldn't miss it, Dad."

"Where is Adelaide?" Frankie asks.

Dad smirks. "She wants to make an entrance. So she's upstairs adjusting her crown."

"Her crown?" I repeat, the horror in my tone so evident that Frankie has to elbow me.

"I know. I know," Dad shrugs, and the ice in his drink rattles. "Apparently, pregnant women wear crowns of flowers at their baby showers. It's a thing."

"It is. I see it on Instagram all the time," Frankie confirms. "It's a whole Mother Earth vibe."

Dad looks like he wants to be as horrified as I am. But can't be. Poor bastard. "She's calling the theme, age of Aquarius but yeah, that's the... wave."

"Vibe," I correct, and he shrugs again and sips his scotch.

"She wants to name the baby Aquarius," Dad announces, and now not even Frankie can hide her horror. "Don't worry. I have vetoed it."

"Aquarius Castera? That's so bad I'm not even sure it's legal," I whisper in case someone might overhear. I have had a rough road with Adelaide, and I don't need to make it worse. "Like the government might step in and rename the poor guy."

"We don't know the sex," Dad reminds me.

"I do," I reply. "It's a boy. Now if you'll excuse me, I need a drink if I'm going to make it through the age of Aquarius."

I kiss my dad on the cheek, and he smiles and pats my back. "Congrats by the way, *ma Louloutte*. It was the age of Lucia Castera on that race track today."

A warm feeling of pride grows in my chest, and I kiss his cheek again. "It was a good quali."

I march straight to the bar and order a gin and tonic. Race day is tomorrow, and I wouldn't normally drink the day before, but one won't kill me. By the time the bartender has finished mixing my drink, Frankie is beside me. She motions for the bartender to make another, and then she leans on the bar, facing me, as I stir the lime in my drink with my straw.

"Don't."

"Don't what?" Frankie asks.

"Don't think whatever it is you're thinking," I brush my hair back over my shoulder and adjust the strap on my dress. "And don't say whatever it is you're going to say."

"What is it you think I am thinking or about to say?" Frankie asks and then turns to the bartender, who just put her gin and tonic on the bar. "Thank you."

"I think it's going to be something that I don't want to hear," I reply and take a sip.

She stirs her lime with her straw and then takes a sip of her own. "I think that we're about to have a sibling named after a zodiac sign. And it will be the wrong sign. The kid is popping out any minute, and Aquarius is from mid-January to mid-February. It's fucking March."

"Pisces Castera is worse," I say, and our eyes meet, and we both start laughing. And then shushing each other because we're laughing.

"You know what's not funny?" Frankie asks when we can control ourselves again.

"If the kid was born in June or early July and she named him Cancer Castera?" I quip and Frankie covers her mouth, trying to contain her giggles.

"Fucking with Nick's feelings," she says softly, and the chipper mood I'm in melts away quicker than the ice in our drinks. Her expression softens, and she looks almost contrite, like she's sorry she's even bringing it up. But she is going to do it anyway. her hand touches my arm. "Louie, he had real feelings for you."

"Had?"

She frowns and pushes her long straight chestnut hair over her shoulder as a breeze picks up the ends. "He still does, but I don't want to upset you with that news flash. And that's why I'm worried. I don't want you to break his heart again."

"His heart wasn't broken," I argue, staring out at the guests and the garden and the pool beyond where Nick and Billy are now talking to our dad. Beyond that, off the stairs to the mini-castle-slash-summer-house, a string quartet is setting up. "His ego might have been a little banged up and his heart slightly... bruised, but not broken. He wouldn't come back to work for us if I broke his heart, and he certainly wouldn't be fucking me again."

"Why do you think that?" She wants to know as the string quartet starts playing.

"Because if someone hurts you badly, like breaks your heart kind of badly, you cut them off like gangrene. There's no second chance on that," I explain, which is silly because she should know. She's the older sister, and she's had way more serious boyfriends than I have.

"Oh Louie," she sighs and wraps a hand around my waist as the quartet gets louder. "I've told you before, not everything is black and white for other people. I know it is for you, but some people... don't have that kind of clarity."

Her words rattle around my brain like pennies in a pop can — loud and annoying. "I want to change the subject."

"Okay," Frankie agrees, but before I can pick the topic she does. "Why are you so convinced that Dad and Adelaide are having a boy? Just odds or something? Like he shot out two girl sperms. Time for a boy one?"

"No. That's not scientific, and I'm not sure of anything. It's just wishful thinking. I'm trying to will it into being. Like the power of thought or whatever."

"Why do you want a boy so badly?" Frankie asks, and all of Adelaide's model friends start waving their thin arms at the guests, getting us to gather closer to the quartet and the stairs. I guess step-mom and her flower crown are making their big entrance.

Frankie and I walk slowly away from the tents and through the rose garden to the stairs. She's still looking at me, waiting for an answer, so I give her one. It's a doozy, but it's the truth. "Because if he has another girl and she's like you, then I look even more differ-ent. More out of place. More... wrong. And before you say a word, my therapist has already explained that I'm not wrong or broken and you and Dad don't love me less because I'm neurodivergent."

I said it. Oh my God, I said it out loud. To my sister.

I stare at Frankie as everyone around us stares up at the doors that are opening at the top of the stairs. But the only thing I want to see is my sister's face. Because I've blindsided her, and she won't be able to pretend. Her reaction to my words will be the truth.

And she looks absolutely clueless. "You're... what?"

Frankie doesn't know. There's an immediate sense of relief that overcomes me, and I stop nervously playing the with straw in my drink, which I didn't even realize I was doing.

"I have ASD. Autism Spectrum Disorder," I whisper as quietly as possible. My secret should be safe, especially because everyone starts clapping.

I turn my head and see Adelaide and her crown have graced us with their presence. She's wearing a long, flowing, white lace gown, that crown of pale pink and dusty purple roses on top of her loose, wavy hair, and very high wedge sandals. "Jesus, those shoes with that belly deserve a medal. Her center of gravity is completely off, and yet she's not even wobbling."

"Why do you think you have autism?" Frankie whispers, pulling me away from the crowd, and they all start to clap again because Dad has joined Adelaide.

"Because have you met me?" I quip back, and then exhale loudly as her frown deepens. "We don't say 'have autism', it's not the chicken pox or covid or something you contract," I reply. "It's a scale. A spectrum. And I'm on it. And I think Dad might know that because Mom had me tested before she died. And I thought maybe you knew it too, and you just were pretending it wasn't true because you didn't want me to freak out, and you were ashamed."

"You thought that?' Now Frankie's pretty face looks more horrified than when she found out we may have a sibling named Aquarius. "You think I'm a person who would be ashamed of you for being on a spectrum or whatever? Are you ashamed of me for having scoliosis?"

Wow. When she puts it that way...I blink and put my drink down on a nearby table. I wipe my hands nervously on the front of my dress. "I don't think you're that person, and I don't want to think Dad is but, look, I was even more blindsided by the news than you, and well, you know how I am. I always go straight to worst-case-scenario. And you and Dad hiding this from me because you didn't want anyone to know, that's worst-case for me."

She puts her drink down on the table next to mine and pulls me into a fierce hug. The kind of hug that would snap my neck if it wasn't so strong from the G-force pressure of racing. "I love you, Louie, and I didn't know, and now that I do, nothing changes. And I would swear on my life Dad doesn't know either."

"Really?" I say as she lets go of me.

She looks me straight in the eye and nods emphatically.

"Girls!" Adelaide calls out. She's standing at the bottom of the stairs now, by the gift table where someone has placed a chair that's decorated with more flowers and ribbons. "Come join the family!"

We both smile and start to make our way over. "Is the quartet playing that old song Age of Aquarius?"

"Yep."

"We're fucked," I whisper. "We are going to have to pay for that kid's therapy."

"And his name change when he's eighteen," Frankie adds.

Nick

LUCIA BANISHED me from her room. She said she needed complete quiet to do her meditations. So I'm standing outside in the narrow hallway, leaning on the wall across from her door, under the metal stairs, waiting patiently. And I stifle a yawn as I do it. The shower yesterday was a trip. Adelaide spent most of it opening gifts, gushing over the guests, and posing for more pictures than I ever thought anyone could in four hours let alone an eight-and-a-half-month pregnant woman in sky-high heels.

And then when we got home, Lucia was in no mood to sleep. No complaints there from me. I would end every evening by sucking on her tits as she rides my cock if I could. It's pretty much my definition of heaven.

I notice Cedric as he walks down the hall. He's in the usual team sweats and matching shirt, staring at his phone as he walks. But then he stops in front of Lucia's door and lifts his hand to knock. "Hey!"

He jumps and spins. His face is a mask of shock, borderline

panic if I'm honest, which seems a little over-the-top. It's not like I'm lurking or anything. He was just too engrossed in whatever is on the paper in his hand to have noticed me. He recovers quickly though and grins. "Nick! Hi. Why are you out here?"

"She's meditating," I explain. "She needs alone time. Did you need to talk to her?"

"No," the one word comes out too quickly, and all of a sudden I know something is off. "I mean, I just was gonna talk to her, but I don't have to. It's not urgent. Tell her I said have a good race."

"Yeah. I will," I say and step away from the wall so I'm kind of blocking Cedric's path out of the building or up the stairs. "Is that all you were going to tell her?"

"Hey, you used to work for Saffron Kent right?" Cedric says, and his thick, straight eyebrows pinch in the middle. "She's singing the anthem today."

"I know. We ran into her already." If this kid is going to ask me to intro them or something, I'm going to laugh in his face. Although it might be a good idea. Maybe then she'll stop texting me, which she still is.

"Who broke up with who?" He asks.

"You mean was I fired or did I quit?" I reply and cock my head. "I quit."

"Because you broke up?" Cedric asks. And then he lifts his phone and shows me a story on the internet. I'm not sure what site, but it's a trashy one, obviously.

It's a picture of me holding hands with Lucia as we walked up to Adelaide's baby shower. We look like a bonafide couple. But the picture beside it is Saffron. And she's standing alone on a sidewalk somewhere... looking... Full. I lean in and squint at the photo. And then I read the headline and jerk my head back like it reached through the screen and bit me.

Bodyguard races off with Lucia Castera leaving pregnant Saffron Kent in the dust.

They don't say I'm the father. That would be an easy libel case for me. But they don't say I'm not. My eyes land on Cedric, and he is blinking. Too much. I don't like it. "Were you going to go in there and show Lucia this? Before a race?"

"I... yeah. I mean... I didn't think it was a big deal," Cedric babbles and tucks his phone away. "She knows right? That you're... you and Saffron."

"There is nothing to know. It's all media bullshit," I growl.

"That belly looks pretty real. I saw it in person like fifteen minutes ago," Cedric replies.

"Where?"

"She's out walking around the garages," Cedric replies.

"Go. And do not show that to Lucia before the race," I say. "She has to focus, and so do you."

"Yeah. Okay. Sorry," Cedric brushes by me and scurries up the stairs to the lounge and cafeteria area like a scared rabbit.

Frankie is coming down the stairs as Cedric goes up them. She gives me a WTF look as Cedric blows by her. I shrug like I have no clue because I don't want to fill her in on these dirty details. She stops at the bottom of the stairs, and I assume she'll head out the door toward the garage because we're starting in twenty, but she walks to me instead.

After kissing both my cheeks she asks in French. "*Ca va?*"

"*Oui.*" I reply and her stare gets more intense. "Lucia is good, and that's what matters."

"But you aren't?" Frankie pushes.

"I don't work for you anymore," I reply and give her as much of a smile as I can muster. "I don't have to answer your questions."

"Yeah, but you will," Frankie replies confidently, and then

she moves us a little under the stairwell, tucked away from any foot traffic. "I saw the piece in the tabloid."

"I was never involved with Saffron. It's not mine," I promise. I think back to seeing her in the airport days ago and how she was wearing that incredibly loose baby doll dress. I couldn't have noticed a bump. "Not even close."

"You don't have to confirm that for me. I know what kind of man you are, Nick. If you had been with her, and this was your baby, I would have found out straight from you a while ago," Frankie says, and then she leans against the wall and folds her arms over her team shirt. "Does she know?"

"That Saff is letting the media think I knocked her up?" I run a hand into my hair, tugging on the ends, before letting go. "No. She is unaware. I think."

"Well, she will not be a fan," Frankie states the obvious. I guess the scowl on my face makes my feelings on that clear because she uncrosses her arms and squeezes my arm, just above the elbow. "She'll be fine though. Eventually. I just... I know that she is important to you, and I'm worried."

"About?" Does she think I can't be with Lucia and protect her at the same time? I'm about to be offended because Frankie should know me better than that. But she clarifies.

"About you," she says softly. "I know she hurt you, and I'm worried she'll do it again."

"She won't," I reply and pause. Frankie can really knock the bravado out of you with her stare. I don't know how Billy walks around with so much swagger with her there to keep him humble. "Well, she might, but it won't be unexpected this time. I know what I signed up for."

"You know, it's funny that for a girl that hates lying, she does it to herself a lot," Frankie replies and glances at her phone. "She cares about you. As much as you care about her."

"Yeah. I know." I rub my jaw and give her a little shrug. "But it doesn't matter if she can't admit it to herself."

"I have to get out there," she motions with her head toward the glass doors that lead out onto Paddock Row. She doesn't move though. She just stands there, studying me. "Did you know that she says she was diagnosed with Autism Spectrum Disorder and she thought that Dad and I knew about it and didn't tell her?"

"Yes." I can feel other words forming on my tongue, but now is not the time to unpack everything that went on between Lucia and me with Frankie. Lucia can and will do it when she's ready. I rub my jaw again. "Has she confronted your dad about it yet?"

Frankie shakes her head. "No. I told her she has to, but you know Lucia. She has her own sense of timing."

"Yeah, and it's usually bad."

"Yep," Frankie gives me a sympathetic smile. "Keep this Saffron Kent garbage from her until after the race if at all possible. I need her focused."

"I'm hoping to."

Frankie nods and leaves. I watch her push the doors open, turn left, and march off like the bad-ass boss that she is. I pull my phone out of the pocket of my jacket and pull up one of the several messages from Saffron. I reply.

> You seen the press? I expect a clarification.
> Thanks.

The door opens in front of me and Lucia steps out. She's ready for the race — hair pulled into a long braid down her back, sunglasses on, earbuds in. Race suit zipped up. She gives me a curt smile and starts for the door. I get there before her and hold it open. She lowers the volume on her phone and stops walking toward the garage. I stop beside her. "Thank you. For just always knowing what I need."

"Lucia, don't thank me."

"Because it's your job?"

I smile. "Because it's my pleasure."

Her cheeks pink a little at that, and then she clears her throat and raises the volume on whatever music she's playing, and continues walking to the garage without another word. Cedric is there, leaning on the back of Logan's chair, headphones around his neck. I lower my aviators just for a moment so he can see me glare at him. His skin tone pales a little. Good. Fucking little shit. I know he didn't mean any harm, but fuck.

Lucia does her usual pacing behind the car, and I tuck myself into my regular corner of the garage behind the tires. My phone buzzes, and I pull it out to see Saffron's reply.

> Sorry, Nicky. No clarification coming. I need the smoke screen at the moment. Cheers!

"That fucking asshole," I hiss. I can't believe it. She's using me as a fucking decoy? Like the consequences to my life don't matter at all? I think less of Saffron than I already did. I shove my phone in my back pocket and try to keep my face neutral. If Lucia looks over at me, I don't want her to worry or ask what's wrong. I can't be a distraction.

I give her a thumbs up as she leaves the garage to head to the starting line, and then I pace in the corner, glancing occasionally at the monitor as I think about how I will fix this shit storm I shouldn't be involved in.

The race doesn't go Lucia's way. On lap fourteen, she collides with Sterling Samuels. It's his fault, but she gets the brunt of the result. I watch with clenched fists as her car slides across the grass toward one of the barriers. She doesn't go straight into it, thank God. She kind of bounces off it, crushing the front left tire. And when she comes to a stop, the car is definitely not going to be able to rejoin the race.

I turn my attention to Frankie, and the words 'Yellow flag' hit the screens. Frankie is gripping the table in front of her so tightly her fingers are white. So is her normal tanned complexion. "Lucia? Talk to me."

Frankie sounds calm, but she's white as a ghost, and when she finally lets go of the table to blindly hand me an extra pair of headphones so I can hear Lucia's response too, her hand is trembling.

"That fucking asshole pinched me. He didn't have the right of way!"

"The stewards will look at it," Frankie sighs in relief but double-checks because Lucia would rant about injustice even if her limbs were severed. "You're okay?"

"Yeah. All good. I mean, mentally my PTSD is off the charts, but I'm fine," Lucia admits, which is a bit shocking. She never talks about the accident in public let alone the effects of it.

"I wonder if she was triggered before the crash?" Logan mutters.

"No," Frankie and I say in unison. I immediately drop the headphones on the table and walk away. It's not my place to speak on this. I don't work for the team. Frankie doesn't notice or care that I did though. She focuses on Logan. "She didn't do a thing wrong there. Samuels got greedy and dangerously aggressive, which we all know is his thing. The stewards better intervene on this one."

"They're investigating," Logan replies.

I wait for Lucia to return. She is going to be hotter than her brakes, and not in a good way. But it's fine. She deserves to be pissed. My phone buzzes, and it's Saffron again.

Come up to the lounge. I'm up here now.
Lonely. :(Let's talk.

I actually growl as I type back.

I don't hang out with people who treat me like a pawn. Don't text me again unless it's to apologize.

Where the fuck is Lucia? I wonder. I glance at one of the monitors showing the television coverage of the race, where the pit crew is gathered. Her car is being towed away. She's nowhere near it. I lean down to one of the guys sitting here. "Where is she?"

"She was walking back but stopped to talk to a guy on the wall. Looked like a reporter or something." He mutters.

Or something. That's why I storm out of the garage and flash my badge at the security to get into the small area between the barriers and the grandstand, where the press ring the track. Because the 'or something' part of that statement scares the shit out of me.

TWENTY-TWO

O-M-G THAT SUCKED DONKEY'S BALLS

Lucia

STERLING SAMUELS IS A GRADE-A, first-class, five-star dick. And he can eat one. I can't believe he fucking hit me! I had the racing line. He should have backed off. I was in front. The track was mine. And even when the stewards make the call and penalize him, it won't matter. The damage is done. I won't get points. I won't finish. I am so mad I could fucking explode.

I decline the scooter ride back to the garage. It's not that far, and I need to walk off some of this frustration. I pass the photographers, and they yell out encouraging words. I don't stop, but I tug off my helmet and give them a quick, curt wave. It's not their fault that Sterling is an asshole, and I need to be pleasant to them.

There's a mostly empty patch of fence right before the stands and the fans, and I pause a minute and take a few deep breaths. I try to focus on the positive. None of this was my fault. I didn't totally freak out when the wall was barreling at me. It wasn't until after the crash, when I was talking to Frankie, that the memories came flooding back. The heat, the flames, the whoosh of the fire extinguishers. The panic of my seatbelt being stuck. The pain of the glove melting away.

I exhale loudly, but not so loudly that I don't hear my name. I look at the stands in the distance. The fans are too far away for it to be one of them unless they have a megaphone which, well, anything is possible. But no. My peripheral vision picks up movement, and I see this guy in all black, including a baseball cap waving at me from the fence. It's part of the track that no one should be in. Is he a photog that got lost or greedy for a new vantage point?

I wave but turn to keep walking. Until he yells. "Maybe you shouldn't be out there with PTSD!"

I stop and my head slowly turns to face him. I don't say anything. I just stare because my brain is having a hard time computing. It hits me I used the words PTSD on the radio. Of course the television broadcast played it or the internet station that allows the users to 'follow' along with whichever driver they want. My brain is running through all of this information, frantically putting together the pieces, so I don't answer him. I can't.

"You gonna get someone killed if you're unhinged out there," he yells.

He looks familiar. Why? From where? My eyes slide down to the lanyard around his neck. I'm too far away to read it, also it's turned around, so I couldn't anyway. I step closer and then think twice and step back. "Take off your sunglasses."

"Nah."

He pulls up his phone and starts snapping my picture, so I look away and start walking again. He's definitely not an accredited photographer for the event. They don't use iPhones. "Seriously. No comment on putting real drivers like Samuels at risk with your unchecked mental health?"

"You are a fuck—"

Something blurs right by me, and I hear the guy swear, and I look back. Nick is there, directly in front of the guy, and there's a heavy cracking sound. He slaps the phone out of the guy's hand. It lands on the outside of the fence, face-down on the small strip of pavement. The guy tries to shove Nick, but Nick slaps his arm away, hard. The asshole swears. "You are going to pay for that phone. Give it back."

"I'm not paying for shit," Nick replies tersely and picks up the cell phone. I can see the screen is cracked. He frowns, and it's the fakest thing I have ever seen. "Damn. That sucks."

"Seriously dude. This is assault!" The guy screams.

"You can tell that to security," Nick replies calmly, and I see two big guys in matching security shirts marching toward us and the fence. "You are going to lose your credentials, and good luck getting them at any race ever again."

Nick is doing something to the guy's phone. And then the guards jump the fence, and the guy tries to run. They grab him, and one of them pulls off his lanyard. He holds it up. "Donovan White from... some shitty internet site I've never heard of."

He shows the lanyard to Nick, who pulls down his aviators to read the thing and then nods. They start to pull the guy away. "He has my phone!"

"Right," Nick hurls the phone over the fence. It lands four feet from the guy, in a puddle so deep that the whole thing is engulfed. "Shit. My bad. I have terrible aim."

I cover my mouth to keep anyone from seeing my smile. Donovan White, the asshole extraordinaire, is seething now. Nick turns away and starts toward me but Donovan's next verbal blow stops Nick and causes the smile to drop from my face. "Shouldn't you be with your baby mama, and not this joke of a driver?"

Baby mama? I would add that to the list of things that make this guy insane, but the look on Nick's face tells me that it's not a joke. Nick is the king of poker face, but right now, his skin is pale, his jaw slack, and his eyes wide.

The guy disappears around the corner of the grandstand with the guards, and I stare at Nick. He hooks my arm and starts pulling me toward the garage. "Let's go."

"What was he talking about?"

"The longer you stand here, the more people will get photos of you on their phone," Nick snaps. "And you look like someone just drowned your goldfish."

"Who did you get pregnant?" I ask, and do the only thing I can, turn my head away from the crowd.

"I've got to alert the venue security about that guy and then update your dad and also look into him myself," Nick says, ignoring my question completely. I know he gets very focused in a security situation, but this is more than that. It's him ignoring me on purpose. Because he doesn't want me to know the truth.

"He's just an asshole blogger or whatever," I say and somewhere in the back of my brain, I'm still trying to remember where I know him from. Donovan White.

Once we're past the grandstand, I grab him and tug him to the side. "Nick!"

He inhales and seems to hold it. "Lucia, the tabloids are saying Saffron is pregnant and I'm the father."

Honestly, if he'd told me Big Bird had impregnated Gonzo from the Muppets I would have had an easier time accepting it. "You..."

"No!" He barks back. "No. I didn't."

"Lucia!" One of the PR team approaches. "Media."

I sigh. It's better this way. I can't look at him right now anyway. I'm reeling, and I don't say smart things when I'm feeling like this. "Coming."

"Lucia," Nick calls my name.

"I'm fine. I'll meet you in the paddock after the interviews,"

I reply, and as we approach the rows of reporters, it hits me. That Donovan asshole was the reporter who asked me about my hair routine.

I don't turn and call Nick back to share that information. I keep walking with the PR person. I can tell him later. Right now, I just need time away. I feel like crying, and it isn't about my DNF in the race. It feels like Nick and I are hurtling toward our own DNF.

I make it through the interviews. It's only fifteen minutes of my life, but it feels like fifteen days. When I get back to the Mirabella paddock, there's a buzz of chatter from the balcony above. VIPs are on the second-floor deck, off the lounge. A few call my name and wave and offer words of condolence. I plaster a stiff smile on my face and nod and wave. When I open the wide glass door to step inside, I glance down the long corridor. I can see the door to my private room ajar. Nick is probably already in there, pacing, waiting to talk to me about this thing. This horrible, outrageous thing.

I hate thinking about him with that pop singer. I hate thinking about him with anyone else. I hate that I hate that. I have no right to act possessively. I'm the one who insists this is a casual thing, and I stand by that. It makes the most sense, and I don't do things based on emotion. I mean... I do. I have, and it's always bitten me in the ass. I don't have the time or emotional capacity for a boyfriend. Nick can't be my boyfriend. I'll hurt him again.

Except, despite that list I just mentally recited, I'm the one who feels hurt. I rub a hand across my forehead, which is starting to ache with from stress, and I start up the stairs instead of to my private room. The lounge runs the entire left side of the paddock's second floor, from front to back. I walk over, pull open the double doors, and step inside. It's filled with celebrities, team members relatives, and old money because you either have to be someone, know someone, or be rich as shit to be in here. Paddock passes that include race day lounge access range between fifteen and thirty thousand euros.

I see a few familiar faces—movie stars, TV stars, a rapper, Billy's mom, Logan's brothers, and Saffron Kent. She is definitely pregnant. I didn't notice it when she was belting out God Save the King because I was focused on the ground. I always stare at inanimate things, not people, right before a race so I stay focused. But now, as I see her and that wretched toad of a bodyguard at a high-top table near the opening to the deck, her little bump is on full display between where were cropped top ends and her flow skirt begins. And she's sipping a clear, bubbly beverage like she was in the airport, which I realize must be ginger ale or Sprite or something.

I walk right over to her. It's not as clear and determined a march as I would like because people keep stopping me for selfies and to tell me I'll 'get 'em next time,' but I reach her eventually. She smiles at me, her big, red-stained lips parting to reveal teeth so white they would make snow jealous. "Lucia! O-M-G that sucked donkey's balls."

"Yes. It did," I nod and try to stop myself from saying what I'm about to say. Like internally, I'm screaming 'Don't do it!' But yet my mouth is moving anyway. "But what sucks even more is the idea that my boy... guard is lying to my face when he says he never hooked up with you."

"I'm sorry your... *boyguard?*" She scrunches up her face in the most exaggerated way. It makes me dig my nails into my palms. "Is that like some new-fangled word for bodyguard you sleep with?"

"Maybe." I snap. "Is that what you called him when you slept with him?"

My voice is remaining shockingly low and chill, but inside I'm screaming these words at her. My face must be doing that thing it does where it shows all my true feelings even though I wish it wouldn't, because Saffron stops acting like a snarky bitch.

"You know Nick better than me, so you should know when he's lying." She leans forward a little and says in a voice barely above a whisper. "And when I say you know him better than me, I mean in every way. Because he was never my *boyguard*. And as much as I desperately want to hire him back, it's not for any other reason than he is excellent at his job, and with this new plot twist, I'm going to need all the help I can get."

The current bodyguard looks up at her with a stunned look on his face. "You're trying to replace me?"

"Yes," Saffron replies without an ounce of remorse in her clipped tone. She turns back to me. "Look, like I told Nick, I need the media to think that he's the dad for a little bit. Because if they know it's not him, they'll figure out pretty quickly that it's my trash panda of an ex. And I am not... I can't deal with him right now. I just need a second to figure out what to do."

"Oh," I don't think I should be mad at her anymore. I mean, I am, but I also feel a little sorry for her. I don't like when two very different emotions fight for space in my heart and brain. It's exhausting and overwhelming. I feel like my engine when the power unit just can't cope anymore.

"Lucia," Nick's voice has me swivel my head to face him.

He keeps his gaze focused entirely on me even when Saffron lets out an all too chipper. "Hey, Nicky! Come join us!"

"Lucia, we should get back to your room," Nick says. His whole body is tense, I can see it in the way his shoulders are pinched and his arms are rigid, "We have stuff to discuss."

"I don't want to discuss anything," I tell him and turn back to Saffron. "I do have to get out of here, though. I'm not in the mood for fans and stuff, and with the race ending, this place is going to be even more packed in a few minutes."

"That Samuels kid better not podium," Saffron says and reaches out to pat my shoulder like we're besties. "Especially after what he said on that radio about you."

"What did he say?' I ask as I step out of reach, so her hand falls off my shoulder. I hate being touched by almost everyone but especially strangers.

"Lucia!" Nick says my name with a harsh clip to his tone. Like a teacher trying to get an unruly class to pay attention. Which of course makes me automatically want to ignore him, which I do.

"What did he say?" I repeat to Saffron.

"He said a bunch of swear words after you guys collided," Saffron says in a gossipy stage whisper. "I don't know exactly which ones because they were blipped by the TV station. But then he said 'That's what we get for letting a woman driver on the track.'"

"Oh fuck," I hear Nick hiss.

"He said that?"

Saffron nods emphatically. "I used to think he was super-hot, but now I think he's a little bitch. We women have to stick together."

"Lucia..."

I finally look at Nick, and I know he picks up on the imaginary daggers I'm throwing his way. "You knew about this, I assume?"

"Yeah. I heard it before I left the garage," Nick admits.

"But you didn't tell me?"

"Other things were happening that took priority," Nick explains. He's doing that super calm, factual tone thing I used to find appealing, but right now it makes me want to scream.

"He pulls misogynist bullshit over the radio, and you think that isn't important for me to know? Before I did interviews where I acted way more polite than I would have if you'd fucking told me," I hiss quietly but fiercely because I am fully aware that we have a couple of people watching us with curiosity in their eyes.

The pregnant pop star, her baby daddy, and the F1 driver who just got humiliated. Yeah, I would be staring too. If I don't get out of here I'm going to meltdown. "I have to leave."

"Good," Nick says with relief.

I stop and glare as he turns to follow me. "Not you. Just me."

"I go where you go," he reminds me.

"Not anymore," I reply, and I don't even realize I'm going to say it until I do. "You're relieved of your duties. Saffron, he's all yours."

"You can't fire me. You didn't hire me."

"We've got the asshole stalker thing figured out now, right? It's that White guy?" I say, and he gives me this half-nod thing that is filled with hesitation.

"It's not exactly a closed case, but it appears that he might be the guy," Nick admits.

"Okay well, you can figure that out. Or give the info to Jack and let him figure it out, but I am no longer in need of your..." services. I was going to say services, but the truth is as angry as I am, I still want him. In all the ways. And that's why this makes me so mad. He's kept important information from me twice today alone. Keeping things from me is the same as lying to me. He knows that's how I think. And now I can't help but wonder what else he doesn't tell me. "I don't need you."

"Like hell, you don't," he whispers back, and there is nothing about work being implied in that statement. His pale eyes hold a wounded glint. Like I just slapped him across the face or something.

"I do not need any of this," I wave a hand toward Saffron who is sitting there watching us while sipping her soda like we're a play being performed just for her. "And I don't need you. So work for Saffron or don't, but you're not working for me either way."

I storm out of the lounge, and by some miracle, I manage to keep the hot tears from sliding down my face until I'm safely tucked away in my private room with the door locked. I peel out of my race suit and throw on my street clothes without even showering. I'm crying the whole damn time. I feel like a wild animal stuck in a trap. I hate everything about today, and I can't change a single part of it. Not the way Sterling clipped my car, the cruel and uncalled-for shit he said on the radio, the fact that the world thinks my Nick knocked up a pop star. I have zero control. And I'm spiraling because of it.

There's a knock at my door a few minutes after the race ends with Billy in third, Jasper Nord in Second, and the younger, non-misogynistic Samuels brother on top of the podium. Good, that will eat away at Sterling's ego like cancer, and he deserves it. I'm fully intending on ignoring the knocking, but it won't fucking stop.

"Go away, Nick! I am not fucking kidding!" I yell.

"It's not Nick!" The female voice calls back.

It's not Frankie either. It's... I walk over, unlock the door and fling it open. "Clara?"

"Hey," She looks kind of upset. "Want a ride back to your hotel?"

"Did Nick ask you to do this?" I wonder out loud.

"Look," Clara's big brown eyes dart down the hallway before they land back on me. "I just really want to get out of here, like yesterday, and I don't want to be alone. Can you come?"

"Yeah," I say because she looks like a no would ruin her. And I've been there. Hell, I am there. "Misery loves company."

I turn and grab my bag off the couch and then follow her out the door.

Nick

"I'M sure she's just back at the hotel," Frankie says with a sympathetic smile. "You know how she gets when she's pissed off. Or overwhelmed. Or both."

"It's not okay that she did this," I reply as we make our way through the V.I.P. parking lot to our SUVs, which are parked beside each other. "It's my fucking job to be there with her all the time whether she likes it or not."

"Oh I think she likes it a lot," Frankie flashes me a cheeky grin, which I don't reciprocate. She leans in as we walk and bumps me with her shoulder. "*Ne vous inquiétez pas. Elle ne partira pas.*"

"You just said she left with Clara for the hotel," I argue, because Frankie just told me not to worry, Lucia wasn't leaving.

"I didn't mean physically," Frankie replies, and when our eyes meet she winks.

"She's saying you'll still get some," Billy elaborates, oh so helpfully. Not. He grins, obviously proud of himself. "I'm learning French. And how to speak Castera sister. One is infinitely harder than the other, mate."

"Yeah. I know." I grumble and purposely avoid eye contact with Jack, who I'm sure is giving me one of his judgy looks. He made it clear that he doesn't approve of me and Lucia. This will only give him more reason to stick to that opinion.

I climb into my SUV, and they climb into theirs. I let Jack pull around me to head out first. I turn on the engine but pause to call her one more time before I start driving. She lets it go to voicemail again. "Lucia, this is your bodyguard. I need you to call me back immediately."

I shove my phone into the holder on the dash and throw the car into drive. I curse the whole way home. She is being reckless, and I won't put up with it. She may think that this Donovan White blogger guy is the one who has been harassing her throughout the season, but we don't know that for certain yet. And she knows that ditching me is not acceptable whether there's a stalker or not. And telling me to go work for Saffron like I'm old shirt she's discarding. She went out of her way to be cruel, which I will not fucking take.

It's my own damn fault on so many levels, I realize as I navigate the streets and get on the A413 for the short drive to the hotel. I shouldn't have come back. I knew I had deeper feelings than she did and that I wasn't over her. It was asking for trouble. And if I couldn't say no to Bash, then I should have said no to Lucia when she wanted to get physical again. I let her walk right through every single emotional wall I had like they were made of Kleenex. And the Saffron thing... well, on top of the fact I never should have taken the job with her to begin with, I definitely should have gotten in front of these rumors, instead of just ignoring them when they first started.

Yeah, I'm furious with Lucia, but I blame myself. That doesn't mean she's off the hook. I am not putting up with her bullshit anymore. This isn't her being different. This is her being mean and irresponsible. And I don't put up with that from anyone.

I pull into the hotel lot and get out of the car. Because the track is forty minutes from London, just about every single F1 team member stays in one of two, side-by-side, countryside hotels. Well, in country terms, that means I can see the other hotel in the distance across a large farm field. I've been particularly worried about this race because of the hotels. There's no way to evade this douche who has been bothering her because he'll know she's in one of these two places. They have extra security on because of the situation, and I know Lucia thinks we caught the guy, but I'm not sure. The police have hauled him into London for further questioning, and I've supplied them with all the information about the previous incidents. That's what I was doing when Lucia decided to disappear with Clara.

I stalk across the parking lot. The light is fading fast since the race took longer than normal. Lucia's wasn't the only crash. Gabriel Allard from Mayflower Racing also crashed, and his car was much more damaged than Lucia's. They red-flagged it and stopped the race while they cleaned the debris. He was fine, thankfully. Maybe that has me on edge too. Crashes bring me back to that moment when I felt the earth shake and saw the ball of fire. To the bile taste in my mouth while I acted like my heart wasn't being shredded by the news it was Lucia. Because my job was Frankie. I wasn't even the boyfriend.

I take a deep breath of the country evening air. It's earthy and sharp, which means it's going to rain. Typical England. But that just further spirals my mood into the dark side. Because it reminds me of that fight Lucia and I had that ended us in Paris.

Fuck. I am going to have to tell her how I feel again. Still. Even if it isn't what she wants to hear. And if this means I go back to just being the bodyguard, then I do. Then I think of Lucia moving on while I'm protecting her, and I realize if she rejects the idea of us as more than bed buddies, I'm going to have to leave again. Or at the very least, protect Frankie. Jack can handle Lucia.

I make my way through the lobby without looking up. The building is an old estate, similar to the one where Adelaide had her shower, that borders on a castle. I keep my eyes glued to the thick stone under my feet and climb the wide, wood staircase to the third floor. Lucia and I have rooms at the very end of the hall. Hers had a balcony, but I switched with her because there are thick ivy vines running up the building, and I worried someone could climb them.

I stop in front of her door and knock.

No answer, so I knock again.

I swear under my breath and yank my phone out of the pocket of my leather jacket. I text her.

> Open the damn door Lucia or I will get security to do it!

I glare at the little dots as they bounce as she types out a reply. Then it stops. No reply. Before I can march down to the concierge and get him to open the door, my phone rings and her name pops up on my screen. It's a video call. I answer it. Her face populates the screen.

She's smiling, which throws me for a loop. "Where are you?"

She's in a car, I can see the headrest behind her. "I'm with Clara. Say hi Clara."

"Hi, Clara!" Clara sings out. Lucia moves her phone so I

can see her partner in crime. Clara is driving, and she grins but doesn't take her eyes off the road. We're going out for a drink. I promise I will be careful. I'm videoing you so you have proof of life. Clara is a badass, she can beat up any possible kidnappers."

"Lucia," I growl. "This isn't a joke. And you and I need to talk."

"Yeah, I don't want to talk," Lucia replies, her eyes growing dark and serious. She takes an audible breath. "But I *am* sorry I tried to dump you on Saffron. And I don't want you to go."

"Well I can't stay like this," I warn her. "And you evading me defeats the purpose of my employment, Lucia."

"It's one fucking night!" She pleads. "Not even a night. I will be back at the hotel in two hours, tops. I'm fine, Nick. That guy isn't going to try anything else."

"We don't know for sure it's him behind everything," I warn her.

"Yeah, but it's likely," Lucia sighs. "I'll drop a pin when we reach the pub, okay? But I'm not coming back yet. If you want to drive here and sit in a corner or wait in the parking lot, go ahead. Do your job, but I don't want it. I need a minute."

She ends the call before I can respond. I swear under my breath and walk from her door to my own. I decide I'll let Bash decide what I should do. He's writing my checks. I'll let him know she's out with Clara, and ask if he thinks I should follow her. The wannabe boyfriend wants to storm over there and haul her out. Have the hard talk and then have the make-up sex. But I have to stay in bodyguard mode.

I fumble with my key as I scroll through my contacts to find Bash's number. I drop the key. Stupid hotel with its quaint, old-fashioned key system. I bend to pick it up, shove it back in the lock and hit send on Bash's number.

He answers immediately, but not with a hello. "Why is that

singer who was at the race telling people you're working for her again? Why did Adelaide tell me that you got her pregnant?"

Ah fuck. I like Adelaide, but she needs to stop reading trashy websites like it's her job. "It's a misunderstanding. Sort of." I get the stupid door unlocked and swing it open. "Your daughter tried to fire me. But she's since rescinded."

"Honest to God that girl…" Bash sighs. "She's been so damn obstinate her whole life. I wish she would just be reasonable for once."

"She manages things her own way," I defend her carefully. "I think you need to have a talk with her. With all due respect, I would advise you don't start by berating her. I know she frustrates you because she handles things differently, but you should ask her why. Try to reach for understanding."

There's silence on the other end, and I start to worry that I've overstepped. I have, and I know it. "Look, it's not my place, and I'm sorry if this is overstepping. I spend a lot of time with your daughter, and she is a really incredible person. I know you two have had some major blowouts, and I'm just trying to give you some thoughts on how to keep it from happening as often. And please don't let it happen over this. I will work it out with Lucia, one way or the other."

I'm so busy babbling to Bash that it takes me too long to realize something isn't right. A lot of things aren't right, and they hit me all at once.

It's too dark.

And cold.

The air is filled with a sharp and earthy scent, like outdoors.

I didn't leave the window open.

I did leave the bathroom light on.

I didn't turn the main light on.

I always do that. I don't ever allow us to walk into a dark room.

"Do you think I'm too hard on her?" Bash asks quietly.

I slowly pull the phone away from my ear, as Bash continues to talk. I take one step. The body hurtles at me from the entry to the bathroom. I hit the wall. The back of my head hits so hard my teeth rattle, and white-hot pain flares in my vision. The phone drops from my hand. I grab him by the front of his shirt. It feels familiar. It's a mix of Lycra and… boom! Now he's slammed against the wall. He's shorter than me, and thinner. This should be easy. But my side is cramping like a mother-fucker. He knees me square in the balls. Hard.

I buckle, and my vision clouds like I could faint as my stomach lurches like I might puke. He pushes me away, and I grab his arm and see a weird shaped greenish blob on his inside wrist, but I can't make it out before he breaks free of my grip and runs out the open door. I try to chase after him, but I only manage to stumble, not run. He's gone down the stairs and out of sight. "Hey! Stop, fucker!"

I scream, but that only brings Logan out of his room at the other end of the hall. I lift my hand and point. "There was a guy in my room! Call security!"

My hand is red. Why is my hand red? Why is my side still cramping? Logan doesn't move. He just stands there looking like he's watching a horror movie when he thought he was going to a Disney flick. "Logan! Call the hotel security so they can inter-cept him!"

"Nick, you're bleeding…" he replies. "Holy shit man."

I turn, intending to return to the room and grab the phone and call them myself. But then the cramping gets worse, and I look down and see blood oozing into my shirt, creating this red circle that's growing at a rapid rate. And fuck, my balls are throbbing, and…

"Nick!" Logan's voice is right beside me somehow. And

there's carpet under my cheek. "Nick, don't worry I called for an ambulance."

"Call the hotel security," I yell and try to sit up, but everything spins, and my body throbs everywhere. "And Bash. My phone. Inside. Call Bash."

I close my eyes and fight to stay conscious.

Lucia

CLARA'S EYES go to my phone, which is on the table between our pints of Guinness, buzzing once again. I flip it over to see the screen. It's Frankie. I roll my eyes. "Now he's got my sister calling."

I put the phone on silent and flip it back over. Clara sips water even though there's a full pint of beer beside her and reaches for the last of the fries on her plate. I've already devoured my fish and chips. "You're not answering any of them?"

"I sent him a pin. He can calm his tits," I reply with a grin, but inside I'm not smiling. I feel sad. I really fucked things up with Nick, and I don't know if I can fix it. "So you going to tell me what has you so... out of sorts?"

Clara leans back in her side of the booth we're tucked into. The pub is in a small village near the hotel. It's got four older gentlemen playing darts at the back who barely looked up when we walked in. The bartender asked for a selfie which I gladly posed for, and then he comped us a free pint each. No one has bothered us since. The place smells of fried food and wood and leather. It's dimly lit and looks like it was built a billion years ago. It's got good energy, and Clara relaxed as soon as we walked in. But something is definitely up with her. "I do. I want to tell you because I feel like I can trust you. And I need to tell someone, but only someone who I can trust."

"You don't trust Billy?" I say, because she's not just his trainer, she's his best friend.

"I can't tell him this. Yet," Clara stares at her beer.

I take a sip of mine. "God, this stuff is awful!"

"I know," Clara giggles. "I've always said Guinness is gross, but it was a nice gesture from the bartender. I didn't want to offend him by turning it down."

"Is that why you haven't touched it?" I ask as I push mine to the side and reach for my water.

"Well, I'm driving you back to the hotel, and I don't want the wrath of Nick," Clara smiles, and then her bottom lip trembles. "So there's that. And the fact that I'm pregnant."

The room gets smaller. Everything in it, the people the noise the smells, lessen as I stare at her and tears fill her big brown eyes. "Oh, shit. Please don't tell me it's Billy's."

My sister's heartbroken face fills my thoughts. But then I look at Clara's face, and she looks positively horrified. "No! God. Gross. No. Of course not."

Okay, so that reaction is a little much. Billy is an attractive guy and very charming and more than a decent human being. It's not exactly an insult to think she would have slept with him. She blinks, and the horror clears from her face, and now she just looks stunned. "You think I would sleep with your sister's serious boyfriend? That I'm that type of person? And that I would then tell you about it?"

"No. I don't think that at all," I promise her. Fucking great.

I'm ruining my new friendship with this girl who just told me her biggest secret. I have to fix this. "Clara, I'm sorry. I just jumped to a conclusion. Because Billy is the only guy I ever really see you with. I'm sorry. I have... I'm neurodivergent, and I don't always react in ways that are considered normal. Especially to surprises."

Clara's wide, straight eyebrows pinch, and she cocks her head. "Is that like autism?"

"Sort of. Autism is a spectrum and I'm on it," I explain. "I just found out, after the crash and everything. My psychologist gave me the official diagnosis, so I'm still trying to figure out who and how to tell people."

"Oh," Clara smiles. "I guess I'm doing the same with this news."

"You can trust me," I promise and lean forward, my palms flat against the grainy wood table. "Tell me whatever you need to. I won't tell a soul."

"I don't know what else there is to say," Clara sighs and slumps a little. "I'm an idiot. I didn't intend for this to happen. Billy... he's going to flip out."

"Okay, well, accidents happen," I say and think about what I would feel if it were me. I would be in mourning because it would mean my career would be over. If I kept it. I'm not sure I would. I look her in the eye again. She's on the verge of tears, and I don't want to make it worse but... "Are you thinking of keeping it or not? I'm not judging. I believe in options."

"I'm keeping it," Clara says, and the first tear falls down her cheek. She quickly wipes it away. "Sorry. I've just never admitted that out loud, and now it feels real, and I'm really freaking out."

"It's okay. Oh, I wish I was a hugger, I would hug you right now," I confess. "Know I'm giving you a mental hug."

"That's better than nothing. Thank you." She huffs out a

little laugh and sniffs. When her small laugh fades, she looks me in the eye again. "Would you keep it? If it were you?"

I open my mouth to say no. But then I close it. Because for the first time in my life, the answer isn't black or white. "I might. It depends on a lot of things. Who the dad is, for one thing."

"You mean, if they'd help?"

I shake my head. "No. Just who they are and what they mean to me. Whether or not they are involved, or I even tell them is something else. But yeah, I mean, I have to have had real feelings for them I guess. And also, it would matter if I thought I could give the kid a decent life."

"I can," Clara says. "I mean, I have support."

"You just said Billy would be furious, so do you think he might fire you?" I ask.

"No. He won't," Clara says with certainty in her voice for the first time in this entire conversation. She takes a deep breath and locks her eyes on mine. "He's my brother."

"Billy? James?" I repeat. She nods. "My sister's boyfriend. The guy I call bro? He's your actual brother?"

"Yeah," Clara nods. "We don't tell anyone because his mother is not a fan of the media finding out her husband had a secret relationship and child with someone else. But Billy has been there for me ever since he found out about me. And I know that he'll freak out and probably be mad at me, but he'll also have my back."

"And the dad?" I ask and then I reach across the table and past her hand. Not something I would normally do, but she looks like she needs it. "I honestly think that you can handle this on your own, I swear, but do you think they'll want to be involved? With you or the baby?"

"Maybe," Clara says, her voice a bit squeaky. "I don't know for sure. I think... I think it would suck for them even worse than for me, so I don't know if I would tell him. It wasn't like I was in a real relationship with this guy or anything."

And that's when it hits me. I'm not in what anyone would call a 'real' relationship with Nick. I'm the person who has called it anything but a relationship since it started. But the truth is, if I was pregnant with his kid, he would be the first person I would tell.

Clara's phone starts buzzing, and she sniffs again and pulls it out of the pouch in her hoodie. "Billy. I have to answer."

"Argh. Fine. Party pooper."

Clara laughs shakily. "If this is your idea of a party, you've got to get out more."

Then she hits the answer button on her phone and says hello. I watch her face fall immediately. "What?"

I feel the hair on the back of my neck twitch and quiver. Something is up. Clara's eyes widen and land on me. "Is he okay? How did this happen? Yeah. Yes. The Pig and the Pickle. That's it. Okay. Yeah."

She ends the call and starts pulling money out of her pocket. She drops two crumpled twenties on the table between our untouched Guinness pints. "We have to go now."

"Why?" I ask as she slides out of her booth and motions frantically for me to do the same.

"Now, Lucia. I will tell you outside. Let's go," Clara says. I slide out of the booth and start to panic. Every single thing about her has changed. She's not sad or vulnerable anymore. She's panicked, and she's making me start to freak out.

I grab my bag, and she takes my hand and pulls me toward the door. I yank my hand away. "Just tell me what's happening. Is it that guy from earlier today?"

"What? Who?" Clara asks and pushes open the door as we reach it.

"The guy Nick had turned over to the police." But then, I step outside and see the black SUV pulling into the parking lot.

Frankie is opening the door before Jack has even come to a complete stop. I can hear Billy yell at her to be careful. Our eyes connect, and something cold starts to seep into my veins. I freeze and stand completely rigid. "What?"

Frankie steps out of the SUV and rushes across the parking lot. Clara turns to me. "It's Nick."

Frankie grabs my shoulders. I shrug her off like her hands are made of fire. "Louie. Someone was in Nick's room when he got back to the hotel."

"Who?" I yell it. I don't know why. I didn't mean to.

"We are trying to figure that out. But there was a struggle, and Nick got injured." Frankie says, and then both she and Clara are moving me toward the SUV.

I'm putting one foot in front of the other, but I'm not sure how. "Is he okay?"

"He will be," Frankie says. "I mean, we think so."

Billy is there now, holding the back door open to the car he and Frankie just stepped out of. "You and Frankie are going to go with Jack to the hospital. I'm going to head to the hotel with Clara."

"Yeah. Okay." I say, but the words feel like they came out of someone else. I don't sound like me. I don't feel like me.

I crawl into the SUV, and Frankie gets in the other side, and the doors close. As Jack starts to drive, I look at Frankie, but her face blurs in front of me as my eyes fill with tears. "Frankie, I think I'm in love with him."

"I know you are," she replies softly. "And it's going to be okay."

I hope to God she's right.

Lucia

I LET Frankie lead the way as we enter the hospital. She and Jack seem to miraculously know where to go. The hallways are too white. The place smells too clean. I still don't know how I'm moving. My legs feel like jelly, my heart is racing, and my stomach is churning. I'm suddenly regretting that fish and chips and everything else I've ever eaten.

I see a sign above a door on the left and rush inside, straight to the toilet. I throw up. And when I'm done, I know the tears streaming down my face aren't just from the violent expulsion of my stomach contents. Frankie is leaning against the sink when I pull myself off my knees, flush the toilet and turn around. "Sorry. I'll hurry."

"Take your time," Frankie says, turning on the tap for me. "He's getting stitched up."

"Stitched?" I echo and feel weak again. She touches my shoulder giving it a brief squeeze before letting go.

"He was stabbed. With a pair of very small scissors,"

Frankie says, and that should reassure me, but I'm not reassured. I won't be until I see him.

I open the door to the restroom and leave, but I don't know where I'm going, so I have to wait for her. Frankie emerges and starts down the hall again, turning right into a large triage area. There are about ten beds, all separated by curtains. We walk right through it and to a short hallway with three private rooms. Jack is standing outside the first one. "In there?" I ask.

Jack nods, and I rush the door like a soccer player going after the ball. I fling open the door. The bed is empty. I spin and find Nick standing in the corner of the room, shirtless. There's a simple white bandage taped to a spot between two of his two lowest ribs.

I rip my eyes from it as he says. "Lucia."

He's staring at me with caution. His shirt is in his hands. He looks tired but good. So good.

"I love you," I tell him.

"I... I hit my head. I have a mild concussion," Nick replies. "And he stabbed me with my own nail scissors, which is a bit embarrassing. But I'm okay. No need to freak out."

"I love you." I insist and my bottom lip starts to tremble uncontrollably.

"I know. Are you okay with that?" He asks and I blink.

"I love you," I repeat. "Are *you* okay with that?"

"It's the best thing that's happened to me all night," Nick quips and I burst into tears. Because he's funny. And charming. And always knows exactly how to diffuse a situation. And me.

The next thing I know he's gingerly wrapping his strong arms around me. I press my cheek into his warm, bare chest and listen to his heartbeat and thank God for the sound. My fingers ghost over the bandage as his hand presses into the back of my hair, cupping my head. "I love you too, Lucia. In case you just need to hear it."

I cry harder. He kisses the top of my head. "I'm sorry. If I had been there, this wouldn't have happened."

"It might have happened to you, and that would be worse," Nick says. "And I'm fine. Honestly. They were nail scissors he must have grabbed from my travel kit. It's deep but small. Doc says I should heal fine."

Frankie enters the room. I only know because Nick speaks again. "*Ne partez pas. Tout va bien.*"

In French, he assures her that he's fine and she doesn't have to leave as I step out of his embrace and wipe at my eyes. Frankie smiles. "You okay Louie?"

"No. Someone stabbed my boyfriend," I mutter.

Nick grins. Frankie laughs. "Guess you both needed a near-death experience to admit you weren't just bumping uglies, huh?"

"After the river of denial you and Billy sailed on for an entire season, do not even think of being smug right now," I warn her, and she laughs.

"Let's get you guys home," she says, and Nick pulls on his shirt and grabs his jacket off the paper-covered bed. He walks out first, and Frankie leans over and whispers in my ear. "Sex is going to be even better now, lucky girl."

"It can't be improved on," I reply with a small smile. "He's a God already."

"Just wait," Frankie replies and winks.

FRANKIE'S RIGHT. Damn her.

When we get back to the hotel, Nick and I both head straight to my room. I want him to rest, but he says he'll only do it if I lie down with him. So I crawl into bed next to him in nothing but a T-shirt and underwear. He's stripped down to just his boxer briefs. I snuggle into his chest, on the side without the bandage, and pull the warn duvet over us. And then his hands begin to roam over my bare thigh, around the curve of my hip, across my stomach.

"Nick, you should rest," I whisper with not one ounce of commitment behind my words. Because his fingers just slipped under the waistband of my underwear.

"Your pussy doesn't want me to rest," Nick argues as his fingers slide through my wetness.

"She's selfish," I whisper back, unable to find my voice as he glides his thumb over my clit. "You shouldn't listen to her."

"I'm not," Nick replies. "But she's got my cock's full attention."

My giggle is cut off by his mouth covering mine. The kiss is long and deep and grows wild with passion within moments. But he's injured, including a concussion, which I know first-hand isn't going to be helped by our usual wild sex session. I pull my mouth from his and move away, making it impossible for his hand to continue to push me to orgasm, unfortunately. "We can't."

"We have to," he argues. "What the hell am I going to do with this if we don't?"

Nick pulls down the sheets and reveals his perfect, long cock, which is rock hard. I smile. "I said we can't. I didn't say I couldn't."

I lean down and wrap my hand around him with a firm grip. Nick moans. I scoot down to settle between his spread legs and I lick his tip. "You just lie still and enjoy yourself."

And then I proceed to suck his cock as if my life depends on it. Because he deserves it, and I want to spend all the time I can making him feel as good as he makes me feel. My tongue swirls, my lips suck and my hand circles his base while the other plays with his balls. I take my time at first and then build up to a steady, strong pace. I feel all his muscles slowly tighten from his thighs to his abs and even his hands start to ball into fists, and I know he's close. So I'm stunned when he suddenly unclenches his fists and grabs my shoulders. He's sitting up, wincing a little as he does it.

"Are you okay?" I ask, panicked.

"No," He growls. "I want to come in you."

"Nick..."

"Lucia," Nick replies his voice stern like I'm pissing him off, but I know by the devilish smile on his lips I'm not. "Take off those panties and climb up on my dick, please."

"Please?"

"I have manners," Nick retorts, and I laugh as I slip my underwear off and straddle his hips. He holds himself up and I start to slide down a little onto him. He moves one hand to my hip, and the other to my clit. "I want you to come around my cock so hard you to take me with you."

Jesus, I will never tire of his demanding and dirty mouth. I stare at him as he leans his back against the headboard and stares with hooded eyes at the place where we're joined together. His fingers are working magic on my clit and I grab my tits, which brings his eyes to mine and he smiles in the most deliciously feral way. "I fucking love watching you."

"Close," I pant and pinch my nipples, He grabs my hip and steadies my pace with his grip, guiding me up and down. His fingers must be slick with me as he rubs and rubs my button and I arch my back and pant his name as my orgasm washes over me.

As I collapse against him he kisses and sucks my neck and pushes up into me slowly, but with force. "I fucking love you, Lucia."

He comes so hard, with a grunt that rattles through us both, that I don't think he even hears me as I say. "I love you too."

After I climb off him and clean up in the bathroom, I crawl back into bed and I think he's already asleep. So I don't expect a response when I say. "I'm so sorry for all the bullshit I've put you through since the crash."

I promise myself to say it again when he's alert, but then he replies in a deep sleepy voice. "I'll forgive you if you do one thing with me before we leave London tomorrow."

My eyes open, and I stare into the darkness of the room, listening to his heartbeat under my ear. "What?"

"Just agree. Trust me, it's not something you'll hate."

"Trusting you is the first favor," I reply. "Now, agreeing is the second favor."

His chest jiggles as he lets out a soundless laugh. "Okay. So I'll forgive you if you do two things for me before we leave London tomorrow."

I hate surprises. I hate agreeing to anything without the full facts and time to process. But it's Nick, and I love him and I want his forgiveness. I think I'd have it no matter what, but I feel like I want to give him this. Even if it makes me a little uncomfortable. "Okay. Fine."

He kisses the top of my head. "Sweet dreams, love."

"No mushy nicknames."

"Whatever you say, love."

TWENTY-SIX
THE WORD IS PATRIARCHY

Lucia

I DRIVE because Nick still has a mild headache from the concussion, and I don't want him to drive. He argues, of course, because he is a control freak, but Frankie sides with me as we eat breakfast together in the hotel restaurant. And when I threaten to call Dad, Nick relents and hands me the keys.

"You are not capable of driving a normal car," Nick announces. "It's like putting a prize-winning racehorse in a pasture with old nags."

I can't help but notice he is gripping the handle on the car door. "Did you just call me a horse?"

I called you a prize," Nick replies. "Slow the fuck down Lucia."

"I'm not speeding, Nick," I argue back. I'm not. I have the Range Rover set to cruise control exactly one kilometer lower than the speed limit.

He punches an address into the nav but won't tell me where

we are going, so I'm just following commands. It adds to the anxiety I have over the unknown, and I'm fighting my instincts to get agitated, but I'm kind of losing. "Can you give me one tiny little hint? I am internally freaking out, and you know that never ends well."

"I'm not close to either of my parents," Nick says. "But I am close to my brother. He lives in West London."

"We... are..." I swallow.

He reaches over and wraps his hand around the back of my neck, under my curls, giving it a little rub. "Going to see my brother. Yes."

He must feel the tension that starts to build inside me because he keeps rubbing my neck and also keeps explaining. He swears it's not a big deal. He hasn't seen them in months between his job with Saffron Kent and now me, and they've been begging him to swing by. But I hate meeting new people. Because I generally suck at it. I never make eye contact, I say the wrong thing a lot. And these people matter because Nick matters.

"Let me into that brain of yours, Lucia," Nick prods as the nav tells me to get off the M1 to head into the city.

"You know that I would normally freak out about someone rubbing my neck like you are?" I ask. "But it doesn't bug me when you do it."

"Good," Nick says and his blue eyes look out the window as the rural roadside turns urban. "But if I ever do something you don't like, always tell me. Don't grin and bear it, okay? I'm open to adapting my habits to you."

"This is me adapting my habits to you," I reply as the nav tells me to turn left up ahead. "Because I suck at meeting strangers, and I hate it, so this is me definitely making an effort for you."

"I appreciate it," Nick replies. "I promise that this will be painless."

I wish I could believe him, but I just smile and keep following the directions.

Fourteen minutes later, I'm standing beside Nick as he knocks on the forest green door of a townhouse in West London. My belly is fluttering like it's a butterfly sanctuary, and the inhabitants are angry. The townhouse door opens, and this super cute, older, rounder version of Nick opens the door. He's wearing a checkered button-down, jeans, and a casual smile. "Nicky!"

He fist-bumps his brother, which is odd and adorable at the same time. And then his eyes, slightly darker blue than his brother's, land on me. "Lucia Castera! Oh man, the guys at the firm are going to be so jealous I'm meeting you. The senior partner, Bruce, has been a fan of Mirabella since your dad started the team."

He makes a fist and holds it up in front of me, so I make one back and we bump them. I guess this is his thing. He moves aside and motions for us to come in. Nick puts a gentle hand on the base of my spine, nudges me over the threshold, and follows me in, closing the door behind us. "Lucia, this is Franklin. He's a lawyer, so that's the firm he's referring to."

"Ah. Cool!" I say and smile. "Well tell Bruce if he wants paddock tickets, we can get them for him next year. And you, of course."

"Is that Uncle Nicky?" A squeaky, little voice calls out. I look down the short hall we're standing in, past Franklin. At the end, it opens up into a kitchen, and the cutest little boy, probably five or six, comes charging toward us, arms up high and a big smile on his adorable face. "Uncle Nicky!"

Nick crouches down and lets the little boy tackle him to the ground. The kid squeals in delight as Nick pretends that he's being bested by The Rock or something and lets the little boy pin him like a pro wrestler. Nick smacks his hand on the oak floors, tapping out. "You win, Lewis! You win!"

Nick sits up, then stands, scooping the boy up and placing him on his hip on his good side, not the one with the stitches. "Lewis, this is Lucia. Do you recognize her?"

"She drives race cars and Mommy says she crushes the pasty-archie too," Lewis announces.

Nick looks as baffled as I am by that announcement. Until a female voice calls from the back of the house. "Patriarchy, honey. The word is patriarchy."

"Whatever," Lewis calls back and turns his big brown eyes on me. "Can you give me a ride in your race car? Can I drive your race car?"

Franklin and Nick laugh, and I grin. "Maybe one day."

"Cool!" Lewis exclaims. He then proceeds to make a fist and I do the same so we can fist bump.

A beautiful blonde woman emerges from the kitchen. She's in jean overalls and a pewter gray shirt underneath. There's another kid strapped onto her chest. I can't see his face, only the tuft of curly blond hair.

"Welcome. I'm Eugenie" she says as she walks closer and turns a little so I can see the face of the child on her chest. He's sleeping, and I'm bad with baby ages, but I think he's maybe two. "This is Charles. I hope you like a good old-fashioned English roast."

"Who doesn't?" I ask and she smiles brighter.

"I hope it's a big one," Nick says as he peels out of his jacket and reaches for him. "This girl can eat."

"Nick!" I gasp.

"We like girls who eat in this house," Eugenie assures me.

"She once tried to stab me with her fork over the last roasted potato," Franklin announces.

Eugenie tells me to join her in the kitchen and Franklin, Nick, and Lewis sit in the attached living room, where Lewis shows his uncle every new toy he's gotten since the last time they hung out. I offer to stir the gravy for Eugenie as she whizzes around doing everything else, including pouring me a glass of wine and one for herself. When she offers one to Nick, I interject. "No alcohol with a head injury."

"Yes, Doctor Castera," Nick replies with a wink. "I'll take a fizzy water or something."

"Franklin, get your brother a fizzy water while he tells us about this head injury," Eugenie commands and Franklin gets up off the couch.

I like this woman. A lot.

Nick goes on to explain a very simple, non-scary version of what happened. I've heard the more detailed version, which he still explained like it was no big deal. But it was, and I think he's downplaying it even more because of Lewis. But he's not even paying attention as far as I can tell. He's absorbed in his Lego starship thing.

Both Franklin and Eugenie look concerned, which is fair. But it makes me feel guilty because I'm the reason he's in danger. "I should have been there."

Eugenie looks at me, and her blue eyes soften. "I bet you wouldn't want him in the car with you when you're on that track. Because he's not trained to be there."

"True."

"Well, he's the one trained for this situation, so it's better for everyone you weren't there too," Eugenie tells me with a sympathetic smile. "So don't beat yourself up unnecessarily. Plus, he seems just fine to me."

"I'm great," Nick interjects.

"Nicky the Great," Franklin adds with a laugh. "He used to

want me to call him that when we were kids and he'd win all those stupid football games."

Nick rolls his eyes. "Only the one time when we won the championship."

Everyone laughs, including me. And the rest of the afternoon goes better than I've ever experienced. I don't feel awkward once, and no one stares at me too long or expects me to carry a conversation. I just interject stuff when I feel comfortable and stay quiet when I don't. Franklin helps with Charlie, who I notice, when he wakes up, has Nick's rare eye color. It's just as stunning on him, even with his fairer skin.

I'm seated beside Nick, across from Eugenie and Lewis, who spent fifteen whole minutes telling me about how tall a giraffe can get and how many muscles it takes to hold up their necks. Franklin is at the end with Charlie in his lap and he feeds him off his own plate.

Charlie is definitely two, I think. He seems big. He's a happy kid like Lewis, and when he sees his Uncle Nick, he giggles and points. He doesn't seem to notice me, and I don't go over and make him pay attention to me, because I hated that as a kid. My mother used to always tell me to 'go say hello' to people who were her friends, when I would hide in the corner, or behind her, at luncheons or dinner parties, and I remember it like it was yesterday. Ugh. I'm not doing that to this little cutie.

When dessert is served, it's one of my favorite local specialties, Eton Mess. "Oh, this is the best!"

"Nick might have mentioned it was your favorite," Franklin says.

"Mine too!" Lewis claps gleefully. "Please come visit more, Lucia, because Mommy doesn't make this lots. And I want it lots."

"I'll see what I can do about that," I smile at him. I am not one of those women that fawn over kids. But this one is a gem, like his brother. I glance at Charlie and notice he's being served two cookies instead of the Eton's Mess.

"Charlie isn't a fan?" I ask and wonder if maybe he's allergic to berries or something else in the dish, like the cream.

"Texture issue," Franklin explains and smiles. "He doesn't like soft, lumpy things like oatmeal or Eton Mess or even ice cream with bits in it."

"Oh."

"And I don't like berries," Franklin explains as Eugenie puts some cookies in front of him. "They are so sweet, and the little seeds…" Franklin shivers. And I know that shiver. I do it when I feel microfiber or rose petals. I look over at Nick. He stares back with a gentle smile and takes my hand under the table. He tips his head towards me. "I get you."

Another hour later, I'm still holding Nick's hand as we say good-bye. Lewis, being a neurotypical toddler, fists bumps us both again and then looks me dead in the eye and asks innocently. "Are you going to be my aunt?"

"Oh my God, Lewis!" Franklin looks mortified.

Eugenie is laughing too hard to speak. Nick just grins at me and then looks down at Lewis. "Never know, buddy."

I should be totally freaked out by that, but I'm not. Holy shit. Who am I? I turn and thank Eugenie, who has Charles strapped to her chest again. He's muttering away in his own little language, flapping his arms. "Come back anytime you're in town. Please. You can even bring Nick if you want."

Nick laughs as we head out the door, and Franklin calls out. "No more scissor fights, little brother. I need you around."

"I know. I'll try my best." Nick calls back. "Love you."

"Gross," Franklin replies smiling. "You too."

I'm silent as Nick punches the directions to the airport into the navigation, and I start driving us there. Every moment of the afternoon cycles in my head. And layer upon layer of revelation starts to build. Nick has always known I'm neurodivergent, probably from the moment he met me. He grew up with a neurodivergent brother who is raising a neurodivergent child. And one who isn't. With a wife who isn't.

"It's a lot, I know," Nick says finally, about twenty minutes into our journey. "I feel bad for kind of just dropping it on you with no context. I'm sorry."

"No that doesn't bother me," I reply shaking my head. I tuck a curl behind my ear and reach for my sunglasses in the well of the middle console because the sun has finally decided to grace us this week. "I just want to know why you never told me that I was on the spectrum before."

"Because I thought you knew," Nick says. "And I knew Franklin hated when people brought it up with him when we were kids. There were much fewer resources back then and virtually no sympathy. He was labeled as 'special' and my parents didn't know what to do with that. I watched him struggle, feel alienated, and develop an inferiority complex. Feel shame."

My heart starts to ache for this man who is a lawyer with a beautiful family. The road to get there, the way Nick describes it, was non-existent. "How did he overcome all those hurdles?"

"Well, luckily, the one thing my parents did know how to do was throw money at a problem," Nick quips. He frowns. "But seriously, my dad had enough common sense to get him a therapist. Well, four actually. It took four until Franklin found one that fit. That man didn't see ASD as a problem that needed to be fixed in Franklin. He made it clear to Franklin that he needed to find his strengths and manage his weaknesses just like everyone else on the planet."

"That sounds like how Carmyn is handling this with me."

"I'm glad you found her," Nick says and reaches over and rubs the back of my neck again.

"I'm glad I found her too," I say, and steal a glance. He looks at me the way he always has — with affection and understanding. "And I'm glad I found you."

He grins. "Me too, love."

"Ugh."

TWENTY-SEVEN

FOR THE FIRST TIME EVER, YOU DON'T GET ME

Nick

IT'S BEEN A WEEK. The jet lag when we move from Europe to North America for races always kicks my ass, but add to that the headaches that come and go from the concussion and the pain in my side. Amazing how much damage a pair of tiny scissors can do. I step out of the shower, and as I wrap the towel around my waist, I glance at the incision in the mirror. The Mirabella team physician told me no more bandages, but he added a butterfly band-aid to it. It's red. And there are lines, like red veins splintering off it. I pull my eyes from the mirror and look down at it. All the flesh around it is tender. It felt like someone was punching the middle of it the whole run we did this morning.

It's race day. Lucia is nervous as hell because, although she qualified fourth yesterday, a new power unit for Allard means he takes a penalty and Lucia moves into third. The Texas track allows for a lot of overtaking, and Mirabella's cars have the strongest DRS on the straightaways of anyone. She has a real chance at her first podium. So this morning, she woke up antsy, and even after I spent a good, gloriously long time trying to orgasm the stress out of her, she still wanted to go for a light run.

I haven't told her about it because I'm sure it's nothing. And she has been in such a good mood all week. Even when a photographer caught us kissing at a restaurant on Thursday night and sold it to a tabloid that produced the lovely headline *'Lucia Castera steals more than an F1 seat.*

And went on to spew; *The female driver who snagged a seat in the sport thanks to her family owning the team, has also stolen popstar Saffron Kent's baby daddy.*

She was offended and annoyed, but she wasn't hurt. She called Jennie and asked her to take handle it. Jennie was Frankie's manager and also did personal PR for Lucia. Jennie was apparently working on getting a retraction, and I'd given her a statement explaining I wasn't the father of Saffron's kid and would gladly take a DNA test.

"You've got snarly face," Lucia says, and I focus back on the mirror to see her standing in the doorway behind me. "What's wrong?'

She's already dressed in a Team shirt and a pair of jeans. Her curls have been pulled back into a tight French braid. Her sunglasses are already on, which is a sign she's about to tune out the world. I am not about to split her focus. I grin at her. "I hate morning workouts."

"Which one? Running or licking my pussy?"

Now I don't feel pain. I just feel my cock twitching back to life. "I love when you talk about your pussy to me."

She blushes. "Shut up and get dressed. Or go to the track like that. I won't complain."

I head into the bedroom and get ready as quickly as I can. I decide I'll talk to the team doctor again once Lucia is doing her meditations and get him to take another look at this stupid thing.

When we get to the track, I realize it's a windy day, which I'm not thrilled with. And not because it's a cool wind either. The chill feels good on my skin. I'm still warm from exercising and rushing to get ready. I'm worried because it was windy in Mexico when Lucia crashed. I know that I can't keep comparing every race to the worst one that ever existed, but I do. The trauma is still too new. Frankie, Billy, and Jack are getting out of their car as we get out of ours. Frankie and I exchange glances. She's the only person I can talk to about these types of useless worries, but I don't because she doesn't need to be consoling me. She needs to focus on the here and now.

"You okay mate?" Billy asks as we walk to the paddock.

"Yeah," I nod. "You?"

"I'm P1," Billy replies. "I'm fucking brilliant. But you're sweating."

"I am," I reach up and touch my forehead. Yep. Damp. What the hell? "I was rushing to get ready."

"Huh," Billy says, and his blond brow furrows. "Any word on the attacker?"

"Haven't heard shit from London police," I reply. "I've called them every damn day, but they are still investigating."

"We know that loser blogger has been released by the London police, he's got a lifetime ban at the track there and no media accreditation ever again," Frankie chimes in and adjusts the sunglasses on her face. They're huge. And encrusted with jewels that may or may not be real. With her, God knows. She still has a ton of people sponsoring her to wear things.

"Well, that's a start," Billy replies.

"He was still in custody with them when I was stabbed, so whoever was in the hotel room wasn't him," I explain and try not to worry too much. I never take my eyes off Lucia so the fucker who did this won't get near her. "They've had security issues at the hotel before, so I'm worried the police will pass this off as a related incident. Like I walked in on one of their usual burglars and the dude panicked."

"That's the easiest route, eh?" Billy says shaking his head as the sun glints off his mirrored Ray Bans. "Instead of putting in the leg work to see if this is the same person who's been harassing her all season."

"Yeah, well," I decide to stop talking about it. Lucia has her headphones in, but she might be able to hear us, and again, I don't want to split her focus. "You just hold onto your position out there today, alright? Unless you want to give it up to your teammate."

Billy scoffs. Lucia glances over her shoulder at us and grins. "He's not going to give me anything. I'll take it."

"Well, well, well," Billy grins. "Someone is feeling ballsy."

Frankie smiles. Lucia laughs, and I wipe my brow again.

WHILE LUCIA MEDITATES AN HOUR LATER, I make my way through the garage to the small office at the back where the team doctor stays before and during a race. I pass the rows of chairs for the pit crew, which are all empty because they're having a last-minute staff meeting across the way. All empty except for Cedric, who is sitting on one chair with his feet up on another, staring at his phone. He doesn't look up as I walk by, so I assume he doesn't see me, but then suddenly, he does stand up. And I have to come to an abrupt stop to keep from slamming into him. He puts out a hand in front of himself, and accidentally jams it into my side. A few tiny inches under the cut. A ball of fiery pain explodes, and I groan. Loudly.

"Shit, dude!" Cedric says. "Sorry! You okay?'

"Yeah," I grunt and try to move around him.

"You sure?" Cedric asks.

Fuck, it hurts so intensely I kind of want to puke. That can't be right. "Yeah. Fine. I've got to talk to the doctor," I mutter and move around him,

"Because of me?" He calls after me, sounding confused.

"No. Not you," I reply, trying and failing to hide the aggravation in my voice.

The kid is just a young, eager, awkward driver. I have to cut him some slack. I knock on the doctor's door, and thankfully he yells "Come in!" I do. Immediately. So I can walk right in, and hurl the contents of my room service breakfast into his trash basket. He stands up. "Jesus, Nick. Is this concussion related or..."

He hands me a piece of paper towel as I lean back against the hospital bed in the corner of his long narrow office, and then he puts a hand on my forehead. His eyes narrow behind his silver-framed glasses. "Let me see that wound."

I lift my shirt and his eyes dart down and then back up to me. And his whole demeanor changes. He walks over to his desk, opens a drawer, and pulls out a small set of keys. "I'm going to give you two shots."

He starts towards the metal cabinet in the corner. "One for nausea and another called Ceftriaxone. Are you allergic to Penicillin?"

"No. No drug allergies," I say. "Is it infected?"

"Worse. I think you have something called Cellulitus," he says calmly as he opens the cabinet and pulls out two small vials of liquid and a sealed needle. "It's a bacterial skin infection, and it can cause serious health problems, including death."

"What the actual fuck," I hiss.

"We've caught it fairly early, so I'm not worried about that," he replies and he fills the needle with a liquid and taps it. "But you'll have to head straight to the hospital after this."

"What? Really?" I don't want to go to the hospital. I can't. This is race day, and it's a big one for Lucia. He levels me with a stare that says he is not fucking around. I know he's not. I feel like shit. "Yeah, okay. After the race starts, I'll get someone to drive me there. I swear."

He hesitates a minute like he's going to argue, and then he leans over my red, hot stomach and side and mutters. "This might pinch a second."

And then he pricks me with the needle, and it feels like he's pumping pure lava under my skin. I exhale a bunch of swear words I don't think I've ever uttered out loud before. The doctor doesn't seem phased by it. He walks over and picks up his cell on his desk. "I'm going to call the hospital and let them know you're coming," he announces and starts to dial. "But first I am calling Lucia and letting her know what's going on."

"Don't!" I bark out.

He doesn't even bother to look at me. "She made me promise that if you came in here for any kind of help, I would let her know. And this is serious, Nick. This can kill someone in forty-eight to thirty-six hours."

"What about HIPPA or whatever? If I tell you not to tell her, then don't tell her," I argue back, because this will ruin her day. Her big race. Her chance at her first podium.

"I'm contractually obligated to tell the team which hired me, about any team member who requires my assistance," he says like he's a lawyer reading the fine print on a contract aloud. "You are, for all intents and purposes, a member of the team. And she's not just a driver. She's the owner's kid, so.. sorry, but she wins."

"You're going to ruin her race," I snap.

"Well, better that than ruin her boyfriend," he replies tersely, and then he hits the send button and pulls his phone to his ear.

I give up and climb up and lie on the table because I'm exhausted in all ways possible. I close my eyes and listen to the doctor ask Lucia to come to the office and explain this cellulitis thing to her. Then I hear him put down his phone and walk back over to me. "Okay, now the shot for nausea. And I'll need you to drop your pants. I have to stick this one in your buttock."

"Of course you do," I mutter and start to undo the buckle on my belt. "Of course."

I yank down my pants and boxer briefs and rollover. The doctor gives me the shot, which is more humiliating but less painful than the first one. "You may feel sleepy."

I just grunt an acknowledgment, and by the time my pants are back on, there's another knock on the door. "Come in, Lucia." I call out for the doctor.

She walks in and focuses entirely on the doctor. "Okay, so you are sure we don't need an ambulance?"

"No. I already gave him a dose of antibiotic, so it's not a panic," the doctor explains and Lucia nods. But her eyes are too wide and her skin too pale. She's upset. Like big-time. "I will call the hospital and tell them you are on your way in and give all the necessary information."

"Thank you," Lucia says and then turns to me. "Let's go, infection man."

"Who is taking me?" I ask and start toward her. "I'm sorry if this throws you out of your zone. I didn't want him to call you."

"I knew if you were having side effects you wouldn't tell me, which is why I made Dr. Kwan promise to treat you like a team member, which means I have to be informed," Lucia explains. "Turns out, I know you as well as you know me. And don't worry about my race." She looks up at me with big, fearful eyes.

"It's going to be okay."

She nods at my words and then opens the door and holds my hand as we make our way through the garage. She honestly doesn't seem agitated, and that's a good thing... I guess? To be honest, it's kind of freaking me out more than if she was agitated.

Frankie is on the wall with Logan and a couple of other top team members. She looks very serious. I worked with her for years, and I don't think I've ever seen her this serious. Except for when she thought Lucia might be dying. "Jack is already in the parking lot, ready with the car. He'll drive."

"But what about you?" I ask because it's her bodyguard. "And please relax. I'm not dying."

"I'm fine here. I'm not leaving this wall for like three hours," Frankie reminds me and reaches out and squeezes my shoulder. "Thank you for seeking out the doctor and not ignoring this. I know a lot of men like to play the tough guy."

"I am the tough guy," I remind her with a smirk. "But I'm also not an idiot. I knew something wasn't right."

Frankie nods and turns to Lucia. Something passes between them, and I don't like it. She hugs Lucia and says "I'll keep you posted."

"Posted on what?" I ask, and a feeling of dread washes over me.

Lucia and Frankie both ignore my question, and Lucia tugs me away by the hand. She's leading me to the private entrance and exit for the teams, where our cars are and where Jack is waiting. "You don't have to walk me to the car, love. I'm fine. I promise I'll get to Jack and go. I want you back in your zone. The race starts in a half hour. You should already be changed into your suit."

"I'm not racing," Lucia says like it's the simplest thing in the world. Like she's ordering extra ketchup for her fries or something.

I stop moving, and she tries to tug me along, but I won't budge. That cool wind feels cold now, which I think means the shot the doctor gave me is already helping with my fever. "You are not missing the race."

"You think I can race knowing you're in the hospital?" She questions. "You think I even want to try?"

"I think that racing is the most important thing in the world to you," I reply. "And I don't want to ruin that for you."

"Nick, really?" Lucia shakes her head. "Wow. For the first time ever, you don't get me."

She lets go of my hand and reaches up and cups the side of my face. "You are the new most important thing in my life. And I'm still as single-minded and obsessive as ever. Multitasking will never be my strong suit, and so if you think I'm going to get in one of those cars when I can't give it one hundred percent, you're completely wrong about me for the first time. And hopefully the last. I love that you get me. So stop arguing, and let's get going. I'm not letting a pair of fucking nail scissors take away the best thing that ever happened to me."

"I would kiss you right now but I threw up."

"Rain check," she says and we make our way to the parking lot.

Lucia

JUST AS DR. KWAN SAID, the hospital was expecting us. We were swept right past the regular emergency and into a private room off the triage. It reminds me of where we were when Nick was stabbed in the first place, even though this is a totally different hospital in a totally different country. The antiseptic smells and the too-bright everything.

Nick doesn't seem to mind. He's so sound asleep he's actually snoring. The doctor who is treating him here mentioned that might happen because of the strength of the intravenous antibiotics. It's fine, I think to myself as I pace the floor at the foot of the bed, my headphones in and my head tipped down to see the screen on my phone, watch the checkered flag being waved as Billy crosses the finish line.

Billy won the Texas Grand Prix. I'm truly happy for him. I'm bummed for me, though. I really felt like this was my day. Like I would do big things today. Cedric, who took my place, finishes fifth. Not bad. I would have done better. I know it in my bones. But as soon as I heard from the doctor that Nick was sick, the race no longer mattered. I wanted to scream and yell for a second. Yeah, my brain wanted the throw a tantrum that I was being derailed from my goal. Because that's how my brain works. I loathe being thrown off course. Admitting I have feelings for Nick means having two courses. And this time, they veered in different directions. And picking Nick was a no-brainer. But fuck, it kind of sucks that I lost out on today.

"It's fine," I whisper to myself.

"What's fine and why are you pacing?' Nick's sleepy voice penetrates my headphones, which I've turned down low.

I spin and see him looking over at me through sleepy eyes. "I'm fine. You're fine. This is fine."

"No. It's not. It's okay to be disappointed, love. I won't take it personally," Nick replies and waves me over to his bed with his non-IV-stuck hand. I walk over and climb up beside him. I lie back next to him, one leg dangling off because the bed is too damn small.

"I mean... yeah I would love to have raced, but I wouldn't want to do it knowing you were in here," I explain. "Anyway, Billy won, so points for Mirabella."

"Good," Nick says and yawns. "And Cedric?"

"He lost a couple spots and ended up fifth," I reply as I pull out my headphones, lay them on my chest, and turn up the volume on the phone so we can both hear. They'll do interviews and then the podium ceremony. "The announcers have talked non-stop about how I dropped out last minute. I wish they would just shut up and not make this a big deal."

"But it is a big deal," Nick argues back softly. "They love a good controversy, and they'd hype this up regardless of which driver. Remember a couple years ago when that guy missed a race to have his gallbladder removed in emergency surgery?

They talked about that like he was fighting for his life when he was just fine. They love drama."

"Yeah, but for me, it's worse," I argue. "Because I'm a woman who gave up a race for a man. It will add to the 'she can't cut it' argument."

"Your dad skipped races when both you and your sister were born," Nick reminds me. "No one balked at that. No one said 'Well a dude with kids shouldn't race. Their head isn't in the game.'"

"Exactly!" I bark and then lower my voice. "But they'll insinuate it with me, and the trolls online will outright say it. Silly girl wants to take care of her man, she should give her seat up and stay home and make him a sandwich."

"I could really go for a ham and cheese. Swiss maybe? Or Havarti."

I look over at him, and he winks. I smile. "Is it petty that I'm glad that Cedric didn't do any better than fifth? If he had gotten on the podium before me, it would just create more proof that I'm not qualified and he should have the seat."

"Hell no it's not petty," Nick replies and tips his head so it's resting on my shoulder. "It's normal. Plus, that kid is annoying. I don't like him."

"He accidentally grates on every last nerve I have sometimes," I admit.

"And for me, it doesn't feel accidental," Nick confesses. "I swear today he stood up at the exact moment I walked by on purpose. Like he..."

"Shh!" I say and crank the volume only phone, as the female reporter starts to interview Cedric.

"You were just thrown into this race last minute," she begins. "Did you have any time to prepare? How do you feel about your race?"

"Yeah, it was a shock, but a welcome one," Cedric grins at

the reporter. "I mean, I'm a driver, I'm up for any race, and I think I proved that I can hold my own. Fifth isn't bad for someone who hasn't had any practice or qualifying sessions."

"And do we know when Lucia might return? How her boyfriend is doing?" The reporter asks. It's an innocent enough question, but I don't like it.

Cedric shrugs, which annoys me further. "Who knows, right? I mean, I can handle all the races she doesn't want to attend."

"She doesn't *want* to attend?" I hiss, and I can feel my blood boiling in my veins. "That fucking asshole."

"Yeah I knew something was off about him," Nick mutters.

"Well, I mean I wouldn't say she made the choice not to attend," the female reporter says, and I nod profusely at the screen. "A hospitalized loved one is something you'd miss a race for, right?"

"I mean…. If they wanted me to, yeah," Cedric says and lifts his arm, scratching the back of his neck nervously. He knows he's starting to look like an ass, and he's trying to figure out how to backtrack. Too late fuck face, I think to myself. And then he speaks again. "It's probably best for her and everyone that she knew enough to step out. I can't imagine her head is in the game much lately with the Saffron Kent stuff and her sick boyfriend and everything. Anyway, I did a good job with her spot. I hope she's happy with my results, and the team is."

"Happy?" I roll my eyes. "I'll be happy when I get to look him in the eye and tell him he sucks."

"If she's still out for Mexico, I'll do them proud again."

"You think she'll still be out for that race?" The reporter questions eagerly, because she thinks she's getting some kind of scoop.

"If she's still distracted because that track is where… well, we all know what happened there," Cedric says ominously. He smiles like he didn't just throw me under a giant fucking bus, and thanks her for her time before moving on to spew garbage to the next reporter.

"Let go of the phone, love," Nick says quietly. "I'm worried you'll crack the screen Hulk-Style with the way you're gripping it."

He wraps his hand around the side of the phone and pulls it out of my grip. I stretch my cramping fingers and stare at the red, smooth skin on the back of my left hand. It's been a year. And I hate that I still have to look at a reminder of the worst moment of my life every damn day. I get off the bed. "Does Frankie know what he's saying? Frankie better know what he's saying."

I reach for my phone, but Nick moves it away. Damn him and his long arms. "Lucia, deep breaths. This isn't the end of the world. He looks like the asshole, not you."

"Fuck Cedric and whoever did this to you," I hiss and start pacing his small room again. "I hate hospitals. I hate misogyny. I hate Cedric. I hate feeling like I..."

"Like you had no choice," Nick finishes for me. "You felt like you had to be here, with me."

"No. I mean I didn't feel like I had to," I shake my head. Everything is jumbled up inside me anyway, so it can't make it worse. I take that deep breath Nick told me to and count to five in my head. "I have a choice. I can ignore how I feel about you. I can push you away. I don't want to. I'm here because you matter to me. I love you. I just wish... I wish that I could control the narrative, you know? And I wish I could punch Cedric in the face. And maybe Saffron too."

Nick smirks. God I love his smile. "I don't advise either, but yeah, I understand all your feelings."

There's a knock at the door, and Frankie pops her head inside. "Are you two decent?"

I make a face. "It's a hospital room. He's hooked up to an IV. Yeah, I'm not getting some."

Frankie grins and steps inside. "With you, Louie, I can't make assumptions. When you were hospitalized after the crash, you had a whole conversation about the power of the pussy and the power of the dick."

Nick lifts his eyebrows and levels me with a shocked look. I shrug. "I was high. Sadly, antibiotics don't make him high."

Frankie turns to Nick. "You feeling better?"

"Yeah," I nod. "Doctor says we caught it very early, and one night on the IV drugs, plus a round of ten days of pills should do the trick. I'm sleepy as all hell though."

Frankie nods. "I'm glad you're going to be okay. Let me take this one for something to eat so you can rest."

"I didn't skip the race so I could go eat," I tell her. She ignores me and grabs me by one of my wrists.

"Lucia, go grab something to eat. In the cafeteria if you don't want to leave the hospital," Nick prods. "You can tell Frankie about Cedric."

Right. "Did you see his interview?"

"I did. On the car ride over here," Frankie says as she opens the door to the room. "I've already got the PR team talking with him."

"That fucker has a four-leaf clover tattoo, but I can tell you it's not going to save him from the hell I'm going to bring down on him," I rant as I step out of the room and Frankie follows. "He's going to wish he was never born. That asshole acted like a friend. Like a team player. He's not a team player. Billy would never sell me out like that. Hell, Spencer Samuels has done a better job defending me in interviews than Cedric. And Samuels is my competition!"

"Cedric kind of is too," Frankie reminds me as I walk down the hall beside her. "He only races if you or Billy don't. It's a hard position for him. He wasn't given a fair chance at his last team, and now his only opportunity to race comes if one of you can't. I'm sure he sees this thing with Nick as lucky."

"Lucia! Frankie!"

I turn around to find Nick standing in the hall, in his hospital gown, holding his IV drip in one hand.

I panic. "Are you okay? What's wrong?"

I sprint the small distance between us, and he puts his free hand on my shoulder. "I'm fine. But you said something when you were leaving. Cedric has a tattoo."

I nod. "Yeah. A four-leaf clover on his wrist. It looks like it was done by an old man with the shakes or something. It's horrible. And he's not even Irish, so it's stupid. And honestly, his luck sucks and is about to get worse if I have anything to do with—"

"Right wrist?" Nick says ignoring my tirade. I nod. "Holy shit. I need to call the police."

"What? Why?" Frankie asks from behind me.

Nick ignores her and turns to re-enter his room. His perfect naked ass flashes us both, since the back of his gown is wide open. I try to cover my sister's eyes with my palm. She's grinning feverishly, so I know she got a look at the goods.

"Nick, you're showing off your assets!" I bark, and he reaches behind him and tries to grab the edges of the gown.

Frankie tries to pull my hand away, but I don't move it until Nick is climbing into his bed again and the door to his room is swinging shut. When I lower my hand, Frankie looks at me. "Nice."

"I know. Now wipe it from your mind forever, please," I replied and push his door open.

My sister and I enter together and stand next to each other at the foot of his bed. He's already picked up my cell and has it held up to his face. He asks for a detective I've never heard of, but I haven't been involved in the follow-up investigation on his attack. I've purposely pushed it from my mind and tried super hard not to talk about it with Nick. I don't have the mental capacity to think about it. I'll get too upset and start obsessing over it.

"Hi, this is Nick Darcy," Nick says into the phone. "Remember I told you about the tattoo or stain on the guy's right wrist? The guy who attacked me?"

Holy... is he saying...?

"Yeah, there's a man who fits that. Who has motive." Nick goes on. "He is part of the Mirabella team."

"Oh shit," Frankie gasps, clearly just putting it all together. Our eyes lock. She pales. "Does he really think Cedric would do this?"

"You know Nick, he isn't going to assume anything," I reply.

We stand there in stunned silence until Nick gets off the call. And then, before he can say a word, I say, "You didn't tell me that you saw a tattoo on the guy."

"I didn't know for sure it was a tattoo. But there was something on his inner right wrist. And you can see it on the hotel security footage too," Nick replies. "As he pushes open the stairwell door he left through. The fucker knew enough to keep his hood up and his head down, but you can see the blob on his wrist."

"I don't know what to do," Frankie replies, still pale. "What do I do?"

"We call your dad. We update him. We let the London police liaise with the local one if need be," Nick replies. "This situation is extremely difficult because of the international thing. But I don't think you should say a thing to Cedric until we have further confirmation. They got a print off the scissors, miraculously, but it didn't come up in their database as a match. But that just means Cedric's prints aren't on file in London."

"They're on file with us," Frankie announces.

Right! All members of the team go through background checks. We need clean records for international travel purposes. I turn to Nick, but I don't have to explain it because he was fingerprinted when he started with Frankie too.

He picks up my phone again. "I'm going to tell the UK police. They can get a subpoena and require the team to turn over the prints to see if they match."

I move to the chair in the corner and sink into it.

"Are you okay?"

I look up at my sister and shake my head no. She drops down and rests her butt on the wide wooden arm of the chair. "I know. Me neither."

Well, at least I'm not the only one. I look at Nick as he finishes up his second call to London. He smiles at me. "Whatever happens, it's okay."

I hope he's right.

Nick

I TAKE a deep breath as I enter the hotel lobby. Lucia, Frankie, Billy and I, stayed behind in Texas while the sting took place. That's the best way to describe it, which is crazy, honestly. It took the UK police less than twenty-four hours to get a subpoena, and Mirabella, thanks to Bash, was ready to ship Cedric's fingerprints to them the second the lawyers got the order.

By the time I got out of the hospital last night, it was confirmed the print on the scissors matched Cedric Pagtakhan. The fucking weasel stabbed me. He's the one who has been harassing and terrorizing Lucia this entire time. Bash was red with rage as we explained the full theory to him. Adelaide had to rub his shoulders and warn him about his blood pressure as the video call went on, and we explained that his motive was he wanted Lucia to be so rattled it affected her driving and she either quit or got dropped so he could get her spot.

But other than the fingerprint, which was enough for a

warrant, we didn't have much else. We needed Cedric to confess. And the warrant wasn't international. We needed Cedric back in the UK. I asked Bash if he would fly Cedric back to London on the false pretense that he wanted to talk about his future with the team. Bash was in a fury and not a great actor, so Lucia and I drafted a text and sent it to him so he could send it to Cedric. Then Frankie, who is an excellent actress, sang his praises and even got Jack to drive him to the airport.

The stupid bastard had no idea that London detectives would be waiting for him as soon as he got off the plane. He landed only fifty-five minutes ago, so I was shocked when my phone started vibrating on the nightstand at four in the morning, our time. I declined the call so it wouldn't wake up Lucia, who was sleeping, threw on some sweats and a t-shirt, and headed into the hotel lobby to call the number back. I had it stored in my phone, so I knew it was the lead detective's desk line.

He explained that they cuffed him as soon as he got off the plane and explained why he was being detained, and he confessed everything while crying on the drive back to the station. Not at all that shocking because men like Cedric have a coward's heart. I called Bash immediately to tell him the good news, but he didn't answer.

Now I make my way back up to our hotel room. We're set to head to Mexico on a mid-morning flight for the next Grand Prix. The first practice round is the next day. Lucia isn't talking about it, but I know this race makes her nervous. I won't push her to open up, but I'm trying hard to read the signs and give her space when she needs it and a shoulder to lean on when that's what she wants.

And now I have to tell her this is over, and I honestly don't know how she'll react. Relieved, but also slighted because he was supposed to be a friend and I know that she has a really hard time accepting injustice. And poor Frankie is going to have to handle the media shitstorm over this too. Damn. The media is going to have a field day with this. Especially after the drama last year where Bash parted ways with his longtime business partner Dario and their other driver Antonio, who it turned out helped cover up Frankie being drugged at a party years ago. Mirabella has spent the last year being whispered about, and it's not going to stop now.

I swipe the key card and open the room to our suite. Lucia is still sleeping peacefully, but when I crawl back into bed she stirs. "Where were you?" She murmurs, lips against my neck. "Your skin is cold."

"I went outside to take a call," I reply, and I can feel her whole body stiffen beside me. I don't make her ask the question. "He's in custody. He admitted to all of it. His goal was to scare you into quitting, or cause you to be so distracted that you got dropped."

"I hate him," Lucia whispers vehemently.

"I know," I reply. Her emotions are big, and rightfully so. "But it's over now."

She doesn't respond. She just curls into me more, and we lay in silence until we both fall asleep. When I wake up next, it's because someone is pounding on the door. Lucia bolts out of bed and throws on a robe and heads to answer it.

"Stop!"

She skids to a halt on the carpet a foot from the door. I walk up beside her. "Sorry love I'm still your bodyguard."

She makes an annoyed noise, but lets me look through the peephole. I see Frankie and Billy there and have a moment of panic we've overslept for our flight. But as I pull open the door, I realize they're both in pajamas with bed head. Frankie is holding up her phone. "They're both here!" She exclaims and turns around so we can see her phone too.

There on screen are Bash and Adelaide and the newest member of the Castera brood. Lucia gasps. "Oh my god, he's here!"

"Last night at around one in the morning," Bash said. "Home birth in a pool in the library with two doulas. It all went swimmingly. Ha. See what I did there?"

We all groan at his Dad joke. He ignores us and continues. "Adelaide was amazing. A real champ."

"Except for the part where, after two hours of pushing, I screamed for drugs or to be bashed over the head," Adelaide admits. She looks exhausted and pale but happy. "Giving birth is not at all as romantic as they make it seem. I should have gone for the drugs."

"But it was worth it, right?' Lucia says. "Look at him!"

"Oh yeah, about that," Bash grins. "It's a *her*, so if anyone made bets with Lucia, she owes you money."

"A girl?" Lucia says, and she is visibly crestfallen.

"Yes. I don't know why you wanted a brother so badly, but you'll have to deal," Adelaide says with a wink. "Her name is Pippa Piper Paisley Castera."

"Is she normal?" Lucia blurts out.

"She's perfectly healthy," Bash replies, not understanding the deeper meaning of that question. "Just like you and Frankie were."

"But I'm not, Dad," Lucia says.

"Maybe you two should talk later," Frankie suggests.

"Right. Of course," Lucia nods. "Sorry."

"Sorry for what?" Bash asks. "What are you talking about, honey?"

"Cedric is in custody," I break in. I want her to have a heart-to-heart with Bash, just not right now. "He confessed to everything. It's a long story we don't have to get into now, but Lucia won't be bothered anymore by ominous threats. At least not from him."

"Good," Bash says.

"I'm glad that's over Lucia," Adelaide says, her eyes on the swaddled bundle in her arms. The baby is all wrinkly, but it has a shock of dark hair very similar to Lucia's color, but straight. "We are going to try and get some sleep. We'll touch base again tomorrow when you guys are settled in Mexico."

"Are you ready for that track, *la louloutte*?" Bash asks Lucia, and she just nods. "Okay then, I'll talk to you later. Love you, girls."

"Love you too, Dad!" Frankie says as Lucia nods again. "And congrats. Can't wait to meet Pippa."

They wave as Frankie ends the video call. She turns to Lucia and says what I was going to say. "You are normal, Lucia."

"I'm not though," she argues. "And that's okay. I'm good with it, but it hasn't been easy. Not understanding why I feel things differently or deal with things differently has been difficult. And I wouldn't want her to feel that way too."

"Well, the good thing about it is now we have a better understanding of ASD if she is on the spectrum," Frankie says.

"And she'll have you to advocate for her," I remind Lucia. "The way my nephew Charlie has my brother Franklin."

She thinks about that and nods. "She does."

"And you need to talk to Bash," Billy adds. "I think you'll feel better if you do."

"Yeah. I will. I just... it's difficult to confront him on this," Lucia admits. "I'm scared he's known this whole time and never wanted anyone to know. Even me."

I wrap an arm around her shoulders and pull her back into my chest, kissing the top of her head. "Since when do you avoid confrontation? Come on now. Also, that's not Bash and deep down, you know it."

Billy and Frankie leave to get ready and pack. We do the same. But then Lucia's phone rings and it's her dad. He's trying to video call her. "Answer it, love."

"Don't tell me what to do," she mutters, but she answers it.

"Hey honey," Bash says with a tired grin. "I did the call all by myself!"

I smile at how proud the old man sounds about his conquering of technology. But I move into the bathroom to pack up my toiletries and give her some space. She glances over her shoulder at me, and the look of vulnerability in her eyes, that seriously breaks me. My gorgeous, strong woman has no idea what a powerhouse she is. I give her a reassuring smile and a wink. She has to do this on her own.

"Lucia?" Bash says. "Are you there? Did I mess this up?"

"No Dad, I'm here," She assures him.

I don't like eavesdropping, but I am worried this will blow up, and I want to be there for her if it goes badly. If Lucia didn't want me to hear, she'd go into the living room or at the very least, close the bathroom door. So I don't feel too bad.

"I wanted to speak to you, now that the baby and Adelaide are resting," Bash tells her. "Are you okay? With everything?"

"Yeah. Don't worry about me, Dad," Lucia says easily. "I'm upset about the whole Cedric thing, and dreading the media. And I'm a little bit worried about being back in Mexico, but my therapist is helping me with all of that. I'll be okay."

"And with the baby?"

"I'm really happy for you, Dad," Lucia says quickly. "And I'm excited to meet her."

"She looks so much like you, Lucia," Bash says, awe and pride swimming in his words. I can hear it from here, and it makes me smile. "I never realized how much of my genes you have, but little Pip proves it. Same chin as you, same dark hair.

Adelaide says she sees you in her stare, even though Pip's eyes are light. You aren't all your mom after all."

"Where did I get my autism from, I wonder," Lucia says and I freeze, the razor in my hand hovering above my travel bag.

That is not how I would have broached the subject, but it doesn't mean it was wrong. I hold my breath as I hear Bash ask her to repeat that. There's a pause, and I wonder if I should go out there, but then Lucia speaks again. "I was diagnosed with autism spectrum disorder, Dad. Recently. And I wonder if you and Mom knew about it when I was a kid. Remember the weekend you guys showed up at our boarding school because you needed to get me tested? Did you know after that? Do you know now?"

"Autism?" Bash repeats. "No. I don't even think that was what they tested you for. It was ADHD or MDNA... some silly acronym. Honestly, Lu, I admit this was bad parenting, but I was still racing at the time, and your mom just handled all of that. I don't know what ever happened to those test results. If she got them, she never told me. She got sick, and we just focused on that. I... don't understand. Why do you think you have that now?"

"I know I'm on the spectrum, Dad, because my psychologist confirmed a suspicion I had," Lucia explains, and her voice lacks its normal power and force. She is talking softly and gently, and it's shame or fear, and I hate that for her so much. I need her to know she shouldn't cower over this. But I do nothing more than lean against the bathroom wall.

"Okay," Bash sounds concerned. "What can I do?"

He sounds so earnest. Lucia sighs. "There's nothing to do. I'm going to keep working with my therapist. Not to *fix* anything. I'm fine the way I am, but because she helps me manage my emotions."

"Okay. Good," Bash replies. "I support whatever you want.

I have to be honest honey, I know nothing about autism. It's a scale?"

"A spectrum," Lucia replies. "I can send you links to sites that explain it better. If you want to understand it."

"I want to," Bash says without a second hesitation. "Is this why you've been so distant? I thought it was the baby. I know you were upset about it."

"No. I wasn't upset about the baby," Lucia replies. "I'm sorry. I just... it was a shock, and I can't handle surprises well. And I was just adjusting to Adelaide, who was also a shock, Dad."

"I understand that," Bash says.

There's a pause where neither of them speaks, and I worry, but then Bash says. "Baby, you know I love you no matter what."

"I know," she whispers so I barely hear it.

"And you know why I'm so excited that Pip looks like you?" Bash questions.

"Because you thought I might be the mailman's and this proves I'm not?" Lucia jokes and I laugh out loud. Shit. Oops. "Get in here, boyfriend."

I slink out of the bathroom. She's sitting on the corner of the bottom of the bed, one leg tucked up under her, and the phone in front of her in her left hand. I take a seat a little behind her and she automatically leans into me. I give Bash a wave. He nods. "Lucia," he says with a grin. "I'm excited Pip looks like you because you were the most entertaining child I have ever met. To this day. You were full of fire and love and yes, you were quirky as hell, but you were so... genuine. And independent. So independent. When you needed me or your mom, it felt like an honor. It still does. So never hesitate to reach out, *ma louloutte*."

I've always liked that little nickname he uses for his daughters. It's a term of endearment in French like how the English say sweetie or honey. I feel Lucia shudder. Oh shit, she's crying. I wrap my arms around her. "I told you he'd have your back."

"She doubted it?" Bash looks offended.

"I never doubt you Dad," Lucia interjects as she wipes at her eyes.

"Good. Now I should let you go and get some sleep myself," Bash says. "Because if Pip is like you when she wakes up, the entire house will know it."

Lucia laughs. "Buy earplugs, old man, and hire a nanny."

"I'm gonna be hands-on with this one," Bash promises. "I wish I'd had more time with you and Frankie when you were little."

"You did great," Lucia replies. "And Pip is in great hands. I mean you didn't name her Aquarius, so you're already winning."

He chuckles and blows her an air kiss and then he looks at me. "Nick, do I have to say it?"

"Is this the speech where you tell me you're glad I'm in Lucia's life, but if I hurt her, you're gonna ruin me?" I ask and he nods. "Nope. I got it. No need to do the whole song and dance."

"Great. Talk to you guys when you're in Mexico. Baci!"

"Baci," Lucia says back. Then she hits end, drops the phone beside her, and turns around. She climbs up in my lap, wraps her arms around my neck, buries her face there, and cries. And I let her, rubbing her back and saying nothing.

"I'm not sad," she manages to croak out after a minute.

"I know."

"Of course you do," she says and sniffs. "You get me."

"Always."

And I hold her tight and revel in the fact that she's mine. This beautiful, wild, brilliant woman is all mine.

Lucia

AND BECAUSE TODAY isn't stressful enough, it's my day to have the entire docu-drama crew follow me everywhere. I wake up with that weight on my shoulders on top of everything else. Nick is already up and walks into the bedroom with a coffee for me. I take it and stare at it for a moment before handing it back. "I can't. I'm worried it will make me jittery."

"Okay," he replies. "Decaf?"

I nod. I like the idea of the routine of coffee too much to say no. He heads back into the living room to make a decaf in the Nespresso machine on the bar. I stretch and pull myself out of bed. I grab my phone and look at the time. Nick wanders back in and hands me the new coffee. "I pushed them to eight-thirty. And when they get here, I can ask them to meet you in the conference room instead of the hotel. I don't give a shit about squashing the director's vision."

God, I love this man. I smile at him and push up on my tip toes to kiss his cheek. "I love you so much. But no. I will let her start the whole interview part here. And you'll be part of it. Like you belong here. Because you do."

"Then the whole world will assume you're dating your bodyguard." Nick lifts one of his dark, thick eyebrows.

"Well, I am aren't I?" I shrug.

He smiles. We're not exactly hiding anymore, but we don't do public displays of affection or anything, so only our inner circle is really sure of our involvement. He plants a kiss on the top of my head. "Only if you're comfortable, love. I don't need the world to know a single fucking thing about us."

"This episode they're filming today is all about me. About coming back to the place I almost died as an F1 driver and conquering fear. Well, I need to conquer the fear of public opinion," I tell him. "I am so sick of worrying what people will think about me. I'm just going to tell them what to think."

Nick nods slowly. "I'm not sure I know what you mean, but I trust you."

I nod and sip my coffee as I walk into the bathroom to shower. He follows without the need of an invitation. We're great at conserving water these days. And a good morning orgasm in the shower is becoming a routine for us I hope never goes away.

An hour later, the film crew is piled into my hotel suite. The director, a woman named Kasey, is barking out orders to her team as I sit on the sofa. Nick is up against the wall of his adjoining suite, trying to blend in like furniture. Kasey positions herself across from me, butt on the coffee table, cameraman over her shoulder so the shot is tight on me. "Okay, you know how this works. I'm going to ask you a bunch of questions. I won't be on camera, and this footage might be interspersed with the rest of the stuff we shoot today."

"Yeah, I know. Let's just go. I'm good."

Kasey nods. "We have had a bit of an issue in the past with

you not looking at me. And I need you to focus on me when you speak. Because the camera is behind me, so we need you to talk to the camera. For the interview parts. It's how we do it."

I sigh. I look at Nick, and he starts to tense up. Like he's going to step in and intervene somehow. And I appreciate it, but I know I need to handle this. Once and for all. I look at Kasey. "Are we rolling yet?"

"No. Not yet."

"Can we be?" I ask. "I'd like my answer to you to be filmed."

"Uh... " Kasey looks completely confused. "Okay. Yeah."

She motions to her camera guy. Another person steps in and snaps that stupid board in front of me. I blink and take a deep breath as Kasey says, "Rolling."

"Okay, so, I know you guys like us to focus right on you. On the camera only when we do these interviews," I start, and my fingers tremble a bit, so I lace them in my lap. "I have autism spectrum disorder, and for me, prolonged eye contact is uncomfortable, so I apologize, but it is what it is. I hope you can understand."

"You... okay. Yeah. Of course," Kasey is completely blindsided, which I get, considering this is the first time I've ever talked about it.

"I know. It's a shock," I add with a small smile. "It was for me too. I was only diagnosed recently. But honestly, along with the shock is some relief. A lot of my life makes sense when it didn't before."

"Do you feel it affects your career?"

"Yeah," I admit honestly. "I don't know if I would be as focused or driven without ASD. Being the only woman at this level, I think that obsessiveness has been an asset. I need to be more focused and more driven than a man in this sport because I get judged more severely. By fans, by media, by a lot of people."

"So you see this as an advantage?"

"Not exactly, but it might help me, yeah," I nod and take another deep breath. "Look, obviously there are drawbacks, like the eye contact thing. But I am talking about it publicly now because I don't want to feel bad about who I am, and I don't want other girls out there who might be like me to think they should feel bad. I met a girl earlier this season named Charlotte who saw me as a role model. And I want to be that for all girls who want to be F1 drivers but also for all girls with ASD who want to be anything. I can't be that role model if I don't talk about it. So I'm talking about it. Make no mistake, though, this doesn't define who I am or what I do or don't do. I don't win or lose because of ASD. It's just part of who I am, like curly hair or brown eyes. Now let's talk about being back in Mexico. Where I almost died. That's the real news."

"Okay. Are you nervous about being back here?"

"As all hell," I admit, and the crew chuckles sympathetically around me. I look over at Nick. He's smiling at me. He mouths 'Love you.'

THE RACE GOES ASTONISHINGLY WELL. I have Carmyn to thank for that. She took a session with me only half an hour before I had to be on track and said something that I repeated in my head over and over as I climbed into the car and as the lights went out on the grid. Those words "it's just another race" were a chant in my mind through every lap, every pit stop. My sister, thankfully, respected my wishes and kept the radio banter to the bare minimum, talking in my ear only when they wanted me to pit or there was a red flag or yellow flag. We had two of both. And those flags, along with my driving skills, moved me from fifth to second on the grid. And that's where I stayed.

I see the checkered flag, and I'm screaming so loud I can

barely hear Frankie yelling on the radio. "P2 Louie! P freaking 2!!! You podiumed! You fucking podiumed!"

I laugh. "Thank you, team! We did it. We conquered the beast. I bested my demon track. Thank you, everyone. I fucking podiumed!"

As soon as I get out of the car, I rush into the wall of crew members who lift me off my feet with their group hug. Clara grabs me next and hugs me. "You did it. I'm so proud of you."

"I'm proud of you too," I whisper back. "And I'm there for you, for whatever you need going forward."

I haven't had a chance to see her alone since she told me her secret. She gives me a nod and hugs me again. When she lets go, Frankie is there to hug me next, and then Billy and Logan, but I only want Nick. I see him in the corner of the garage, and I drop my helmet and everything and charge at him. He is grinning as he catches me and swings me around.

"You're amazing, you know that?"

"I am!" I laugh. "And I fucking love you."

"I love you too," he assures me. "Now get up there and get your trophy."

I go through the weigh-in, and the media, and then step onto that second tier beaming with pride, my eyes on Nick standing in the swarm of Mirabella crew below. I feel so happy like my world is finally complete, and it has to do with so much more than just this trophy.

When I get off the podium, the docu-drama crew is right there, in my face. I know they filmed the whole scene with Nick in the garage so our relationship is officially public. Kasey is smiling as she walks beside me, just out of the frame of the camera held by the guy walking backward in front of me. "How good does that feel?"

"It feels incredible," I say and fight tears. "I've conquered a hell of a lot more than just my fears of this track over the last year. So this trophy, this win, it's more than just my first F1 podium. It's more than just overcoming a fear of this track. It's... it's proof that I am where I need to be and who I need to be. And I know I wouldn't be here without the people who always believed in me. No matter what. Like my boyfriend, Nick. And my dad and sister."

I pause and force myself to look right into the camera. "I'm lucky to have the support system I do. And I will never take that for granted again." I continue walking and see Nick up ahead. "Now if you'll excuse me, I need to go kiss my boyfriend."

I run into Nick's embrace again, wrap my arms around his neck, careful not to clobber him with the trophy I'm holding, and kiss him with all I've got.

ACKNOWLEDGMENTS

I want to thank my friends and family, for supporting my journey in life, and this profession. Big thanks to my agent Kimberly Brower and her team at Brower Literary. Thanks Kelly Green for your P.A. services and your general 'ray-of-sunshine' attitude that always makes me smile.

Thank you to my loyal readers, who always one-click my books, even if they didn't fall head-over-heels in love with Formula One (because of Drive to Survive) like I did. Thank you to Kelly Keating for, not just being a dedicated reader but also a friend, to both me and my mom.

Also thank you to the League ARC team and my small but dedicated personal ARC team. Thank you to fellow authors like (but not limited to) Sierra Hill, Kat Mizera, Lasairiona McMaster, Sarina Bowen, Leslie McAdam, Regina Kyle, J.E. Birk, and others who are always there to brain storm, cross-promote and share tips and tricks. Thanks to Mignon Mykel for the lovely custom cover. You never disappoint. Katie Kenyhercz, thanks for being so accommodating and moving my editing deadline multiple times and still getting it back to me early early. You are a rockstar.

Lastly, thanks to my now-departed fur ball Gus. I was blessed to have loved you for almost sixteen years. I miss you every day.

ABOUT THE AUTHOR

Victoria Denault is a proud Canadian, and former Californian, who lives in a 223-year-old house with her husband and more spiders than she cares to think about.

Victoria's hobbies include; performing stand-up comedy and watching scary movies and true crime shows then wondering why she has anxiety. Victoria has never met a beach she doesn't like, but her favorite beach will always be Ocean Park, Maine where she has gone every summer since she was four months old.

Fast Track is Victoria Denault's seventeenth book. For more on her other novels, go to www.victoriadenault.com

www.ingramcontent.com/pod-product-compliance
Lightning Source LLC
Chambersburg PA
CBHW071426200726
48294CB00002B/534